The Messenger Adrift

book two of the Messenger Trilogy

by Joel Pierson

iUniverse, Inc.
New York   Bloomington

iUniverse books may be ordered through booksellers or by contacting:

iUniverse
1663 Liberty Drive
Bloomington, IN 47403
www.iuniverse.com
1-800-Authors (1-800-288-4677)

Because of the dynamic nature of the Internet, any Web addresses or links contained in this book may have changed since publication and may no longer be valid. The views expressed in this work are solely those of the author and do not necessarily reflect the views of the publisher, and the publisher hereby disclaims any responsibility for them.

ISBN: 978-1-4401-8884-8 (sc)
ISBN: 978-1-4401-8885-5 (ebook)

Printed in the United States of America

iUniverse rev. date:11/11/09

Acknowledgments

Once again, I could not have done this without the help of my writing group, Jamie, Melissa, Holly, Christy, and Andrew, who kept me motivated to write all along. Thanks also to Juliet, the unofficial member of the group, whose insights and ideas allowed me to decide that the book was done and ready to go to press.

Thanks go out to my legal advisor, the Honorable Kate Dyer (and she really is), who made all the lawyer-type stuff sound authentic.

And thanks, of course, to Dana, who understood the time constraints of creating three books, and always displayed the utmost patience when it was writing night.

About the Author

Joel Pierson is the author of numerous award-winning plays for audio and stage, including *French Quarter, The Children's Zoo, The Vigil, Cow Tipping,* and *Mourning Lori*. He also co-authored the novelization of *French Quarter*. How he has time to write is anyone's guess, as he spends his days as editorial manager at the world's largest print-on-demand publishing company. Additionally, he is artistic director of Mind's Ear Audio Productions, the producers of several popular audio theatre titles and the official audio guided tour of Arlington National Cemetery. If that weren't enough, he also writes for the newspaper and a local lifestyles magazine in his hometown of Bloomington, Indiana. He stays grounded and relatively sane with the help of his wife (and frequent co-author) Dana, and his three ridiculously loving dogs.

The Messenger Trilogy

Don't Kill the Messenger
The Messenger Adrift
(Coming Soon) Messenger in a Battle

And as the new days commence, from the west shall come Hamesh, keeper of the word of Hosea, he who will bring wholeness to The Nine. Upon the tail of a mighty wind will he arrive, fresh-steeped in grief and newfound wisdom. And by his side shall come Persephone, fair of face and possessed of fire.

Brief shall the unity be, for the true sins of one father and the false sins of another shall align. Oil and water shall combine with blood, and set the messenger adrift into battle.

—Found in a cave outside of Jerusalem, 1763
Author unknown

PROLOGUE

TORNADO DAY

CEDARSBURG, KANSAS

3:58 PM

INSIDE THE ENCOUNTER VEHICLE

"Contact! Visual contact. Funnel heading 275." Paul makes the announcement from Tiny's driver's seat.

"Confirmed," Shafiq says, his eyes transfixed on the Doppler radar screen at his station in the middle of the vehicle. "Heading 275, range six miles. CBDR."

CBDR. It's an old naval term for constant bearing, decreasing range. In other words, it's heading straight for us.

"Is it on the ground?" I ask from my current location aft.

"Stand by," Shafiq says. "Checking. I can't tell yet."

"I can," Paul interrupts. Being at the windshield has its advantages. "It's just touched down. Large funnel, and from the looks of the downdraft, it's picking up strength. It'll be a wedge by the time we get there."

"Time to intercept?" Delia asks as she makes adjustments to the photographic equipment.

"Under present conditions," Paul replies, "eight minutes."

"I have to warn the others," I remark, picking up the two-way radio. "Rebecca, do you copy?"

Her voice tells me she's all right. "We copy." *Thank God.*

"We have visual on a funnel cloud," I report. "Bearing 275, range six miles. It's a funnel now, but it's building strength. We're likely to see a wedge by the time it gets here."

"Okay. What does that mean?" she asks. *Newbies. Gotta love 'em.*

"It means get the fuck out of Dodge! We're going to intercept."

"Roger, we copy. Just be careful, please."

"Ten-four. Go south. Go now."

The hailstones are relentless. Larger than golf balls, they plummet from the sky with enough force to crack windshields and leave enormous dents in the sheet metal of ordinary vehicles. But Tiny is no ordinary vehicle. The powerful stones provide a staccato soundtrack to our little adventure, but pose no threat to the vehicle's safety—or ours.

"Are we really going to intercept?" Paul asks. The others look at me. The fate of four lives and a multimillion-dollar vehicle rests in my answer.

"I say we go for it. This is the best chance we'll ever get."

"Copy that," Paul says. "Continuing on intercept course."

My heart races a little at those words. *Intercept course. An EF4 tornado, right where I want it.*

"Wind speed increasing," Shafiq announces. "Seventy. Eighty. Ninety." The increments are coming much faster than I'd like. I can feel the head wind pushing against the vehicle, trying to impede our forward progress, but Tiny's engine is strong, and we push forward.

"What's the wind speed at the funnel?" I ask.

"It looks like 170 to 175."

"Still cameras and digital video functioning perfectly," Delia says. "I'm getting amazing footage."

"Keep filming," I tell her. "Paul, any damage to report on Tiny? Any loss of handling?"

"That's a negative," he replies. "She's taking it like a star."

"Cool. Maintain course and speed. And watch out for debris as we get closer."

"Range three and a half miles," Shafiq says. "The wedge is forming, and we're still CBDR."

There are a dozen things to prepare, but my station has no windows, and I have to see this monster. I dash forward to the passenger's seat and get my first look at our quarry. It is beautiful and unspeakably terrible. Pitch black from all the soil it has picked up, the tornado is a blight on the horizon, building in width from the more common funnel into a wedge, a wall of inescapable destruction. And we're driving toward it.

A steady stream of vehicles is heading the other way, some of them honking their horns and flashing their lights at us to warn us, ignoring the fact that Tiny is very obviously a tornado encounter vehicle. I can't blame them, though. If I were anyone else but me, I'd convince people to head the other direction too.

A full minute passes, and I realize that I have been staring at the cloud when I should be doing my job. "I have to get ready to take readings," I tell the others. "Stay strong, and shout out if we've got something to worry about."

"You mean other than an EF4 on an intercept course with us?" Delia asks with a little smile.

"Yeah. Besides that little detail."

I dash back to my station and launch the software I've spent eleven months developing. In conjunction with Tiny's barometer, radar equipment, anemometer, and a host of other tools, the software will measure the tornado's outflow and downdraft. Exactly the measurements I need. "Paul, be sure to keep us out of the suck zone. Find a way to get us behind it. I want to follow it for as long as I possibly can."

"Check. I'll do what I can."

As my computer screen comes to life and the first readings come in, I am running on pure adrenaline. The two-way radio is within reach. I have to know that the others made it to safety.

"This is Tiny. What's your location?"

Again, I am deeply relieved to hear Rebecca's voice. "We're a half mile south of town. "Where are you?"

Ignoring our exact location, I give the only answer that fills my mind: "In paradise!"

My name is Kavi Abhishek Ariashi, and thanks to Rebecca Traeger and Tristan Shays, this is the most exciting day of my life.

PART ONE

A WOMAN SAYS *GOOD MORNING*

As Rebecca tells it

48 HOURS EARLIER

Chapter 1

It began like nothing has ever begun for me before, with a stranger carrying a message for me in his mind. He entered the club in Key West where I worked as an exotic dancer, but unlike the hundreds of other men who populate that place day in and day out, he was there to *see* me, not to look at me. Tristan Shays, the man who changed my life with a single message. Now we are on the run together—away from some things, toward some other things. I thought I could leave him, simply accept a ride back to my father's home in Ohio and then never see him again. I realize now that I was wrong.

What followed were four of the most harrowing days I've ever known. I watched a man die in an explosion; I watched Tristan get accused of his murder. Fortunately, I had the knowledge and training to help him beat the rap.

Beat the rap? Good, Rebecca. Way to sound like a 1930s detective magazine.

That's my name, by the way. Rebecca Traeger. For the first eighteen years of my life, I was Persephone Traeger, a name I carried like a lead weight around my soul, because I knew it wasn't who I was. It was who my father wanted me to be. My father—I haven't even talked about him yet. God, so much has happened. It was my father who sent Tristan to Florida to bring me home, only Tristan didn't know it. He gets *assignments,* I guess you could call them; instructions in his mind to go and help people in trouble. Strangers, people he's never met. And he does it! He drives for days and warns them about whatever danger they're in. Of course, if he doesn't do it, he gets terrible pain all through his body, so it's not totally out of the goodness of his heart. Well, he *does* have a good heart. He can be socially awkward sometimes, but I blame that on a solitary lifestyle. Because he really does mean well.

Earlier today, he told me that he loved me. I haven't even known him a week and he said it—right in front of my father—right *to* my father. (Who almost shot him for saying it, but that's another story.) It's been a very long time since anyone told me they loved me and meant it. I honestly don't know if I love him. But I know that I honestly could.

"Penny for your thoughts."

His voice startles me; I've been wrapped up in what I'm thinking. "Even with all your money, my thoughts are only worth a penny?"

"Humor me," Tristan says. "I don't have the luxury of peeking inside my companion's mind, like *someone* here does."

"Hey, gimme a break on that, huh?"

"So what's on your mind?" he asks, easing off on the ribbing.

"Everything. I imagine after two years of doing this, you're used to this frantic pace, but it's all new to me. I feel like I barely have time to catch my breath before we're headed somewhere else."

"That's why I insisted on a leisurely sit-down lunch today," he says. "A chance for both of us to catch our breath."

We're at a corner booth in a little café in Palisade Heights, Ohio— my former hometown until I left college two years ago and decided I couldn't live with my father's rules anymore. But then he tricked me, deceived Tristan into bringing me back here so my father could use me to help him make money.

This is hard to explain, mostly because I've just realized it myself and it sounds absolutely crazy to say it—but I have ... abilities, I guess you could call them. Skills with my mind and my thoughts that most people don't have. I wish I could explain better, but I literally found out about it today, and with everything that's happened, I can barely keep it all straight.

"Are you thinking about me?" he asks.

"It'd be a little hard not to."

"Any thoughts about ... you know ... what I said this morning?"

"It's *private*," I tell him.

"Even if it's about me?"

"You really haven't spent much time with women, have you?"

He looks sheepish. "No." After a few moments of silence, he adds, "You took a big chance back there." *I knew he'd bring that up.*

"My father had a gun to your head. I wasn't going to let him hurt you."

"But standing in between us? How did you know he wouldn't hurt *you?*"

I take a sip of water and tell a half-truth. "Because I know him."

"Do you think he'll have us followed?" Tristan asks.

"I don't know. I guess it depends on how much he needs my help in finding that oil reserve. He can follow us all he wants. We're going to Kansas to help those people."

Kansas. Our new destination. There's a town there called Cedarsburg, with 11,000 people in it, and on Tuesday, in two days' time, a tornado will devastate it. An hour ago, Tristan got the assignment to go to Cedarsburg and warn as many people as possible so they can get to safety. I saw the horror in his eyes when he told me that—the magnitude of it, the burden of having to save so many lives. That was the moment when I knew I had to say no to my father and stay with Tristan, at least until this assignment is over.

"Yeah," he says solemnly. "Those people. How are we supposed to do this? How are we supposed to get all 11,000 people out of town in time?"

"We've got two days, and because we're flying there, we have time to coordinate our efforts. We can contact the local authorities, and I'll call my friend Kavi to help us."

"The storm chaser?"

"That's right. He's been through a lot of tornadoes, up close and personal. He'll do it just for the chance to know exactly when and where one is going to hit. I believe we can do this, Tristan. Otherwise I wouldn't have come with you."

As we wait for our food to arrive, we have time to strategize. We'll have to fly from Dayton to Kansas City and then rent a car to meet Kavi in Lawrence before heading to Cedarsburg. I'm optimistic, but I can feel the anxiety pouring off of my companion. Breaking a promise I recently made to myself, I open my mind up enough to peer into his thoughts, and inside I find overwhelming insecurity and self-doubt. He doesn't think he can do this, but he has no choice. I have to be strong for him, because I *do* think we can do this. And what an opportunity; a chance to save hundreds, maybe even thousands of lives. *Hell, yeah, I'm in.*

"You don't have to come with me, you know," he says, but I know what he wants me to reply.

"Yes I do," I tell him.

He hesitates a moment, then says, "I'm glad you're here. The thought that I would never see you again was pretty upsetting."

He says the sweetest things sometimes. "I think it makes the most sense to wait until tomorrow before we contact the authorities in Cedarsburg," I suggest.

"Why not today? Why not give them a full two days to prepare?"

"Credibility. The storm system we're warning them about hasn't even formed yet. By tomorrow, the front will be approaching, and there'll be some indicators of trouble that a meteorologist might pick up on. Tell them tomorrow and we sound like experts; tell them today and we sound like fortune tellers."

"You are so goddamn smart, it scares me," he says.

"Thanks, I think."

The waitress brings our lunches. I'm starving, so I ordered a personal pizza (as opposed to an impersonal pizza, I guess) and a Caesar salad. Tristan ordered a turkey club with bacon, home fries, and cole slaw. We continue the conversation as we begin eating.

"So what do we do today?" he asks me. And suddenly I get the distinct feeling that I'm leading this mission. I like that.

"Well, we have to get there, and I can't imagine there's too many flights from Dayton to Kansas City each day, so we'll have to take what we can get. Once we get there, we'll pick up Kavi in Lawrence, which isn't far from KC."

"How well do you know this Kavi?"

I laugh a little. Memories stir. "Kavi Ariashi. We went to high school together. He's quite a character. He made me laugh all the time. And smart. Wow, if you think I'm good, wait till you meet him. Makes me look like serious shortbus material."

He smiles at that. "What can he do for us when we're there?"

"Keep us from dying, if all goes well. You ever seen a tornado up close and personal, Tristan?"

"Can't say I've had the pleasure."

"I have," I tell him. "Once. I was about thirteen, and a big one came through town. It passed about two blocks from where I was living. I don't know if I've ever been as scared as I was that day. The sound of it ... people compare it to a freight train, but it's worse than that. It's like this unearthly screaming and tearing sound. Like it's ripping up everything and spitting it back out. You can't look at it, not when it's that close, because you're hiding. You're in your basement, in the cellar, hiding like it's a monster, and if you can't see it, it can't get you. And you keep hoping that it'll miss you, because you know that if it doesn't, nothing will ever be the same again."

He looks intently at me as I relive this memory, pausing as he takes in the full implications of it all. "And after all that, you'll still willingly put yourself in harm's way to do this with me. Why?"

"I don't know. Maybe I'm getting back on the horse. Maybe I want to be the big hero. Maybe I just want to face it one more time. The reasons why are between me and my demons. Fair enough?"

"Fair enough."

"And we're on equal footing this time. No macho 'save-the-girl' shit. Clear?"

"Clear."

I think about it a moment. "Unless, you know, I really do need saving. Then it's okay."

"Hey," he says, "same goes. Don't worry about emasculating me psychologically. If something heavy is about to fall on me and you have the chance to pull me to safety, go for it."

"Deal."

Lunch is good, very satisfying. Even more satisfying is the growing feeling of excitement in me. I feel like I'm on the most bizarre, most exhilarating vacation of my life, with an open-ended ticket in my hand and a close friend at my side. At that thought, I look up at Tristan. He really is a close friend, even though I've only known him less than a week. The things we've been through together have convinced me that I *would* risk my life to save his, just like he would do for me.

"You're staring," he says, snapping me out of it. "I'm the one who's given to staring off into space, remember?"

"Sorry. Just thinking about stuff."

"Stuff?" he kids. "Sounds serious."

"Oh, you know it. Don't let the pretty face and the hot bod fool you; inside is the soul of a philosopher."

This earns a little snicker. "Eat your pizza, Aristotle. We've got places to go."

"Speaking of which," I interject, "shouldn't we be making travel arrangements?"

"I've got a guy."

"You've got a guy?"

"I've got a guy. One phone call and we'll have tickets."

"Must be nice being rich," I tease him.

"Gets me all the hot girls," he retorts without missing a beat. I throw a crouton at him for that one.

Our waitress stops by. "Behave, you two," she chides.

"She started it!" he says, pointing at me with a mock-wounded look on his face.

"You be good," the waitress warns, "or no dessert. And when you see the peanut butter pie, you'll wish you'd behaved."

I like her. She's getting a good tip.

Once we're finished eating, Tristan pulls out his cell phone and selects a contact from his list. I watch as he works his magic. "Vincent, it's Tristan. ... Doing fine, thanks. And you? ... Great, glad to hear it. Listen, Vince, I'm on a business trip, and I need some last-minute airline tickets for today, next available flight. ... I need two tickets, coach class, from Dayton, Ohio to Kansas City, Missouri, any carrier." There is a significant pause as his travel agent checks availability. "You can? That's great. What time does it get in? ... Why so late? ... Oh, I see. No, that'll work. Book me two seats together and put it on the AMEX. I want to pick it up at the American ticket counter in Dayton. ... Second passenger is Rebecca, standard spelling, Traeger, T-r-a-e-g-e-r. ... Thanks, Vince. I owe you one."

He puts his phone away. "We're set."

"When do we have to be at the airport?"

"Flight leaves just before 3:00, so we should leave soonish. We'll get there almost five hours later, courtesy of a fairly long layover in Chicago."

"But you haven't answered the important question," I remind him. "Do we have time for pie?"

"Could I possibly say no to pie? Come on."

The pie is everything the waitress promised and more. We leave the café quite satisfied and feeling better about our assignment, knowing that we have transportation. And so we climb back into the rented Chrysler Sebring convertible that has transported us from Key West to Atlanta to Wyandotte, Pennsylvania to Dayton. Truth be told, I'm actually going to miss it a little.

Tristan volunteers to drive us the half hour to the airport. We put the top down for one last feeling of the wind blowing through our hair. Arriving at the airport, we begin with the rental car return desk. The attendant looks surprised at the huge deviation from Tristan's original rental agreement, and then puts on his best "soften-the-blow" voice as he informs us that it's going to be an extra $332 more than the original agreement stated. Tristan doesn't even blink as he pulls out his credit card and authorizes the charge. I couldn't even begin to guess how much my traveling companion is worth, and the funny thing is, I don't even care.

Sure, I grew up in a wealthy family, and I've dated a couple of guys just because they had a lot of money, but it was extremely superficial, and I didn't like myself very much by the light of day. But it's different with Tristan. It feels respectable. And the difference in our ages doesn't bother me; it's easy for me to forget that he's fifteen years older. He's just *him,* and he doesn't treat me like a kid or anything just because I'm twenty-one. Watching him in moments like this, when he's so calm and in control of the situation, makes me wish I could look into the future, the way he can, and know how long this man is going to be a part of my life.

As he finishes up with the rental car company, I try to call Kavi on my cell phone. After five rings, it goes to voice mail. "Kavi, it's Rebecca Traeger. I know this is a surprise, but I'm on my way to your area right now, and I need to speak with you on a very important matter. I can't go into detail over the phone, but this is big. I'll be in Lawrence tonight. When you get this, please give me a call. Looking forward to seeing you."

Tristan walks over to me. "Anything new?"

"I can't reach Kavi yet, but I left a message. You done handing your money away?"

"My darling, I've only just begun."

A few minutes later, we are riding in relative comfort in the rental company's shuttle to the terminal, our bags safely tucked into a rack in the middle of the bus. I reach over and hold Tristan's hand, partly because I want to reassure him about what lies ahead, and partly because I really like holding his hand. He welcomes my touch and gives my hand a gentle squeeze. I focus on how this feels—the warmth of his hand, the way our fingers lace together. I'm reminded of how he made me feel in the hotel in Atlanta, the night we made love. I wish I understood my own feelings well enough to know if I'm really in love with him. Once upon a time, I would have had no doubt. But that's the problem—I used to fall in love too quickly and it hurt me sometimes. So now I'm not so quick to say it. Or to feel it. I want to, honestly I do. I want to stand up and tell a bus full of strangers that I've met an incredible, caring, thoughtful man and I've fallen in love with him. First I have to convince myself that it's true. And second, the two of us have to survive our time together. Given what we've already faced and what's on the horizon, I don't want to be too quick about declaring a love that will last a lifetime.

We arrive at the terminal and take our bags to the American Airlines ticket counter. There's a short wait, after which we make our way to the next available agent. "Afternoon, folks," he says pleasantly.

"Good afternoon," Tristan replies. "My travel agent arranged for two tickets to Kansas City to be available for us here today. They'd be under Tristan Shays, S-h-a-y-s."

The ticket agent types the information into his terminal and waits a moment for it to appear. "All right, I have it here." A look crosses his face. "Shays?" he says. "Tristan Shays?"

"That's right. Is there a problem?"

Rather than answering, he calls to his associate. "Allison, could you come here for a second?"

A young woman steps over from another workstation. "What's up?"

"I'm not sure," the first agent says. "It's coming up with an E7."

My mind is racing at all the possible things an E7 could mean. I look over at Tristan, worry evident on my face. He still looks calm, and his expression is clearly encouraging me to maintain mine. But I have to wonder—did my father pull some strings as retribution for my refusing to help him with his business? Did he call the police or the FBI or the FAA?

"Hit alt-F3," the second agent suggests. "That'll give you the explanation code."

By now, the other passengers in line are looking at us with annoyance and a touch of concern, courtesy of the widespread paranoia that accompanies air travel these days. Before that paranoid fear can seep too deeply into my mind, the first agent says to Tristan, "There's a problem with the credit card your travel agent used for the tickets. The security code number on the card doesn't match with what American Express has on file. Do you have the card with you, Mr. Shays?"

Relief washes over me as Tristan gets the card from his wallet and hands it to the man. "Ah, there we go. The last two digits were transposed. Give me just a minute to fix that." He types in the correct information, and the printer spits out boarding passes. "All set. I'll just need to see your photo IDs and you'll be set to go."

We produce driver's licenses and display them for the man, who looks at us and our pictures and decides that we are who we say we are. "Very good then," he says, handing them back. "So we have two bags to check, and two to carry on. Flight 716 to Chicago leaves from gate B-16. In Chicago, you'll catch flight 2210 to Kansas City at gate A-9. Have a good flight."

"Thank you," Tristan says.

With that, we gather our carry-on bags, breathe a mutual sigh of relief, and—after a lengthy and very thorough inspection by the TSA—make our way through the terminal to gate B-16.

The flight to Chicago is mercifully uneventful, a word I haven't been able to use to describe the past four days. Once we get settled into our seats, neither of us feels much like talking. Tristan contents himself with looking out the window, taking in the panorama of the Midwest as we rise above it all. I choose to close my eyes and reflect on what's to come.

I suppose if I give it too much thought, I should be scared. Not just of facing the tornado, which is frightening enough in its own right. But on a bigger scale, I should be scared of the decisions I'm making for my future. I'm the first to admit that being an exotic dancer (I hate the word *stripper*) in a men's club in Key West isn't a career move, but the pay was damn good. Even with all my current bills paid, I have enough saved up to live on for a year if I need to. Tristan doesn't work; he doesn't have to with all his money. I need to be doing something, whether it's helping him on his assignments or earning a living. I just can't be idle; it drives me crazy.

Stupid thing is, when he told me I had to go back to college, I was actually excited at the prospect. I've missed my life there and the pursuit of a career in law. For a few days, I had it to look forward to. Then I realized it was all a trick by my father, and I watched those dreams fly away again. I'm so pissed at him, more than I've ever been before. But at the same time, knowing there are people out there who want to hurt him, maybe even kill him—I don't know what I'd do if I found out they succeeded.

So what do I do now? I feel like I've been making it up as I go. Accepting a ride to Ohio with Tristan was easy. It had a destination, an end point. But when I chose to stay with him, it changed everything. Now it's all open-ended, and as exhilarating as that is, it's also more of a commitment than I've made in years.

He turns to me. "You okay?"

"Yeah," I answer. "Just thinking too much again. I do that sometimes."

"You should try to sleep," he suggests.

"Oh, I don't think so. I don't sleep well on airplanes."

I wake up as we are taxiing to the gate at O'Hare Airport. I look over at Tristan, who is smiling at me, a smile that I truly want to believe is not self-satisfied. "Feel better?" he asks.

"Yes, actually. How much time do we have before our connecting flight?"

"A little more than an hour," he replies. "You hungry?"

"I could stand to eat."

"I just happen to know of a place right here in the airport that serves the best Buffalo wings. Interested?"

"Hell, yeah," I answer enthusiastically. "I wouldn't have thought of you as a wing fan."

"Silly girl. Haven't you learned yet that I'm full of surprises?"

We grab our carry-ons and deplane, heading for P.J.'s, a little sit-down place in terminal B. He's right—the wings are as good as he said they'd be. I use the opportunity to try to call Kavi again, and again I get his voicemail.

"Still no luck?" Tristan asks.

"No, and it's not like him not to return my phone calls."

"He's not pissed at you for anything, is he?"

"I can't imagine he would be. We parted on good terms. God, I hope he isn't on vacation or something."

"Even if he was," Tristan says, "his cell phone would probably go with him."

"I guess we may have to wait until we get to Lawrence and just go see him."

We finish our winging and make our way to the gate in time to board our connecting flight to Kansas City. Thanks to the sleep I got on the last flight, I'm able to stay awake for this one, and Tristan graciously gives me the window seat. It's been a few years since the last time I've flown anywhere, and it's good to look out at the clouds again, peeking at the world below as it passes by my window.

The flight lands in Kansas City just before 7:00 PM and we get our luggage quickly and head to the nearest rental car agency. When we get to the counter, I put in my request. "I'd like to get a convertible again."

He looks at me for a few seconds, then says, "Think about where we're going and what we're doing. Do you *really* want to feel that much wind in your hair?"

"Okay, point taken. No convertible, then. So what are we getting?"

"A nice, big SUV," he answers, facing the attendant again. "The heavier the better."

"How long do you want the car?" the man asks.

"Two days, with an option to extend."

"And how many drivers?"

"Two," I answer.

"All right. Is everybody over twenty-five?"

The question stops both of us in our tracks. "Ooh," Tristan says, "no. I guess just one driver then. Sorry."

"Not a problem. Just fill this out, please."

I have to admit, I feel a little disappointed as we leave the rental desk with keys to a GMC Yukon in hand. For the first time since our travels together started, my age is a hindrance. Tristan shrugs it off without a second thought, but suddenly I feel young, and not in a good way. More of a "you can have it when you're older" way, which does nothing to lift my mood.

We pick up the Yukon, which is almost the size of the territory it's named for, and painted a shade of covert federal agency black that gives it the perfect balance of soccer mom and fucking badass. I'm definitely rocking the latter.

He-Who-Is-of-Age takes the wheel, and I once again get out the cell phone and hit redial, hoping to connect with the uncharacteristically absent Kavi Ariashi. His cell phone rings five times, and for the fourth time today, I hear his message: "Hi, it's Kavi. I can't take your call, so leave a message, and if I want to talk to you, I'll call you back."

After the prompt, I leave yet another try, this one a bit more urgent than the others. "Kavi, it's Bec. Dude, where are you? We've landed in Kansas City and we're on our way to Lawrence right now. I sure hope you still live in the same apartment, because that's where we're going. We'll be there in about an hour. If you get this message before then, call me back. It's really important."

I end the call and my concern is very evident. Tristan tries to lend comfort. "We'll find him."

"God, I hope so. This'll be so much harder without him."

We proceed west under skies that are darkening because of sunset and heavy cloud cover. The winds start to pick up, and a light rain falls as we drive. It feels like an appetizer for what is to come.

The rain lets up as we pull into Lawrence, home of the University of Kansas. It's been three years since I was last here visiting, but I remember the way to get there; I have a good memory for directions.

We get off the highway and travel another mile and a half to the Four Oaks apartment complex, parking in front of building J. As we get out of the Yukon, I'm hoping against hope that Kavi hasn't moved or left school or gone to Costa Rica, or any of a dozen possible scenarios that could put him anywhere other than right here where I need him.

I hurriedly lead the way to apartment J-118, Tristan scrambling to keep up. Saying the closest thing I have to a silent prayer, I knock anxiously on the door. Then, for reasons I don't even know, I start counting the seconds as they pass; five, ten, fifteen. From behind the door, I hear someone approach. The door opens, and I'm looking at a stranger, a guy about twenty years old, with light brown hair, a scruffy goatee, and a fashion sense that favors sweat pants and KU T-shirts. He looks at me without recognition and then smiles. "Sup?" he says.

The sight of him disheartens me, but I have to say something. "Umm ... hi. I— I don't know you." *Odd thing to say, but okay.*

He seems unconcerned. "I'm Riley. Who're you then?"

"Rebecca," I answer. "I'm Rebecca."

He glances over at Tristan. "So, is this your dad?"

My companion is displeased at the suggestion, and is less than a second away from an unkind retort, but I stop him by saying, "We must be at the wrong place. I'm looking for my friend, Kavi."

To my surprise, Riley brightens at this. "Yeah, I'm his roommate. He's not here. You wanna come in?"

"Thanks," Tristan says, now ready to put aside the earlier resentment.

We enter and he closes the door behind us. Though the roommate is new, the décor looks about the same as it did when I was last here three years ago. College boys; God bless 'em, they can't keep a room clean to save their lives.

"It's very important that we talk to Kavi," I tell Riley. "We're only here until tomorrow. Do you know what time he'll be back?"

"You must not have heard, huh?" he replies.

"Heard what?" Tristan asks, a hint of worry in his voice.

"Dude, Kavi's in jail."

Chapter 2

For several seconds, we stand there in disbelief. Finally I say, "He's in *jail?*"

"Yeah," Riley says calmly. "He got arrested two days ago."

"For what?" Tristan asks.

Riley pauses and gives it what appears to be some deep thought. "A bunch of stuff. I don't remember like the exact details right now, cuz I'm kinda fucked up."

"This doesn't make sense," I reply. "If he got arrested two days ago, he should be out on bail right now."

"He didn't wanna be," Riley says. "I remember that part."

"It wouldn't happen to be for possession of *marijuana,* would it?" Tristan asks, clearly annoyed by Riley's stoner detachment.

"No, not for that."

I'm growing tired of this. "Where are they holding him?"

"Douglas County Jail downtown," he answers. As we turn to leave, Riley adds, "Hey, if you see him, would you ask him where my new guitar strings are?"

We leave the apartment without answering. *What in the world could he have been arrested for?* I've known Kavi for several years now, and he's done some stupid things in the past, but nothing worth landing him in jail. And why *now,* when we need him?

"You're not taking this well," Tristan observes as we get back into the SUV.

"I'm pissed. It's bad enough that he got himself arrested, but then to stay in jail without getting released on bond."

"We don't know the whole story," he reminds me. "Let's go hear it from him and then judge."

I try to shelve my annoyance until I know the facts, but I remain sullen as Tristan drives us the three miles to the Douglas County Jail. We park in the visitor lot and make our way to the front desk of the jail area.

"Help you?" a desk sergeant says.

"We're here to visit a ... *prisoner*." I am embarrassed to note that I say the last word quietly. The sergeant doesn't seem to care.

"Prisoner's name?"

"Kavi Ariashi."

This gets a reaction out of the man. He gives a little half-chuckle and calls his co-worker over. "Hey, Kellogg."

Another cop walks over to the sergeant, who proceeds to whisper something in the man's ear. Considering this to be extremely rude, I choose to look into the desk sergeant's thoughts, and realize that he is whispering the words, *"They're here to see Gandhi."*

It is only through the deepest of restraint that I don't call him on it. The lawyer-bitch instinct in me is bubbling just beneath the surface. God help them if they're messing with his civil rights.

"Wait here," the sergeant says. "I'll bring him to a visiting room."

After he leaves the room, I turn to Tristan and tell him quietly, "I've got a bad feeling about this."

"We have to play it cool," he reminds me. "Even if we can't get Kavi out of here, a lot of people in Cedarsburg are going to need us very soon. So no grandstanding, okay?"

I know he's right, but I just hate injustice. "Fine."

After a few minutes of waiting, the desk sergeant pokes his head out of a nearby room and calls to us, "Visitors for Arachi?" I have to wonder if the mispronunciation is ignorance or disrespect; either is possible.

We go to him and enter the room. "You got twenty minutes," he informs us. With that, he leaves the visitation room, leaving another uniformed officer to supervise. Mercifully, it's not like what you'd see in the movies—people talking through a glass window over decades-old telephones, with sobbing women promising to stay faithful to their incarcerated thug men, while the men are hoping their visitor will flash them quickly for a cheap thrill.

Instead, the room looks like a room. There's a rectangular table in the middle with six chairs around it. And in the room is Kavi, dressed in an orange shirt and pants with a six-digit number stenciled on the lapel in black ink. Apart from the hideous outfit, he looks just like I remember him. Overcome with relief, and forgetting where I am, I rush over to him and put my arms around him. The officer quickly steps over and separates us. "That's not allowed here," he says politely but firmly. "No touching the prisoner."

He directs us to sit at the table, with Kavi nearest the officer, and Tristan and me opposite. Kavi is, understandably, surprised to see me.

"So, Bec, what are you doing here? I thought you were in Florida."

"I was. It's a long story, but I had to leave there."

"And ... umm—" He gestures toward Tristan, and I'm embarrassed to realize that I have been completely rude and overlooked the necessary introduction.

"Oh my God, I'm sorry. This is Tristan Shays. Tristan, this is Kavi Ariashi."

"How ya doin'," Tristan says.

"I'd shake your hand," Kavi replies, "but I think they'd get out the nightsticks." There is obvious contempt in his voice; whatever got him here was clearly an affront to him. "So, Bec, I repeat: what are you doing here?"

"We'll get to that in a minute. The better question is, what are *you* doing here? You've never been arrested before."

"The *charges*," he says with a sneer, "are disturbing the peace, trespassing, and resisting arrest, two of which are total bullshit."

"Which one isn't?" Tristan asks.

"The resisting arrest part," he answers quietly. "I kinda did that."

"But what happened to get you arrested in the first place?" I ask.

"Two days ago, I was doing a chase. Supercell hit just south of Lawrence. It was perfect. I had good intel on the storm's track and I was out with the chase team. We were able to track it from state highways, but then the thing took a left turn and headed through a farmer's field. And I sort of followed it."

"Kav—"

"I knew what I was doing. But then the funnel just disintegrated, blew itself out right there in that field. And there I was, with my car in the middle of this guy's just-harvested field."

"And the farmer came out," I venture.

"Yeah. With plenty to say. He called the cops as soon as he saw my car pull into his field. Then he ran out there with his shotgun in hand—talk about cliché—and told me not to move. The cops arrived, and he told them he caught a Muslim terrorist coming to destroy his farm."

"What?" I respond in disbelief.

"I made the obligatory effort to tell everyone that I was born in Ohio and I'm of Indian descent, but welcome to Kansas, where 'evolution' is a four-letter word and ethnic diversity means going out for chop suey on a Tuesday night."

"You resisted arrest?" Tristan asks.

"I was trying to explain to them that I was on a scientific mission to help protect the people of this county, and all they wanted to do was put me in handcuffs, so I kept pulling away from them until I could finish my explanation. Well, they disregarded that and added resisting arrest to the charges."

I give the matter a moment's thought. "You can probably plea bargain down to disorderly conduct, pay a fine and get off with time served, and then get this wiped from your record in a year if you stay out of trouble."

"That could work," he says.

"You've already had a bail hearing and they set a trial date, right?"

"Yeah."

"When's your trial date scheduled?" I ask.

"In five days. I'm still deciding if I want a public defender or whether I'll represent myself."

"But why won't you pay the bail and spend those five days free?"

"I'm making a statement. I'm not going to give them five hundred bucks just to walk around free when this whole arrest is a crock."

I exchange a worried glance with Tristan. The man we need by our side is one indignity away from staging a hunger strike, and he seems very well dug in. We only have one piece of ammunition, and it's time to present it.

"You asked me why we're here," I say quietly. "We're here because we need you. But we need you at your liberty, and we can't have that if you're locked up in here."

Now I have his interest. "What's so important that you came here from Florida just to see me?"

"I can't give you *all* the details here, but you have to trust that everything I'm about to tell you is true. The day after tomorrow, a tornado is going to hit Cedarsburg, an EF4 …"

He interrupts. "The Fujita score doesn't get applied until *after* the tornado hits. It's a measure of the damage inflicted. Which means that you wouldn't be able to know that number unless you had advance knowledge of the storm …"

It's my turn to interrupt. "Including exactly where and exactly when it's going to strike."

He looks in my eyes for confirmation and sees that I am serious. "Holy shit," he says. "How—?"

"That's the part we can't tell you here," Tristan answers. "But if you'll let yourself be bailed out, we can go somewhere and talk, and we'll tell you everything."

"You know *exactly* when and *exactly* where?" he says.

"To the minute and the mile," I answer.

He stands quickly. "Then what are we waiting for?" He takes a couple of steps, then stops suddenly and turns around. "Oh, umm … you wouldn't happen to have five hundred bucks on you, would you?"

Tristan just smiles and nods a little.

Outside the jail, we make our way to the parking lot and the waiting SUV. Kavi looks relieved to be free and just as glad to be rid of the orange clothing that marked him on the inside. As we were checking him out, there was obvious animosity between Kavi and his captors. I could tell without a doubt that he had been a thorn in their side since his arrest. Was it because they knew deep down that he was right? Or, more likely, was it simply a matter of having to deal with a troublemaker? Whichever it was, we have him and he's intrigued.

"Let's go somewhere and talk," Tristan proposes.

"Can it be somewhere with food?" Kavi asks. "I'm starving and jail food sucks."

"Where do you have in mind?" I ask him.

"Olympus Gyros," he says, "over on Seventeenth. I can guide you there." We arrive at the car, and he does a double take at the enormous black vehicle. "Nice car. You two aren't feds, are you?"

We drive to Olympus Gyros and select the most out-of-the-way table we can, to facilitate private conversation. Kavi orders a deluxe gyro with fries and a Greek salad. Tristan contents himself with breaded mushrooms and a plate of flaming cheese. I get the chicken shish kebabs with rice and an order of stuffed grape leaves. Once the food arrives, it's time for the explanation part of the evening.

"So," Kavi says between bites, "you want to tell me how you know exactly where, when, and how severely a storm is going to hit, and what this has to do with me?"

Tristan takes a breath, prepared to give the explanation he's given so many times already. I stop him before he can begin. "No, you've told it plenty of times. It's my turn." He nods at me and I look at Kavi and begin. "I met Tristan last week down in Florida. He came to deliver a message to me that I had to leave my job, leave Key West, and go back to Ohio. I asked him for a ride and he gave it to me. But on the way there, he kept getting messages to deliver. He warned a fisherman in Florida that his boat might sink if it wasn't repaired. He warned a man in Atlanta that someone was trying to kill him, but that man didn't listen, and he died. He warned a couple in Pennsylvania that their house was just a few hours from collapsing, and we helped them get out safely. Then he got the warning about Cedarsburg—that the tornado will hit in two days, and we have to warn as many people as we can ahead of time and get them out of there. So you see now why we need you? Your storm-chasing skills will help us to stay out of the tornado's direct path, and your background will give us credibility with the local authorities. And in exchange, you get to know where this storm will hit, and you can do all the research and testing you need to do when we're there."

Kavi has been sitting there silently during my explanation, not even biting into the gyro that he was so craving. When I finish, Tristan and I look at him for many seconds, anxiously awaiting the expected response of disbelief. What Kavi says surprises us both. "So, you're an actual honest-to-God messenger."

Now the disbelief rests on this side of the table. "Excuse me?" Tristan says.

"Where did you hear that term?" I ask him.

"From a friend of mine at KU—Jason. He's a psych major, but his focus is on parapsychology. He's been documenting case histories of people who were rescued from tragic situations before the tragedy hit. Seventeen or eighteen of these cases, and every time, they talked about a stranger coming to see them beforehand and warning them not to do something that would have caused the catastrophe. A few of them described these people as angels, but every time they were described as having human form and human mannerisms. The word that kept cropping up was *messengers.* Jason's been waiting a long time to actually meet one, but he's never been there at the right time and place. And now here you are. Would you be willing to talk with him?"

I'm floored by our luck. Finally, after all of his assignments, someone might have some answers for him about why he was chosen for this task. "Yeah," he says, "I suppose so."

"You suppose so?" I respond. "This could be big. This could give you the answers you've wanted for so long."

"I know," he says quietly. "And I do want to talk to him, to learn everything I can. At the moment, my mind is on this assignment, and it's hard for me to concentrate on anything else until it's done."

"That makes sense," Kavi says. "We should wait until after Cedarsburg. If this thing is hitting the day after tomorrow, we've got a lot of work to do between now and then. We shouldn't do anything tonight as far as notifying anyone there, because it's likely that the supercell hasn't even formed yet, and there'd be no way we could know it was coming."

I give Tristan a proud little smile; those words sound awfully familiar.

"Tomorrow morning, we need to head into the meteorology lab," Kavi continues. "I want to check radar and get readings for about 300 miles to the west. Maybe if we're supremely lucky, we can even use Tiny."

"Tiny?" Tristan asks.

"The university's tornado observation vehicle. Built like a tank. Best place to be when a storm is nearby."

"Forgive my ignorance," Tristan says, "but storm-chasing. What's the goal? What do you get out of it and what do others get out of it?"

"Well, a lot of people are amateurs, in it for the thrill of the chase. They don't know what they're doing; they just go out during tornado season and hope to get lucky. They try to get as close to the funnel as they can, and they take pictures or video. Some of them sell the video to local news stations; make a few bucks doing it. I've provided some video to news programs myself, but that's not my primary goal. I have university backing and support, so I'm in it for the science. A lot of the chasers you see on TV and in movies are always trying to get ahead of the storms and release sensors into the funnel to take readings. Well, that's great, and it makes for good TV, but guess what? They've succeeded, and they've gotten about all the data they can get from inside a tornado, short of exactly how it gets you to Oz. Me, I've got a different goal. I've watched dozens of tornadoes die. Just fizzle out of existence when you think they're about to wreak more havoc. And I want to help them do that."

"How's that again?" I ask.

"Everybody else out there is looking to make a breakthrough in early-warning systems, giving cities more time to prepare for an oncoming tornado. I want to figure out the precise atmospheric conditions that lead to the dissipation of an existing funnel cloud and try to find a way to recreate those conditions artificially. Create a weapon, if you will, to blast a tornado out of existence minutes before it would naturally dissipate."

He returns to his gyro as Tristan and I contemplate the implications of what his success could mean. "Shit," I say quietly. "That's pretty exciting. Do you … do you think it could work?"

"Sure I think it could work. Otherwise I wouldn't be doing it."

"Are you close to succeeding?" Tristan asks.

"There's the problem," he replies. "In order to succeed, I have to be there precisely in front of the funnel cloud, especially at the moment when it dissolves. That's why I was in that farmer's field two days ago. I had some equipment with me and I was taking as many readings as I could."

"And that equipment did nothing to keep you from looking like a terrorist," I tease. "You scary, brown-skinned person you."

"Exactly. You may not know this, but Kansas is not exactly crawling with Indians. Not my flavor of Indian, anyway."

"But didn't he kind of figure something was up when a tornado came tearing ass through his field?"

"He probably thought I created it with my evil terrorist weapons. This state has its head so far up its own ass, it can spit and give itself an enema."

I look over at Tristan, who was poised to take a bite but stopped short at the mental image.

"Sorry," Kavi offers. "Subtlety isn't one of my strong points."

"So the Cedarsburg twister could be a dream come true for you," I suggest.

"It could do wonders to further my research, yeah. What time is it supposed to hit town?"

"At 4:06 PM," Tristan replies.

"Any idea how long it'll be active?"

"Not exactly. I know the path it'll take through Cedarsburg, and given the size of the town, it could be active for fifteen minutes or longer."

"That's enough time to get some significant data. That trajectory is going to be very important. I don't have a mobile Doppler unit, so I'd be at a disadvantage."

"This *tank* thing," Tristan says, gently ill at ease. "Do we have to be in it with you?"

"No. Not unless you want to be. The way I understand it, you're there to warn people, help them get out of town. You can be in your SUV, and I can be inside Tiny with my team. We'll keep in contact through cell phones and walkie-talkies. Bec, you want to ride with me in Tiny?"

I don't know what to say. It sounds like an amazing opportunity, but the reality of being that close to a funnel cloud scares me more than I want to admit to him. "I'll let you know," I answer.

"We'll need to start pretty early tomorrow morning," Kavi says. "Do you two have a place to stay tonight?"

"Not yet," Tristan says, "but it looks like there are plenty of options."

"You could stay with me," he offers.

"That's very kind," Tristan replies, "but we couldn't put you out."

"Oh, it's no trouble. You could use Riley's room and Riley can sleep on the couch. Most nights, he falls asleep there anyway. Some days, too."

Suddenly a hotel sounds pretty good to me too. "Thanks all the same, Kav, but we'll be fine at a hotel. We can take you home first and then meet up again for breakfast in the morning before we get started." I suddenly remember. "Shit, you don't have classes that you have to go to tomorrow, do you?"

He gives a dismissive little wave of his hand. "I was planning on being in jail anyway. This is much more interesting."

Thirty minutes later, we drop Kavi back off at home, going back into the apartment with him to say our good-byes for the night. When we enter, Riley looks genuinely surprised to see his roommate. "Dude, I thought you were in jail!"

"I was, man. I decided to fight the system from without, instead of within."

"Cool," Riley responds, still clearly enjoying the buzz of the evening. "Oh, hey, two people were here earlier looking for you. They didn't leave their names, I don't think, but I told them where you were. I hope that's okay."

Tristan and I look at each other in disbelief. Kavi looks at me and signals the question, "You two?" I nod, and he gives a knowing look.

"That's fine, Riley," Kavi tells him. "I'm sure they'll call back eventually."

I turn to face my old friend. "We're heading out."

"Okay. Thanks for, you know, springing me."

"We need you there," Tristan tells him.

"And I'll get the 500 to you after the hearing."

"It's fine. We know where you live. Which is more than I can say for your roommate at the moment."

"He's just rockin' the ganj right now," Kavi says. "He'll sleep it off and be slightly less disoriented tomorrow."

"See you here at eight in the morning," I confirm.

"I'll be here."

Tristan and I make our way back to the car and find a hotel about a mile away, the Admiral Benbow. "Funny name," I observe as we pull in.

"It's a classic," he tells me. "*Treasure Island*. It was the inn where young Jim worked before he set sail."

"Never read it." I realize that this is an aspect of his life that I know very little about. "So, you were a college boy, then?"

"Harvard," he says with no fuss or immodesty. "Bachelor's in economics."

"No MBA to follow it up?" I ask, teasing only a little.

"Thought about it, but didn't want to invest the time. Quite honestly, I didn't know what I wanted to do with it."

"Still, Harvard. So you're super-smart, then?"

"Couldn't you tell by all my stunning discourse over the last four days?"

"Naturally, but I didn't want to presume."

We park outside the main office. "I'll go get us a room," he says, opening his door.

"Wait," I say. "I want to get this one."

"You know you don't have to."

"I know, but I want to. You've paid for so much already, and I can afford it. So if you don't mind, I'd like to buy tonight."

"Okay," he replies with a smile, "but if you think this means you can take advantage of me sexually, you're probably right."

The place is clean and bright, and not terribly pricey. After all, it's Lawrence, Kansas. A little more laid-back than the big city. We get a room on the first floor and bring our things inside. The king-sized bed looks very comfortable and inviting. We've decided that we're past the "two queens" phase. We can share a room, we can share a bed. Though secretly, I'm hoping that his desires don't run toward the romantic tonight, because I'm damn tired. Considering that I woke up this morning in a hospital bed after a night of fighting off exhaustion, sleep is what I truly need now. I don't want to hurt his feelings, since our relationship is so young and uncertain, but I don't know how amorous I could be for him right now.

We put our bags down and he walks over to me, wrapping his arms around me. I dissolve into his embrace, feeling the strength and comfort of him and breathing in the scent of him, a scent that seems to change each day to match things that I crave—favorite foods or aromas from pleasant childhood memories. I don't know how he does it; I don't think he wears cologne or anything like that. But tonight—right now—I'd swear he smells like warm sugar cream pie.

I pull back after many blissful seconds and look him in the eyes, seeing so much affection there. We both look like we have something we want to say, but neither wants to go first. He breaks the silence tenuously. "I have something to ask you, but I don't want you to feel bad or get the wrong idea."

"Just ask me."

"Would you mind too terribly if we just went to sleep tonight? I'm so tired."

I have to physically stop myself from emitting a relieved laugh, lest he think I'm laughing at his request. "That's fine, Tristan. It's been a hell of a day, and I think the most wonderful thing in the world would be if you would hold me close to you while we fall asleep together."

"I'd like that very much," he responds with a smile.

Following much-needed and very relaxing showers, we strip down and climb between the blissful coolness of clean hotel sheets. He stretches out on his back, and I burrow myself into his shoulder, pulling my body tight to his.

"God, I'm wiped," he says.

"Me too. I really hope we can get some decent sleep tonight."

"The way I feel, I don't anticipate any trouble with that."

"What do you think we'll be able to accomplish tomorrow?" I ask.

"The big thing is giving the authorities in Cedarsburg some advance warning. Apart from that, it'll be a good chance for your friend to do some calculations about this tornado. We know when and where it's going to hit, but not for how long. If he can help get rid of it sooner, that'll mean less damage."

"Tristan ... what Kavi said earlier about his friend Jason and his research— Do you think you'll talk to him about what you've been through?"

"I don't know. I guess. He certainly sounds like a good resource. And what Kavi was describing sounds like what I've been through."

"Maybe he can help you," I suggest.

"How do you mean?"

"Help you to understand why it happens. How it happens."

"I'm not sure that would help me much," he says. "Rebecca, I know that what I do seems heroic and exciting to you, and I'm very glad you're with me now. It's just, right now, I'd give almost anything never to get another assignment again."

Chapter 3

Tristan's announcement doesn't surprise me. I know how much pain he goes through when each new assignment arrives, and I know that the past two years have disrupted his entire life, leaving him at the mercy of forces he doesn't even understand. I'm a little disappointed to hear it, mostly for selfish reasons. Being here with him is a tremendous high for me, and I want him to share in my enthusiasm. But I can't force him to feel that way, and I won't. Maybe if we can save all those lives in Cedarsburg, it will bolster him. It's that hope that sustains me as I let sleep carry me away for the night.

Seven hours later, I awaken to daylight filtering in through the drapes. Another new day, another new town. I'm not sure how he does it day after day. I look over and see that Tristan is still asleep. He must be dreaming; his eyes are moving and he's making muffled sounds. *What does he dream about?*

It takes me about four seconds to remember that I don't have to confine that thought to wonder and speculation. With the slightest effort, I can visit his dreams. It is a supreme invasion of privacy, I know, but it is an amazing opportunity. But just because I can, does that mean that I should? And yet I don't want to be invasive.

Just this once. He probably won't even know I'm there. I close my eyes and open myself up to his thoughts.

Remarkable—that's the only word to describe it. Entering his dream is like stepping into a room, right through the wall. I see him there, standing in a haze, like a smoky mist. His back is to me, and he's watching something in the distance. I take a step closer and he turns to face me, clearly very surprised to see me. "What are you doing here?" he asks. "It isn't safe."

"I had to see," I tell him apologetically. "I had to know for myself." As I step closer, I see a house on fire in the distance.

"They wouldn't listen," he says. "And she's still in there."

"Who? Who's still in there?"

"Sara. She's only eight, and she's all alone. I have to go in after her."

The look on his face breaks my heart. Even in his dreams, he can't stop. He's always on a mission. I want so much to hold him, to give him the peace that even sleep won't. "You don't have to," I say quietly.

"How can you say that? I can't leave her in there to die!"

"Tristan, it's not real."

Disappointment darkens his features. "I thought you of all people would understand."

That's when it hits me: he doesn't know the dream isn't real. For him, this is actually happening, just as it must every time he goes to sleep. I have to help him. At least I know I'm not in any real danger.

I hope.

"Let's go then," I say, taking a few steps toward the burning house.

"You can't just go—"

"Hell I can't! Keep up if you can."

With that, I sprint to the house. I can feel the heat, smell the acrid smoke. I hear a young girl sobbing in an upstairs room. Though I am perfectly aware that I am in someone's dream, every aspect of it feels perfectly real. I try to concentrate and accomplish what we came to do.

"Sara!" he calls out. "Can you hear me?"

A child's voice calls, "I'm in my room. I can't get out!"

"We're coming to get you," I add. "Stay where you are. Keep talking so we can find you."

"I'm upstairs," she says. "I'm upstairs. Please hurry."

The fire is on both floors of the building, but the staircase is solid and intact. We rush up the stairs, following the sound of the girl's voice as she repeats, "Please hurry, please hurry!"

The sensation is unlike anything I've ever felt before. Every one of my senses is filled with the reality of Tristan's dream world. I can feel the adrenaline rushing through me, though my conscious mind knows my physical body is lying safely in a bed in a hotel room in Lawrence, Kansas. I see everything he sees; I hear every sound. It makes me wonder—if he were to awaken suddenly, where would it leave me?

With Tristan close behind me, I reach the top of the stairs, following Sara's cries until I find her room. The upstairs corridor is filled with smoke; instinctively, I crouch, staying low, despite the knowledge that it can't hurt me. Tristan follows suit, not blessed with the same knowledge. To him, this is another assignment; perhaps one from his past, maybe even one from his future. *Could this be his training ground for an assignment yet to come?* There isn't time to speculate. I make it to the child's bedroom door and try to push it open; it won't budge.

"Something's blocking the door," I tell Tristan.

"Let's work on it together," he says. Shielding our faces with our clothing, we stand and team up against the door. Time and again, we shove against it with our shoulders. I feel the pain as it resists. On the fifth try, the object against the door moves aside and the door opens. Inside, the room is filled with dark smoke, courtesy of the window curtains that have ignited. I see the chair that was blocking our entrance, and for a moment I wonder how it got there. Then I remember that this is a dream, and the rules of how things happen don't always apply. Sometimes obstacles happen for dramatic tension.

I look across the room and see young Sara taking cover under her bed. I'm startled by her appearance, because for reasons I don't understand, it changes. She becomes several different children—probably standing in for the many Tristan has been called upon to help in the past. I have to wonder if he sees her the same way.

He kneels and calls to her. "We'll get you out of here. Come to me."

The terrified child scurries out of her hiding place and goes right to him. "Let's go," he says to me. With that, we make our way swiftly down the stairs, seconds before the staircase collapses. The front door to the house is in sight, and we're running for it. Though it's less than fifteen feet away, the physics of the dream take over, and suddenly, no amount of running gets us there. Impossibly, it recedes into the distance, placing foot after foot of smoke-filled room between us and safety. It is Tristan's anxiety and frustration kicking in, and it isn't helping anything. But maybe I can manipulate it.

"Focus on the door," I tell him. "Picture us getting to it."

It works, and the anomaly disappears. We're out the door in a matter of seconds, into cool night air.

With a start, Tristan opens his eyes in the hotel room and looks right at me. I sit up in bed and offer a gentle, comforting smile. "You were there," he says in disbelief. I nod in confirmation. "How?"

"I wanted to see your dreams."

"This shouldn't be possible."

"A lot of things we've been through shouldn't be possible," I remind him. "We're rewriting the rules every day."

The last part of what I said appears to be lost on him. I watch as he stares intently at my face—not in the way a man does when he's with the woman he loves, but in the way a man does when the woman he loves has something on her face that shouldn't be there. I try not to worry as he licks two of his fingers and reaches out to me. His fingers feel cold and wet as he rubs them against my right cheek.

"What?" I finally ask him. "What's there?"

He stares at his fingers for a few seconds, then looks at me in disbelief as he turns them to show me. The fingers are coated in a deep black powder. "It's soot," he says quietly.

Now it's my turn for stunned silence. I stare at the physical evidence before me, and many seconds later, I reach out to take some of the soot from his hand. It feels gritty on my fingers. "This shouldn't be possible," I say in response.

"You saw what I saw," he says. "You were there, by my side, communicating with me."

"I know. I saw the house, the fire. We rescued the girl together."

"Only," he says, holding up his fingers, "you brought some of it back with you. We're treading on dangerous ground with this. I don't think you should be visiting my dreams. Not until we know what's happening, and how you did this."

"I'm sorry."

"It's all right. Just be careful. What time is it?"

"Almost 7:00," I answer.

"We should get up. Lots to do today." He sniffs the air. "Take a shower first. I can smell the smoke on you."

The shower feels good, but as I let the water rain down on me, all I can think about is how it came to be that I carried the soot and smoke with me from out of a dream that wasn't even mine. I think I need to meet Kavi's friend Jason and ask him what he thinks of it.

Soon we are both dressed and out of the hotel. The ride over to Kavi's apartment is fairly quiet, right up to the moment when we park in front. Then Tristan says to me, "Don't say anything to him about what happened this morning."

"Okay." But then I have to know. "Are you mad at me for what I did?"

He hesitates before answering. *Does he have to think about it or is he trying to find a gentle way to say yes?* "It's just going to take some getting used to, that's all. I know that nothing about our situation is normal. I'm just … adjusting. So I'll need you to be patient with me. And I'll be as patient as I can too. We've got a lot to accomplish today, so I think the best thing to do is to focus on Cedarsburg."

All I can do is nod. I really *do* want to talk about this, about the shared dream and what it means, and about the level of intimacy that comes from knowing your partner's thoughts. I want to say something to make him realize that I'm not a nosy bitch who spends her every waking moment poking around in his brain. But those words aren't coming. Not at the moment anyway.

Kavi opens the door to his apartment at this awkward moment and greets us with genuine enthusiasm coursing through him. "Hey there, you two. Who's ready for some fun with the weather?"

"You're awfully upbeat this morning," I observe.

"Thrill of the chase, my dear. Thrill of the chase. Usually, nature has the upper hand, but this time around, it's Ariashi one, nature zero. And I don't know about you, but I am craving the shit out of pancakes this morning."

We climb back into the Yukon and make the short trek to the local pancake house, where Kavi satisfies his craving. Tristan settles for coffee and a bagel, and remains quiet in his seat. I want to ask him what's wrong, but with Kavi sitting there, it would be awkward. Forgetting myself, I start to reach into his mind, then very firmly stop myself, realizing that it's this very inclination that probably has set him off. The temptation is just so great, every time he keeps his thoughts to himself. And he's done that so much since the run-in with my father. *Am I that insecure that I have to know what he's thinking all the time? Do I care that little for his privacy and his feelings?* It troubles me deeply to know how close to *yes* my answer is to both those questions.

I distract myself from these thoughts by talking to Kavi. "Do we have a plan for the day?"

"Well," he says, indulging in his short stack, "it starts at the lab, where we'll check the radar, check with NOAA for any existing watches and warnings for the area. After that, I'll put together a chase team and try to sign out the encounter vehicle."

"Are you going to tell the other members of the team how you know what you know?" I ask him.

"Probably not a good idea. I've been known to follow hunches before, so they trust my instincts. Besides, about 75 percent of a chaser's work is spent on false alarms and wild geese. I should have no problem getting them to follow me to Cedarsburg tomorrow. The hard part is going to be keeping them from starting the chase today."

Tristan breaks his silence. "What if we do start it today? Think about it. Our goal is to stop the destruction of Cedarsburg tomorrow. What better way than to keep the tornado from ever coming there in the first place? You said you're working on a way to dissipate funnel clouds. Let's meet this thing out in the middle of nowhere and blast it to hell before it comes anywhere near the town."

"The key words in this equation are *working on*. I'm still a long way from being able to point a ray gun at a twister and banish it to the nether worlds. It's going to take a very specific set of precise measurements before I know the exact atmospheric conditions that lead to dissipation. That's why tomorrow's storm is so important. I get to be there at the moment it forms, track it as it makes its way through town, and be there as it dissipates. I'll be taking readings constantly, and I'll have amazing data to analyze when this is over."

Tristan looks disturbed and disappointed. "But the whole reason we need you with us is to keep the town of Cedarsburg safe. You have the tools to protect the town."

"I have the tools to help protect the *people*," he corrects. "Early detection and warning will give them a chance to get to safety. But nothing you, I, or anybody can do will stop that tornado from making its way through the town. A big portion of Cedarsburg, Kansas is going to die tomorrow. We're here to make sure 11,000 people don't die with it."

The disappointment and dismay are etched into Tristan's face. Beyond warning the residents of Cedarsburg, he must have allowed himself to contemplate the possibility of preventing the tornado altogether. Kavi's being realistic, which is what we need in all of this. I only hope that realism doesn't stand in the way of Tristan's ability to complete his assignment.

Forty minutes later, we arrive at the University of Kansas Atmospheric Science and Meteorology Lab on campus. Kavi escorts us in past throngs of students and professors. I'm feeling a definite twinge of longing, being back on a college campus; the sights, sounds, and even the smells are all so familiar. This wasn't my school, but it's a school, and the excitement I felt at the prospect of returning to college, followed by the letdown when it got taken away, is welling up inside of me, making it very hard to concentrate on thunderstorms and funnel clouds.

Kavi, by contrast, is entirely on task, knowing exactly where he wants to be. He leads us to a computer terminal that's already turned on and displaying a Pulse-Doppler radar image of the Lawrence area. Tristan and I watch from behind him as he visits screen after screen, showing first the immediate area, then pulling out to the whole state and then the Midwest. The screens begin to fill with color, first greens, then blues, yellows, and reds. Kavi's face is rapt, focused intently on the images. He is silent at first, but as each new image appears, he gets more and more vocal. "Oh, baby, this is a live one," he says.

"What do you see?" Tristan asks.

"Take a look at NEXRAD," he replies. "It's a classic. Textbook case. High-pressure system meets low-pressure system. You see these images here? Cumulonimbus clouds with large-scale rotation. That indicates rear-flank downdraft and mesocyclonic activity."

"English, please," I request.

"Okay, look here. See the area of bright green adjacent to the area of bright red? Those indicate imminent tornadic activity. It's called a tornado vortex signature. The storm to our west is big and it's heading this way."

"Tell me this," Tristan says, "is it imminent enough that we can call the authorities in Cedarsburg today and not sound like we're talking out of our asses?"

Kavi thinks a moment, checks his screen, thinks some more. "If we present it right. If we go in there, guns blazing, and tell them to get out now, we sound like the boy who cried wolf. Remember, this is Tornado Alley. Eight months out of the year, these people live their lives on yellow alert."

"I don't understand," Tristan says. "That should make it easier to convince them."

"In theory, yes. In practice, no. Damn near every house in this region that isn't on wheels has a basement or a storm cellar. Tornado warnings come, and people are trained to head to those shelters almost by instinct. Which is fine if an EF1 or 2 comes through. But tomorrow's storm is going to be a 4."

"How bad is the damage from that?" I ask.

"I'll show you," he replies. With a few mouse clicks, he navigates to a folder called Storm Damage, and a subfolder called EF4. Inside is a gallery of horrors. Picture after picture shows neighborhoods, towns, and cities after an EF4 has passed through. It looks like photos of a war zone. Entire buildings lifted off their foundations; others splintered and scattered. Every now and then, a single room in a house is spared, almost as if the tornado had a sick sense of humor. But everywhere I look, the devastation is total.

"Holy shit," I say without thinking.

"So you see, even if people go to their storm cellars, there's a greater risk of death or severe injury. We have to try to convince people to get out of town, even for the day; go north or south of there. They'll lose their homes, but they'll be much more likely to survive."

"Okay," Tristan says, "so what do we do?"

Kavi returns to the Internet. "Let me get the phone number for Cedarsburg's police department. We don't want to use 911 at this stage, but we want to talk to someone in charge. Here it is, here's the number. The chief of police is named Carl Haversham."

"Great. You ready to give him a call?"

Kavi hesitates. "Uhh—well …"

"Well what?" I say. "You're the one with the knowledge and the credentials. It should come from you."

"That's lovely," he says, "but you forget that until last night, I was in jail. Local jurisdictions have access to that information. With the things I was charged with, all that chief of police would have to do is run my name, and we'd lose any hope of convincing him that this is legit."

"So what do we do?" Tristan asks.

"One of you should make the call."

"Us? What would we say?"

"All right," Kavi says, "we can do this. We'll go to a private room and get on speakerphone, so I can hear everything that's said. I'll tell you what to say. When you call, use this name." He writes it down.

Tristan looks at it. "Charles …"

"Shhh, don't say it here. The way to make this work is to sell it. The more we believe it, the more they'll believe it. Are you ready?"

"I guess so," Tristan says.

Kavi spends a few minutes giving us the basics of what to say and what not to say. After that, we move to an empty office with a telephone and close the door behind us. Tristan takes a deep breath and prepares to make the call. Kavi hits the speakerphone button, gets an outside line, and dials the number for the Cedarsburg Police Department. It rings twice, and a woman's voice answers, "Cedarsburg Police, may I help you?"

"Good morning," Tristan says. "This is Professor Charles Comstock, head of the department of atmospheric science and meteorology at the University of Kansas. May I speak to Chief Haversham, please?"

"One moment, please."

We hear hold music, which strikes me as unexpected while calling the police. It's so generic, too. They could at least have theme music, like "Wanted Dead or Alive" or something like that. I let that thought amuse me for the brief period before the music ends and an older man's voice comes on the line.

"This is Carl Haversham. What can I do for you, Professor?"

"Well, sir, I wanted to call you today to let you know that our team here has been tracking a supercell due west of your location that's showing persistent activity. We're watching its speed and projected path, and it appears to be on course to impact Cedarsburg tomorrow afternoon."

Kavi smiles and gives the thumbs-up sign. Tristan sounds convincing.

"We saw that storm off to the west," Haversham says, "but we were hoping it would peter out before it gets too close to us. You're thinking it's likely to remain strong?"

Tristan looks to Kavi for what to say, then repeats the words that Kavi whispers: "It's a stalled front with plenty of hook echoes. There's always a chance it could lose strength, but for safety's sake, I think it would be wise to let the people know that this might be coming their way."

"We've got the tornado sirens, of course. In the past, we've given folks a good five to ten minutes to take shelter."

Straying from Kavi's prompting, Tristan continues on his own. "That may not be enough, Chief. I'm wondering what would be involved with organizing an evacuation of the town."

"Evacuation?" he repeats, sounding surprised. "That's quite a tall order. How much wind are we talking about?"

"If our projections are correct, it could be upwards of 150 miles per hour."

"Well, that's … that's definitely serious, you're right. But still, an evacuation. These people have stayed put through some rough stuff. A lot of them are older; been here a lot of years. They won't be too keen on abandoning ship."

"Even for a day," Tristan says. "If there's a way to encourage them to leave town tomorrow for just one day. Please, Chief Haversham, I know this sounds drastic, but with this magnitude of a storm, if it hits Cedarsburg directly, the loss of life could be significant, even with people in storm shelters."

"I'll see what I can do," he says. "But I can't guarantee anything. People tend to dig in when it comes to their home."

"I'm sending a team of experts to you tomorrow morning," Tristan tells him. "Will you be available to meet with them?"

"I'll be here. Maybe when they see you arrive, they'll take the threat seriously."

"I sincerely hope so, Chief. Our goal is to protect the lives of your citizens."

"I appreciate that. We'll see you tomorrow."

Kavi ends the call, remarking, "That went as well as can be expected. We gave him something to think about, and he doesn't think we're kooks."

"But wait a minute," Tristan says. "What happens when I show up there tomorrow with this voice and I'm not Professor Charles Whatsisname?"

"It was a speakerphone call," he replies. "Nobody sounds the same in person. Besides, by the time we get there, we'll all have plenty to keep him occupied."

"And why didn't we just have the real Professor Charles Whatsisname make the call?"

"Oh, he can't be bothered with something like that. I've just found it's easier to impersonate him in situations like this. Come on."

Kavi leads us back to the lab, where a small group of students is working. He calls out to them. "Can I have your attention, please? The NEXRAD team is tracking an active system 220 miles to the west that's likely to produce tornadoes in the area of Cedarsburg tomorrow. I'm looking for a chase team to accompany me and help me take readings for Project Wind Shear. Do I have any volunteers?"

Three hands go up. Kavi smiles in appreciation; these are clearly people he knows and trusts. A young woman asks him, "Will we get to use Tiny?"

"I'll clear it with Comstock today," Kavi says. "But with the intel we have, conditions are very favorable for a close-range encounter, so I suspect our dear professor will let us take Tiny with us." This news invigorates the chase team. "I'll also need a spotter vehicle. We have two guests with us for this chase. This is Dr. Tristan Shays and his assistant, Miss Rebecca Traeger. They're experts in early detection and tracking of storms, so they're taking point on this chase. The team will report to me, and I will report to them. Tristan and Rebecca, this is your team for tomorrow—Paul, Shafiq, and Delia."

The team gives us a wave. I feel very official. And I try very hard not to laugh at the "Doctor" part. The students are all about my age, but there's a look to them—it's like a hunger for knowledge and experience, and it makes me feel good about having them with us.

"Doctor Shays," Kavi says, "would you like to address your team?"

Tristan steps forward and takes a moment to decide what to say. "Thank you, first of all, for volunteering for this assignment. As Kavi said, we're working off of good information about the storm system's track. At present, it's in largely unpopulated farming areas, but tomorrow afternoon, we have reason to believe that it will hit the town of Cedarsburg with considerable force. You'll be free to conduct scientific study and take any readings you wish. Miss Traeger and I are going to be working with local authorities to help get as many people to safety as possible. It's why we're in this region, to see how effective the early detection and tracking is at saving lives. I think it's important to mention that there's a degree of risk to this operation. The storm system we're tracking has very high winds and the potential for devastating damage. We'll do everything we can to safeguard the members of the team, but there's still the possibility of injury or worse. If you would rather not be a part of it, please tell us now, and you'll be excused with no questions asked."

The team members look to each other as Tristan makes his announcement. They share a moment, a decision. Then Paul says, "All part of the chase. We're in."

As the chase team returns to what they were doing, the three of us huddle up. "So what now?" I ask.

"We could call it a day," Kavi suggests.

"It's 10:15 in the morning," Tristan reminds him. "I think we have time for a field trip."

"Cedarsburg?" I ask.

"Exactly. When we get there tomorrow, I don't want to waste a minute figuring out where everything is. I want to hit town and immediately start evacuation efforts. So today is all about recon. We go there, we look around. We see where the police station is, where the fire station is. We pay attention to all roads out of town. Gather as much information as we can about the place, and make extensive notes. You two with me?"

"Hell, yeah," I answer.

"Good to go, boss," Kavi adds.

Armed with pens and paper, we pile into the Yukon for the trek west. Kavi estimates it'll take us almost two hours to get there in good weather. We pay close attention to the distance, the directions, and any alternate routes, in case they're needed. Tristan is at the wheel, of course, with Kavi riding shotgun. This leaves me the spacious back seat. It takes a little while for us to loosen up and shake off the tension of the morning, but within a half hour, Kavi and Tristan are sharing what I might almost call camaraderie.

"Is he a TV actor?" Kavi asks.

"Yes," Tristan replies.

"Is he on TV now?"

"No."

Inspiration lights Kavi's face. "Is it Pernell Roberts?"

In a moment I'll remember for years to come, Tristan gets a look of sheer delight, and actually high-fives him. "Yes! Well played, sir. Well played."

"It's all about knowing the right questions to ask. Guess that means I'm up. Rebecca, you sure I can't lure you into the game?"

"I wouldn't," Tristan warns. "Word to the wise—she cheats."

I reach up and slap him gently on the side of his head. "Eat me. I don't cheat."

"That's not how I remember it," he teases, clearly trying to get a rise out of me. "Go ahead, try her. See how many questions it takes her."

"Okay," Kavi says, thinking a moment. "It's a place."

I sigh and give in to this exercise. "Is it in Europe?" I ask, already knowing the answer.

"Yes," Kavi answers.

"Is it Montenegro?"

He actually looks cute with his mouth open and his eyes wide. Tristan is loving it. "Do another one," he prompts.

"It's a person this time," Kavi says.

43

"Is it a woman?" I ask.

"Yes."

"Madame Curie."

Now he's looking for a scientific explanation. "It's a historical site."

"Arlington National Cemetery."

"Person."

"Who the hell is Meadowlark Lemon?" I ask.

"How are you doing this?" he asks me.

"I'm not sure," I answer honestly. "I just realized a few days ago that I can do it, and I can't do it all the time. But I guess I can with you."

He's smiling now, a look of amazement all over him. He turns to Tristan. "So you can see the future." Then to me. "And you can read minds. Damn, I want a superpower too!"

"Cute."

"I see why twenty questions with you would get old pretty fast. So, you can read my thoughts, then?"

"It's easiest when you're focused on what you're thinking, like the answers to those questions. I can't read your general stream of consciousness."

Tristan interrupts. "I think it's important that we stay focused now. There'll be time to talk about this after we do what we need to do in Cedarsburg."

"Sure, sure," Kavi replies. "I'm just thinking of ways we might be able to use this to our advantage tomorrow. If knowing the thoughts of the people we're trying to help could allow us to work better."

"Come up with anything?" I ask.

"Not yet, but I'll let you know."

The miles pass and I watch the weather. There are a few clouds, but the sky is blue and the winds are calm. Knowing what's coming, it feels deceptive. I think back to the pictures Kavi showed us of EF4 tornado damage and I picture the landscape outside devastated. Suddenly, everything we have to do feels monumentally important and I feel like my actions in the next day will make an enormous difference to the people of this town.

We pull in to Cedarsburg just before noon. I can't say the town is beautiful, because it isn't. Like so many of the towns we've passed through, it's just … *there.* It's a nondescript cluster of homes on the outskirts, followed by a downtown area that's made up of little stores and businesses, dotted with the occasional fast-food place or chain store. It's the kind of place that annoys you on long road trips, because it's totally irrelevant to you, and yet you have to slow down to fifty, then forty, then twenty-five, just trying to get through it as soon as you can and be on your way. And yet, for the next thirty hours, this town and the eleven thousand people in it are going to be extremely relevant to my life. Just as we will be to theirs.

"There's a diner up ahead there," I say, pointing to the right. "I think we should stop in and meet a few people."

"I thought we were being low-impact on this trip," Tristan says.

"Low-impact doesn't mean no-impact," I retort. "Pull us over. We should do this."

He finds a parking spot in front, which isn't difficult here in the land of ample parking. Main Street (and I'm actually amused to note that it's actually called Main Street) is starting to get busy in its small-town way. Retirees are visiting the shops, and businesspeople are making their way out to lunch, including at our destination, the Cornflower Café. The place is adorable, and as I look at it, I catch a quick grimace on Tristan's face and realize that he must be doing the same thing I'm doing: trying very hard not to picture it in ruin tomorrow afternoon.

We enter and I lead us to the counter to find three seats. Tables are for isolation; the counter is where you talk to people. The boys look puzzled at first, but before long, they catch on to what I'm thinking and sit with me. A waitress approaches, a woman in her fifties with graying hair, a little too much makeup, and earrings shaped like panda bears. She pours us each a glass of ice water as she greets us. "Welcome to the Cornflower. I'm CJ. I'll be taking care of you. Don't think I've seen you three around here." She says it pleasantly enough, not with a *"what're y'all doin' in our town"* darkness to it.

"We're from Lawrence, from the university," Tristan explains. "Here for a couple of days to do some field research."

"Well," she says pleasantly, "we got plenty of fields. You studying the farmland?"

"The weather, actually," Kavi answers. "We're doing some storm studies."

"Heck," she says, "you oughta be out in Hays today. Way I hear it, they're getting hit with quite a storm. Might even see some tornadoes before the day's out."

"Actually," Tristan says, "the system that's in Hays right now is supposed to make its way here tomorrow. That's why we're here, to watch it approach."

"What're they callin' for?" CJ asks.

"It's still pretty far away," Kavi says cautiously, "but, uh—it's a powerful system. Not showing any signs of letting up. We'll see some heavy rain, probably some hail. Maybe some tornado activity."

"We get a lot of warnings around here," she says. "Then it blows through or it blows over."

"But what would you do if a big one hit?" Tristan asks. "Right in town?"

CJ suddenly gets quiet and serious. "We do what we always do. We go underground to safety, and then we get on with our lives." She looks intently at him. "You know something, don't you? Something that's coming here tomorrow?"

"Yes."

"Come with me," she says. "All three of you. We need to talk about this."

She leads us to a back room in the café and speaks to us in hushed tones. "I had a dream last night that something was going to happen here tomorrow. It was bad—a strong storm. Houses got knocked down, people got killed. My daughter's house caught fire, and my granddaughter was trapped inside."

Tristan and I share a knowing look. "Your granddaughter?" I ask. "How old is she?"

"Sara's only eight."

A penetrating chill sweeps through me, and I am on the verge of an audible gasp. I look to Tristan, and a single thought rushes from his mind to mine: *Say nothing.*

"CJ," Tristan says, "the tracking system we have is very good, very accurate, and you're right. We have every reason to believe that a tornado, a powerful one, will come right through Cedarsburg tomorrow afternoon. We're here to help save people's lives, but we don't want to start a panic. What would it take to get people to leave town for the day?"

She looks stunned. "We've never evacuated. Everybody's got storm cellars; we always figured it'd be enough. But getting everyone out? There's 11,000 of us."

"We know," Kavi said. "But if this storm is as strong as we expect it to be, cellars will only provide limited protection."

"We're strangers here," I tell her, "but you know these people. You know this town. They'll listen to you where they might not listen to us."

"I'll need some time," she says, sounding frightened. "I have to figure this out, find a way to get the word out."

"We're going to do some scouting work today," Tristan says. "Drive the streets of town, see what our options are. Then we'll go back to Lawrence and get our gear together for tomorrow. We plan to be back here with a team of meteorologists tomorrow late morning. That will give us a few hours before the storm hits. Is there a phone number you can give us where we can reach you tomorrow?"

She writes it down on a guest check and hands it to him. Tristan smiles reassuringly at her. "Thank you, CJ. You may just be the biggest hero this town will ever know. With your help, we can save a lot of people tomorrow."

She is on the verge of tears. "I just don't want anything to happen to my family. I know that sounds terrible and selfish, but they're all I've got."

"Tell them what's coming. Encourage them to leave town tomorrow for the day. Keep what you saw in your dream from happening to them."

"I'll try. Thank you for telling me this."

Tristan surprises me a little when he tells her, "Sometimes, CJ, God puts people together who were meant to work with each other. I think he sent you to us for a reason."

"Amen," she says sincerely.

"We've got a lot of work to do today," he continues. "Would you make us up some sandwiches and get us some cold drinks to go?"

"Sure. What kind of sandwiches?"

"Whatever ones you like the best. We'll take them with us and do what we can to help the people in Cedarsburg."

"Thank you," she replies, losing the battle with her tears.

"We'll be out front at the counter."

"Wait, I don't even know your names."

"I'm Tristan. This is Rebecca and Kavi."

She smiles, and the fear starts to subside. "It's good to meet you."

Chapter 4

We return to the lunch counter and sit in our original seats. By now, I can't keep the eerie feeling inside of me anymore. "Jesus Christ, Tristan. Her granddaughter."

"I know," he says calmly. "It may be a coincidence."

Kavi looks confused. "What? What am I missing?"

"Tristan had a dream this morning about saving a young girl named Sara from a house fire."

"Shit," he says. "Do you think it was her?"

"I don't know," Tristan answers.

"Have you had prophetic dreams before?"

"I can't really call them that. I sometimes have dreams about assignments I've completed, and others about assignments I haven't yet faced."

"There's more to it," I say.

"Rebecca, don't."

"He needs to know! We're in this together, and the more information Kavi has, the better we can work together as a team. I was awake when Tristan was having his dream, and I looked into his thoughts. I was able to enter the dream and interact with him. I helped save the girl from the fire."

"Damn," he says. "You two just keep getting weirder and weirder."

"You haven't heard the weirdest part yet," I tell him quietly. "When the dream ended, I was sitting in bed and there was soot on my fingers."

He looks amazed. "Soot?"

"I could smell the smoke in her hair," Tristan says.

"You're sure you weren't dreaming at the time?"

"We were both wide awake," I answer. "It was very clear."

"I am *way* out of my comfort zone," Kavi says. "Jason would be eating this up. God, I wish he was here. This means something; it has to. The two of you meeting each other. Tristan's visions, Bec's psychic abilities coming out. And now the two of you not only dream-share, but you bring physical manifestations out of the dream with you? If you take requests, I'd love it if you could dream about huge stacks of money."

"Kavi, be serious," I insist.

"Sorry, sorry. Just a joke. But look at it—here we are, in a place where we know a disaster is going to hit, and we happen to go to the one place in town where somebody dreams the same dream you two shared this morning. It's too many coincidences. Something's building here, and you two are a part of it. Now we just need to figure out what it means."

CJ emerges from the kitchen with a bag full of sandwiches and canned beverages. "What do we owe you?" Tristan asks.

"It comes to $22.50 with tax," she says.

He hands her forty dollars. "The rest is for you," he says. "Do everything you can. We'll be in touch, and I promise you we'll be here tomorrow."

She nods as we rise and take our lunch out to the Yukon. We return to our previous seats and each begin on a sandwich as we make our way through the streets of the town. Tristan drives, I call out the pertinent details, and Kavi takes them down on paper; it's a very efficient system.

"Downtown, corner of Fourth and Elm, fire department," I call out. "One block away, Fourth and Maple, police department."

As we continue winding our way through the streets, we take note of the medical clinics and doctors' offices. There is no hospital in town, which we decide is a good thing, given how difficult it would be to evacuate patients. We note the location of old fallout shelters, which could serve as storm shelters for those who can't or won't leave. We record the names and locations of major north/south exits out of town, since the tornado will almost certainly attack from the west.

On the edge of town, a building catches Tristan's eye. "Rebecca, look at that. Radio station."

"Radio station," Kavi repeats.

"Should we go in?" I ask.

"Yeah," Tristan says, "I think we should."

We park and enter the headquarters of KVKC-AM, a tiny station that looks like it's been around since Marconi invented the medium. The floors are covered with dingy old tile, the walls are made of cinder blocks painted a pastel yellow, and the ceilings are that spongy white material that just begs to have pencils shoved into it. There is no receptionist to greet us when we enter, so Tristan calls out, "Hello?"

Over the speakers, a country song from some bygone decade is playing. I couldn't name it if my life depended on it. Even Tristan shows no recognition, despite being—as was previously discussed—old.

From out of the booth, a man as old as the song he is playing emerges. "Hello," he calls back in response. "Help you folks?"

"We're in town for a couple of days," Tristan explains, "on a sort of scientific mission, talking about safety procedures during severe weather. We'd love it if there was a way we could spend a couple minutes on the air with you, talking to the people of Cedarsburg. Is that something you could make happen, Mister …?"

"Delmar. Arnie Delmar," he says, offering his hand. "Well, sir, I'm the program director, such as it is. We're a very small station, only 5,000 watts. Barely gets outside of Cedarsburg."

"Quite all right," Tristan says. "There's some strong storms headed this way tomorrow, and we'd like to inform as many people here as we can."

Arnie grabs a sheet of paper from the control room and looks it over. "Today's booked pretty tight," he says. "Some music, then farm reports, then Paul Harvey."

"Isn't he dead?" Kavi asks.

"Aw, hell, that don't stop him." He continues to gaze at the sheet. "Yep, it looks like a rich tapestry of entertainment for the next few hours. Any chance we could get you on tomorrow, neighborhood of 1:15 in the afternoon?"

"That could work," I answer.

"That's cutting it close," Tristan says discreetly.

"It might be a more effective message when things are about to happen," I point out.

"Arnie, you've got yourself a deal," Tristan tells him. "We'll be here at 1:15 tomorrow. Will you be on the air?"

He gives a little laugh. "Pretty much if the station's on the air, then so am I."

Arnie's a charmer, and I'm touched by his dedication. Then I realize—if he's going to be able to broadcast to this community, he'll have to stay in this building through it all. "Arnie," I say, "does the building have a basement?"

"Yeah, but it's pretty full of old junk. Why?"

"Just curious," I reply. "I'm a fan of old buildings."

We bid him farewell and return to the SUV. "Why didn't you tell him?" Kavi asks me.

"Because it's still privileged information. Telling CJ was a big enough risk. If we start predicting the future on a wider scale, there's no telling what could happen. Tristan's right: This is a scouting mission. The bulk of our work happens tomorrow."

Once the three of us are back in the vehicle, I ask Tristan, "How much more scouting do you think we need to do today?"

"Not much," he answers. "We've got a good sense of what's where in town. We don't want to stay out too late."

"May I make a suggestion?" Kavi asks. "The storm is currently in the area of Hays. We could be there in a couple of hours. What if we did some advance research on it today?"

"I don't like it," Tristan answers quickly. "It's risky."

"But it could be beneficial," Kavi suggests.

"There's too many dangers. We could get stranded; the SUV could be damaged; or we could get hurt, and then Cedarsburg will have nobody tomorrow. I'm sorry, Kavi. I know this is important to your research, but I can't take that chance. Besides, I think we'll all have plenty to see tomorrow. I propose we head back to Lawrence and make an early night of it."

Tristan's plan makes sense, and we decide to take what we've learned and return to Lawrence. There's an important piece of business to attend to, so we return to the lab, and Kavi goes to speak privately with Professor Charles Comstock—the real one. He's in there for about fifteen minutes, and when he returns to us, he's wearing a big smile and holding up a set of keys. "Lady and gentleman, we have Tiny. Shall we go meet our girl?"

He leads us out of the building to a garage in the rear. Outside the garage door is a covered black plastic box mounted to the wall. Kavi flips open the cover and enters a five-digit code. Slowly, loudly, the door rises. I swear I'm disappointed that there's no heroic music to accompany this sight. The afternoon sun is behind us, and it dramatically seeps into the garage as the door creeps open. And there she is—Tiny—and she is anything but. She may be more beautiful than me, but she's certainly not more petite. The tornado encounter unit is built on the frame of an RV, but looks like it is tricked out for combat. The wheels are protected by steel plates; the side panels are reinforced as well. There is an area over the driver's cab that was originally designed to sleep two, but it has been fitted with steel as well, leaving a row of turret holes for still and video cameras. It's a thing of monstrous beauty.

Even Tristan looks impressed. "I shudder to think of the gas mileage," he says.

"Well," Kavi replies, "there's a reason she has a 300-gallon tank. But don't worry, I have the company credit card. You want to see inside?"

"Hell, yeah!" I answer for both of us.

He opens the main door, and the inside surpasses the outside in wonder. Up front, there is room for a driver and a navigator. The navigator's station has two LCD-screen monitors and a host of maps for Midwestern states. The bathroom has been left almost as it was from the factory, but the rest of the interior has been outfitted for the task at hand. Two computer stations are in place to monitor the radar and other pertinent conditions. There is a small table with two-way radios on it. The walls are lined with charts and printouts. It feels like a mobile command outpost, and in many ways it is.

"So," I say to Kavi, "four of you will be in here tomorrow?"

"Or five if you'd care to join us. Paul drives, I navigate and take readings, Shafiq mans the radar station, and Delia is on cameras. It's quite a view from in here."

"How safe is it?" Tristan asks.

"Tiny weighs in at just over 16,000 pounds without the fuel. All exposed glass is shatterproof, the rest is steel-reinforced. Tires are impervious. She's gone head to head with an EF3 and remained unscathed."

"We're facing an EF4 tomorrow," he reminds us.

"Yeah, well, we haven't taken one of those on yet. In theory, she can handle it."

"In theory?" I repeat.

"We've yet to see if it'll happen. That's why tomorrow is so important. We have to know what Tiny can handle."

"And if she can't take it?" Tristan asks.

"Plan B is, we get the hell out of the path of the storm."

I've made my decision. "If it's all right with you, I'd like to ride with Tristan tomorrow. He should have somebody with him, and I feel like I'd just be in the way, with the four of you here."

He seems fine with it. "No problem. You're right. Tristan needs someone to interpret my notes while he drives. While we're here …" He reaches out and picks one of the walkie-talkies out of its cradle. "Have this with you in the SUV tomorrow. We'll be able to communicate with each other."

Tristan takes it. "Thanks."

For many seconds, we stand there inside the vehicle, nobody knowing what to say. Tomorrow feels so inescapable, even though we could just as easily choose to stay away; treat it like somebody else's problem. Leave those people in Cedarsburg to their fate and concentrate on protecting ourselves. At the moment, it sounds very enticing, but I know there's no way in the world we can let that happen.

We drop Kavi off at his apartment and return to our hotel room, which we've decided to keep for another night. Dinner is obligatory and forgettable, shared in near silence. I'm scared about tomorrow, and—owing to my promise of respect for Tristan's thoughts—I can now only imagine what's going through his mind. The responsibility for so many lives.

My voice sounds strange, even to me, as I break the pervasive silence of the room. "We did good field work today."

"I guess," he replies quietly.

"CJ will help us, and getting on that radio show tomorrow will make a difference. By that time of day, the storm will be close enough that we can appeal to people to evacuate, and have the authority to back it up."

"But what if they don't?" he asks.

"Then we use the hours following the radio broadcast to go through the town—house to house, if we have to—and get people out of there. In their cars, by carpooling, whatever it takes."

"Some will want to stay. You heard CJ today; people have storm cellars."

"All we can do is our best," I tell him. It sounds weak, even to me.

He doesn't respond, but instead turns on the TV and looks for a weather report. It doesn't take long to find, and the results are what we expected: a powerful storm in western Kansas, making its way east, leaving heavy rain, hail, and wind damage in its wake. The forecaster describes the expected path of the storm, but doesn't mention Cedarsburg by name. How I wish he had.

The evening feels like a blur, which is strange, because the days since I've met Tristan have made me feel hyper-aware of everything around me. But tonight, it feels like we're prisoners marking time before our execution tomorrow. I try very hard not to feel that way, but I can't escape it.

By 10 PM, we're in bed together. Right now, I want very much to be held, to have a feeling of safety and warmth, to know that there's someone who'll protect me with his life. Tristan welcomes me to his side and holds me securely in the crook of his arm. I love the way he smells; today, it reminds me of soup that my grandmother made when I was a girl. I inhale it deeply as I melt into his body. He turns and kisses me; his lips feel good against mine, and I welcome the kiss, initiating the next one. Before long, I become aware of the unmistakable evidence of his arousal. His free hand explores my hair, then my face and neck. When he brushes my right breast, I utter, "Tristan, I …"

Instantly he stops, withdrawing his hand. "I'm sorry. I didn't mean to assume— If you're not interested …"

"No, it's not that. Everything felt very good and very tempting. I just have so much on my mind tonight, and I'm pretty scared about tomorrow. Right now, the most loving thing you could do for me would be to hold me all night long."

"Then that's what I'll do," he says, without a trace of disappointment in his voice. He brings his body closer to mine, and I positively nest in him, wrapping myself in his comforting strength as I close my eyes against the future that awaits us. At this moment, an unexpected thought comes to me, words I haven't heard, said, or even remembered since early childhood.

Now I lay me down to sleep. I pray the Lord my soul to keep.

I would say that we awaken eight hours later, but that suggests that we spent those eight hours sleeping. It's closer to the truth to say that we decide to get out of bed eight hours after getting into it. There was some sleep in between, but much more restless turning and staring at the ceiling, and thinking far too much. When one of us would realize that the other was awake, there were brief periods of conversation, but they always had the same inane theme.

"You awake?"

"Yeah. You too?"

"Yeah."

"Can't sleep?"

"Nope. How about you?"

"A little, but not much."

Counterproductive and obvious; the dialogue of the damned. It must suck to be an insomniac, because there's no useful chatter to be had at 4:17 in the morning. We talk around the truth of the matter— that both of us are afraid of what's to come. For me, it's not even a fear of dying in the storm. It's a fear of failing, particularly of failing Tristan. This is my first assignment after deciding to stay with him, and even if he's not actively judging me by my accomplishment, I'm certainly judging myself.

By 6:30 in the morning, sunlight is starting to filter into the room, and we are wide awake. "Across the street," Tristan says, "there's a park."

"Yeah."

"I want to walk through it. With you. Will you do that with me?"

"Just walk?" I ask.

"Yeah. No planning, no strategizing, just walking and watching the sun come up, and appreciating being alive."

"I'd like that."

It takes us just a few minutes to put some clothes on, after which we walk across the deserted street into a good-sized city park. We have the place almost to ourselves at this hour. The occasional jogger passes by; we see a couple of people with their dogs. Everyone smiles and says hello. They don't know us; they don't know why we're here. They're just pleased to meet us, even briefly, as we strangers share this place on this gently foggy morning. There's an autumn crispness to the air, a suggestion that winter isn't too far off. Here in Lawrence, there isn't even a breeze; it's disquietingly calm, and I'm trying very hard not to think about wind.

"It's beautiful," Tristan says, interrupting my thoughts. "So many times, I don't get to stay in one place long enough to see the beauty. But right here, right now, I'm seeing it."

"In Lawrence, Kansas," I say. "Who would have thought?"

"Not I, certainly. Maybe after all of this is over, if I don't get another assignment right away, we can stay for a few days."

"That sounds good." A few seconds of silence pass between us as we walk a paved path. Despite myself, I utter the words I've been trying not to say. "It's tornado day, Tristan."

"Yeah. It is."

"Can we do this? I mean, can we really do this?"

He answers honestly. "If the answer was no, I don't think we would have been asked to come here."

"I'll try my best not to fall apart today."

"I'm not worried about you falling apart," he says.

"Thank you. What time are we getting on the road?"

"No later than nine. I want plenty of hours before zero hour."

We walk on for thirty pleasant minutes, taking in the tranquility of this place. As the sun climbs higher, it paints the morning sky a rich red. *Sailors take warning,* the old rhyme whispers through my head. Take warning, indeed. Before this day is through, there's a toll to be paid. When I was nine, my Sunday school teacher tried to tell us that hurricanes and tornadoes and lightning storms were God's punishment to the sinners of the world. Even at that age, I didn't want to believe it. Punishment? Fuck that bullshit. I'm supposed to believe that God made this amazing world, filled it with humans, who are his ultimate and greatest creation, gave us all free will, then unleashed storms to punish us, like a petulant child breaking his toys when he can't get his way? Not my God. Not in my world. Storms are storms, and nobody's punishing anybody. Like everything else in this world, it just *is.*

We are close to the edge of the park, ready to return to the hotel, when we see an old homeless man on a bench. At his feet is an ancient dog, smelling as bad as his master. As we draw near, the man looks at us and an expression of need and despair clouds his features. He puts out a hand to us, silently asking for a contribution. Tristan reaches into his pocket and pulls out ten dollars. As he reaches out to hand the money to the park dweller, the man suddenly grasps Tristan firmly by the hand and then speaks. His voice frightens me, because it sounds like it doesn't belong in this battered old body. It is young, rich, and strong, like it's coming to us from someone else—somewhere else. "Save them, Hamesh," the old man says to Tristan.

I am ready to spring to his aid, but he waves me off with his free hand. "I plan to," he says to the man.

"They will not want to leave that place," the man continues. "You must show them."

Tristan doesn't bat an eye at this. Not the strange name or the strange message or any of it. Instead, he engages the man in a conversation. "Do you know what I can do to help them?"

He looks at Tristan, but not into his eyes. Instead, he looks just over his shoulder, as if the answer is written in the clouds behind us. "Train them up in the way that they should go."

"Train them?" Tristan repeats. "How can I do that?"

"Yes, train them up in the way that they should go. You alone are their salvation, Hamesh."

"How do you know this?" I ask the man. "How do you know who we are?"

He turns to me, looking just past me as he did with Tristan. "You must cleave to him, Persephone. You who will turn from him. Keep vigil while others sleep, and bring with you more than you possess."

"I don't understand," I tell him.

"Will we succeed today?" Tristan asks.

Without answering, the man lowers his gaze until he is looking Tristan in the eyes. He loosens his grip and realizes that he has been handed money. He then takes the money and puts it in the pocket of the tattered jacket he wears. Looking down at his dog, he tells us, "This is Amos."

At the sound of his name, the dog slowly stands and wags at us. Tristan reaches out and pets the frail old animal on the head. "Hello, Amos." He then pulls out fifty more dollars and hands it to the man. "Eat well today."

A look of surprise and delight positively glows on the recipient's face. "God bless you both."

"Let's hope so," Tristan says.

Swiftly we return across the street to our hotel room. I sit down on the bed and am surprised to find that within a few seconds, I am crying openly. Equally surprised is Tristan. "What's wrong?" he asks me.

"What's wrong? How can you ask me that after what we just saw?"

"He didn't try to hurt us. He's just hungry and homeless."

Still sobbing, I raise my voice. "Oh, oh, and did you miss the part where he told us our future?"

"Yeah, I caught that. That was unexpected."

"How can you be so fucking calm about all this? All this weird shit is happening, and yeah, I'm tired and I'm scared, but what happened out there—you could at least be a little freaked out about it. For my sake?"

"I'm intrigued, I'll admit. Somehow, he knew who we were, and what he said sounded important. Train them up. What does that mean? How do you train someone to leave town?"

I'm starting to get the tears under control, but I'm still a long way from calm. "What did he call you? Honish or something?"

"It was Hamesh," he corrects. "No one's ever called me that before. I don't know what it means. Train them. Hmmm."

"He ... he told me to cleave to you."

"I like cleavage," he jokes, and I laugh a little, despite myself.

"He told me I would turn from you. I don't want to turn from you."

He smiles at me. "Then don't."

"But if he saw the future ..."

He reaches out to me and gently holds my face in his hands, drying some of my tears with his thumbs. "Maybe he's like me. He sees things that might be, and he gives warnings to prevent bad things from happening."

"You really think so?"

"I'm starting to believe that all things are possible, Rebecca. We're so busy helping others. Maybe this time, someone's helping us. I mean, look at it. Something made me want to go to that park this morning, and we passed by that very bench. We could've walked by without giving that man a thing. But we didn't. And what he gave us might well be much more valuable than all our money put together. Don't be scared by what you saw, love. Be inspired by it. Be encouraged by it. I think we were given a gift out there just now."

His words drain the fear from me and make me want to believe everything he says. "We were?"

"I really think we were." He steps away from me and gets a pen and a piece of hotel stationery from the desk. Quickly, he jots something down.

"What are you writing?"

"His words. He told me 'Train them up in the way that they should go.' Here, while I get ready, I want you to look at those words. They don't mean anything to me at face value. But we should see if it's ... I don't know, a code or an anagram or an old saying or something we can use. His message will only be useful today if I know what the hell to do with it."

I take the paper and stare at the words as Tristan heads to the bathroom to prepare for what comes next. Because this is it; practice time is over. This is tornado day.

Within fifteen minutes, we are back in the Yukon and headed to pick up Kavi at his apartment. As Tristan drives, I continue to look at the written words. "Anything yet?" he asks.

"I've tried re-arranging the letters, but I don't know if what it spells means anything."

"What do you get?"

"I get words like hear and rain and air and man, but there's no meaningful sentence that I can get using all these letters. Actually, the sentence as it's written makes the most sense."

"Yeah, but what could that mean? Train them up in the way that they should go? To train is to teach, but I really don't think of a group evacuation being a teaching exercise. It's more like, 'Hi, everybody. Tornado's coming. Get out of town fast.' Unless he means that we should get there early enough to have an evacuation drill first."

"But if you're going to have a drill," I reply, "why not just use that opportunity to make it the real thing, and get them all out of town?"

"You're right; that makes sense. We could *say* we're having a drill, and when they're leaving, tell them not to come back for a day."

"Yes, but then you undercut your message. If they think it's a drill, they might not want to participate."

He acknowledges that I have a point. "Then we're back at square one with what this means."

"Maybe Kavi will have some insight."

Ten minutes later, we know that Kavi is just as clueless as we are. He reads the words several times without a glimmer of recognition.

"You're supposed to be the brilliant scientist," I remind him.

"I just do weather," he says. "Puzzles aren't my thing. I'm still trying to wrap my brain around homeless guys giving you messages from God. All they give me are dirty looks."

"Nobody said anything about God," Tristan replies.

"Oh, I'm sorry. He must've been drawing from the collected musings of homeless guy prophetic lore. 'Clean your windshield, sir? Spare some change? Oh, and by the way, beware the ides of March.'"

"So, what then?" I ask. "You think he was crazy?"

"Maybe," Kavi says. "I didn't see him; you did. Who's to say he wasn't crazy *and* accurate? Look back at the Bible. All the people who claimed to talk to God? Most of them were outcasts who most people thought were insane. Maybe they're the ones who know the truth. Maybe you have to be a little crazy to distill the one true voice."

Suddenly it hits me, how I know those words. "The Bible," I say quietly.

"What?" they both reply.

"I knew I've heard those words before. At Sunday school, years ago. Train up a child in the way that he should go. It's from the Bible, the Old Testament, I think."

"That's great," Tristan says, "but what does it mean to us?"

"I don't know. I really don't."

The conversation is cut short by our arrival at the meteorology building on campus. It's time to meet up with the team and get on the road to Cedarsburg. Paul, Shafiq, and Delia meet us in front of Tiny's garage, as Kavi enters the code to open the door. The three students look and sound perfectly calm. I can't decide if it's because they've been on so many chases before or because they don't know the magnitude of what's to come today.

There's plenty of chatter, which suggests they've done their homework. "You picked a great day to be here, Dr. Shays," Delia says with excitement in her voice. "We're likely to see some heavy activity."

Tristan, meanwhile, is relishing the persona he gets to play. "It's Delia, isn't it? Well, Delia, I think you're right. Our mission today is going to have two parts. Kavi will lead your team as close to the action as possible, to get readings for Project Wind Shear. Rebecca and I will be testing some protocols for the evacuation of a town of about 10,000 people."

"So we're going to Cedarsburg, is that right?" Shafiq asks.

"Right," I answer. "Projections indicate that the storm is headed straight for it later this afternoon."

Before anyone else can speak, there comes a mighty growl and roar from inside the garage. Kavi has started Tiny's engine, and it sounds as if a battleship should be motoring out to greet us. Everyone stands aside as he pulls the vehicle out of its mooring and into the muted sunlight of mid-morning. It's an impressive sight, I have to admit, not just in its sheer size, but in its efficiency and functionality. Tiny was built for a single purpose: keeping her crew alive while they penetrate places where humans shouldn't go. For a moment, I actually consider changing my mind and riding with Kavi, but then I remember. *Tristan needs me there.*

Kavi puts Tiny in park and climbs out of the vehicle carrying a two-way radio. "Let's check 'em," he says.

Tristan gets our radio and turns it on. "Test, test, can you hear me?"

"I hear you fine," Kavi says. "We'll take point, because we've got real-time monitoring of current conditions, and we can alert you to any trouble ahead." He pops back inside the RV and emerges with a yellow-domed light. "Go ahead and put this on top of the SUV and plug it into the cigarette lighter. While you're on the chase, it'll alert motorists that they should give way. You can't run red lights or anything, but it'll help you be seen, especially when the skies get dark. So, any questions?"

"Do you have everything *you* need?" Tristan asks him.

"Seems like."

"When we get there, we've got work to do, so we may not be right where you need us at all times," he reminds Kavi.

"That's cool. Just always keep your radio on and with you, and keep us apprised of where you are. And if I get on that radio and tell you to move your ass, you move your ass. I don't care if you're carrying a paraplegic grandmother and her pregnant cat. You move."

"Fair enough."

"Saddle up, people!" Kavi calls out. "Safety first, and never leave your wingman."

And with that, we head west to face the most frightening moment of my life.

Chapter 5

The further west we go, the less sunlight bears down on us. Clouds thicken and congregate overhead, as if welcoming us to our assignment. Ahead, Tiny fills the lane. In the Yukon, it is all business. Tristan focuses on the road ahead, while I go through Kavi's notes. Everything is well laid out and easy to read. He's made maps of the central areas of town and detailed notes about the residential districts. Considering that we only had a day to prep, it's amazingly thorough and complete.

"What's our first stop when we get there?" I ask.

"Police station. I want to see how far along things are. Then I'd like to bring the fire department into it, make sure they're ready."

"What about CJ?"

"We'll call her. I'm hoping she's left town with her family. I'm hoping a lot of people have left town with their families."

I look over at him, at the determination on his face, and I decide to tell him. "I'm proud of you."

He smiles in surprise. "Of me? I haven't done anything yet."

"Yes you have. You've made this happen. And this town is going to owe you big. Even if you save only one person today, that's so significant. And what we're doing today could impact the future of thousands of people. That's something to celebrate."

"I'll let you know when I feel ready to celebrate."

Further west still, a light rain falls on us for about twenty-five minutes, then gives way to completely overcast conditions. Just before 11:00 AM, we pull into Cedarsburg. At first glance, everything looks about the same as it did yesterday. People are still going about their business. I guess I had hoped that CJ or the police chief would have been able to get a portion of the population evacuated early. It seems we're to have no such luck.

Kavi's voice comes over the two-way radio. "What's our first stop?"

"Police station," I answer.

"Copy that."

The two vehicles pull into the parking lot of police headquarters at Fourth and Maple. Tiny is getting a lot of attention from the locals as we drive through town, and as we park, people stop to gawk. Tristan and I get out of the Yukon as Kavi exits his vehicle. A man in his early sixties, dressed in a police uniform, comes out of the building to meet us.

"I'm Carl Haversham," he says to the group, waiting for one of us to step up and be the leader.

Tristan accepts. "I'm Tristan Shays, and this is my team. My assistant, Rebecca Traeger. Can we talk inside?"

"That's fine," the chief says. "This way."

On the way to the building, Tristan instructs Kavi, "Get the team ready. Make the most of your time. If people start asking questions, don't hold back. Tell them a tornado is on its way and recommend evacuation as quickly and safely as possible."

"Right."

Hearing this, the police chief takes a contrary position as he walks with us into the building. "Now just a second. I'm wondering if that might be a bit premature."

"Chief," he replies, "I understand the importance of acting on proper information, but I need you to believe me that the data we have on this storm shows that it will be here later this afternoon, and the destruction is likely to be extensive, with a strong chance of loss of life."

"We've been monitoring weather conditions as well, Mr. Shays, and we've seen the storm you're talking about. Based on everything we've seen, it doesn't look like we'll even see any severe weather for another five hours. With that much time, there's plenty of opportunity for the storm to die out or change course."

I can hear Tristan trying to keep his patience. "This is true, sir. You're right. That's why our team is here. We're monitoring the storm in real time, and we're going based on projections of past weather patterns. Everything we've seen indicates that the current atmospheric conditions are likely to put the storm over Cedarsburg just after 4:00 this afternoon, with the likelihood of a funnel cloud of EF3 strength or greater."

"Chief Haversham," I add, "we know that this town sees a lot of severe weather and there are safety precautions in place. But our research is telling us that what's coming here today is stronger than anything the town has seen in the past hundred years. For safety's sake, we want to evacuate as many people as possible, even for a day. If we're right, a lot of people can be saved. And if we're wrong, we've interrupted people's lives for a day."

"It's not that simple, Miss Traeger. To evacuate the town, we'd have to close all the businesses, get people out of their homes. It's a coordinated effort that takes time and resources."

"Are you telling us you won't help?" Tristan asks him.

"No, of course not. All I'm saying is that we need to be prudent and wait until we're sure that there's an immediate danger."

I can see the objection in Tristan's eyes, the desire to argue, but it is a losing battle. Before he can say anything else, I respond, "Thank you, Chief Haversham. I'll have the team take more readings throughout the day, and we'll report back to you. In the interim, would you please coordinate your efforts with the fire department and EMS?"

"I'll get on that," he says.

With that, I lead Tristan outside, out of the hearing of the chief and his people.

Safely outside, Tristan releases the anger he's been containing. "Damn it. Why did you give in so easily? How the hell are we supposed to do this now?"

I look him straight in the eye. "Listen to me. You weren't going to win that argument. All you were doing was making an adversary out of him. You don't have his support yet, but as that storm gets closer, you will have it. *If* you stay on his good side. We have almost five hours before it hits. We've got airtime on the radio, and we've got access to the people of this town. Let's go make the most of that."

He nods, and in his eyes I see that he understands me.

Kavi approaches us. "Status?" he asks.

"Not good," Tristan answers. "They think we're too early for any evacuation. They want to wait and see."

"Doesn't surprise me," Kavi says. "That's the problem with tornadoes. Most of the time, you don't know you're in danger until the damn thing literally drops out of the sky on you. Does this mean we don't have police support?"

"Not exactly," I tell him. "It just means we don't have it yet."

"So what do we do?"

"Go someplace in town, someplace very public," I reply. "Get out your equipment and take readings. Make phone calls; fake ones if you have to. Be seen by as many people as possible, and get the word out that there's danger here and evacuation would be the best plan for the day."

"Can do," he says. "What are you two going to do?"

"Pretty much the same thing. We'll start by going to see CJ."

As Kavi and the team head out in Tiny, Tristan and I return to the Cornflower Café. As soon as we enter, CJ rushes to the front to greet us. "I'm so glad you're back," she says.

"We're here for the rest of the day," Tristan tells her. "Do we need to go someplace private to talk?"

"No," she says, "we can talk here." With that, she raises her voice to address the more than twenty people in the diner. "Y'all, these are the people I was telling you about from the university." A murmur passes through the crowd. "They're the ones who told me a tornado is coming here later today."

The announcement is not what I was expecting, but it's useful all the same. "If anyone has any questions," I announce, "you can ask us."

A middle-aged man asks, "What CJ told us is true? This thing is for sure coming here this afternoon?"

"Yes," Tristan says. "We've been tracking it since yesterday. It's a bad one, with the potential for very damaging winds. Even underground storm shelters may not be enough to protect you."

"You really expect everyone to evacuate?" an older woman calls out.

I answer this time. "It's what we're recommending. By tonight, things should have passed through. The most dangerous time will be between three and six this afternoon. We're not asking you to pack up your homes and go. Just please consider getting yourselves, your family members, and your pets to safety, either north or south of town, for a few hours. As for possessions, take only the medications you need and anything that's irreplaceable and easy to transport."

The murmur starts up again, some of it positive, some doubtful. CJ speaks up again. "Y'all need to listen to what they're saying. I asked God what to do, and he said to get the people of Cedarsburg to safety. That's why I told you about this ahead of time. Just for tonight, people. Be somewhere else."

A younger man asks, "Is this evacuation mandatory?"

"No," Tristan answers. "It's entirely voluntary, but I can't express strongly enough how important it is to trust us on this. We have a tornado encounter vehicle in town taking measurements, but it won't be able to stop this from happening. We'd be very grateful if everyone here would tell at least ten other people in town what we told you, and ask them to do the same. Have them leave by 3:00. We'll be on the radio at 1:15 with more details. Please tell everyone you know to tune in."

I see some people nodding as they return to their meals. Tristan looks at CJ. "You know these people. Did they take it to heart?"

"Many of them did," she says. "And they'll tell others. So you're going on the radio?"

"That's right. Arnie's going to put us on his show. Any advice?"

"Stay on as long as you can. Appeal to their sense of family. The men here don't want to look cowardly by running away. But they don't want to put their women and children in danger. See if you can reach 'em that way."

"Thank you. We'll try that."

"What about you, CJ?" I ask. "Will you leave town?"

"As soon as I can," she says.

"We have things we need to do. I don't know if we'll see you again before … well, *before*."

"You two go," she tells him. "Do what you can for these people. And thank you. I don't know who sent you to us, but I think a lot of people here will owe you their lives before this day is done."

She squeezes our hands and sends us on our way. With almost two hours before our radio broadcast, and not much more we can do with the local police, we make a concerted effort to interact with as many people as possible on the street. Tristan and I split up, covering as much of the downtown area as we can, telling groups of two, four, and even individuals of the danger that awaits them. Several have seen Tiny in town, and our explanation helps drive home the urgency of the situation. I feel like it's working; people are listening to us, and many agree to get their families to safety and tell others in town.

Minutes become hours; I've never known an afternoon to pass so slowly and yet so quickly at the same time. Over and over, I repeat the same words to person after person, until I feel like they've lost their meaning. As yet another passerby walks off, I feel Tristan touch my shoulder. For a moment, I just look at him, as if wondering where he came from. His words rouse me from that moment. "We have to get to the radio station."

I shake it off and nod slightly in agreement.

"Are you all right?" he asks.

"I feel strange."

"Do you need anything?"

"Let's just walk there. I think that'll help."

Together we walk the four blocks to KVKC. Tristan holds my arm the whole way; whether it's affection or support, I don't know. All I know is that I like it, so I make no effort to discourage him.

Arriving at the station, we go directly to the broadcast booth, where Arnie Delmar is, of course, on the air. He waves us in and we enter. "Hey there," he greets us.

"Hello," Tristan replies. "I take it we're not on the air yet?"

"Nah, the 1:00 network news feed is still on. Once that gets done, we'll go live. Have a seat."

He's set up chairs at a small table and wired two microphones for us to use. "So, what's the plan? You going to talk about tornado safety and why you've come here?"

"Yes," Tristan says, "but there's more to it. The storm we were tracking yesterday is going to be here this afternoon, and we need to let people know."

"How bad is it?" he asks.

"Bad," I answer. "Probably an EF4."

"How long do we have?"

"Maybe three hours," Tristan says.

"And you're gonna warn people?"

"That's the plan."

Arnie thinks about it for a moment. "All right. But please be careful of what you say. We can warn them, but I don't want to start a panic."

Again those words return, holding us back from what we have to do. The ever-present fear of panic. The people of Cedarsburg need to get a little panicky over what's to come.

Arnie confirms our names and then prepares to put us on the air. The network news feed ends; he turns a dial and it fades away. He then flips three switches, and a red light turns on in the room. "It's 1:14 here at KVKC radio. Arnie Delmar with you at midday, hoping you're having a good one. Currently fifty-two degrees under very cloudy skies. The barometer is at 29.44 inches and falling. And I've just got word that the National Weather Service has issued a tornado watch for a dozen counties in the area, including ours. So keep an eye out for some rough stuff. Speaking of which, I have guests in the studio today who might just have some additional information about that. Tristan Shays and Rebecca Traeger are in town from the University of Kansas at Lawrence. And if you've seen the heavily armored recreational vehicle from *Stripes* cruising around town, that's theirs too. Looks like we might see some twister activity later today. Folks, welcome."

"Thank you," Tristan and I answer.

"So I see the NWS has issued a tornado watch already, but that just means conditions are right for tornadoes to form. Do you think we'll see a tornado warning later?"

"Very likely," Tristan says. "We've been tracking a major storm to the west that's done a lot of damage in the area of Hays, and we have reason to believe that it'll be in Cedarsburg by 4:00 this afternoon."

"That's pretty serious. Any chance it might change course and head some other way?"

"There's always a chance of that," I answer, "but the track of this one has been steady, and we're here advising people to take every precaution."

"An afternoon in the storm cellar, then?" he asks with a smile.

"That may not be enough," Tristan answers, minus a smile. "We're actually recommending that everyone in Cedarsburg evacuate the town by 3:00 today, and remain in a safe location until at least 6:00 PM."

The silence that follows suggests that Arnie wasn't expecting that answer. "Well, that … uh … that's certainly serious. I've been here a lot of years, and I can't recall that we've ever evacuated the town."

"We wouldn't recommend it if we didn't think it was necessary," Tristan says.

"Well, folks, of course we here at KVKC want you to do what's best for your family. If you're in a place that, uh, that you can arrange to take a little day trip this afternoon, it might be a good idea. If not, be sure to get to a place of safety if this tornado watch becomes a warning. And of course, we'll keep you up to date with all the live reports, just like we always do. We'll be back in sixty seconds with more from our guests from the University of Kansas."

After the commercials, we get back on the air and talk for six more minutes, telling Arnie and his listeners about the importance of heading either north or south out of Cedarsburg. There's no subtlety to it, just the emphasis that's needed. Arnie thanks us, repeats the tornado watch, and puts on some music. When he stands up to show us out, his face is deathly pale. Looking in his eyes and then into his mind, I realize why. "Oh my God," I say to him, "you can't leave here when it comes, can you?"

"I'm on the air this afternoon. It's my responsibility to keep the people informed as long as I can."

"But your own safety has to come first," Tristan says.

"Mine ahead of 11,000 people's? That's not the way I see it."

"Arnie, please," I say to him, "you have to do something. Clear a safe place in the basement. Stay on the air as long as you safely can, but when it gets close, please, *please* get to safety."

"I'll try," he says, trying to sound brave. "Believe it or not, I'd really prefer not to die today. I've seen this town through some pretty bad stuff. Somebody's got to keep them informed."

For reasons I can't even explain, I put my arms around this man and say the closest thing to a prayer that I can muster at the moment. "Be careful," I whisper.

"You too," he says.

As we return to the radio station's parking lot, I feel like I want to cry. Tristan's face shows that he's not doing much better. I'm trying to keep despair at bay as I stare at the concrete beneath my feet. My concentration is disturbed by a sound coming from around us—car doors, lots of them. Tristan and I look up at the same time to see families in dozens of houses surrounding the station piling into cars, some carrying overnight bags, others ushering pets.

"My God," Tristan says quietly, a smile creeping back to his face.

"They're listening," I reply, smiling as well.

We throw our arms around each other, knowing that each family who listens to our warning is a family that is likely to survive this day.

"Flyers," Tristan says out of the blue.

"Huh?"

"Damn it, why didn't I think of this earlier? There's a copy shop in town. We go there right now, make up a couple thousand flyers warning about the tornado, and get as many people as possible to deliver them house to house."

"It'll take time and manpower," I remind him.

"I think it's the most efficient use of our time," he says. "And as for manpower, we'll recruit everyone who's willing to help. Never underestimate the power of a small town to band together."

Within half an hour, we have two thousand one-page flyers that warn of the imminent approach of a powerful tornado, advising them to leave town no later than 3:00. We are able to muster a volunteer army of almost forty people just from the downtown area, each of whom will make deliveries to fifty homes, ringing doorbells and leaving the information. And with each minute that passes, I see more and more cars getting onto route 11 southbound out of Cedarsburg. It's really working.

As the afternoon wears on, the skies continue to darken. By 3:30, a sickly green pervades, casting an awful hue over everything. The winds are picking up, twenty maybe thirty miles per hour already. It's coming soon.

Tristan and I are outside the Cornflower Café, handing out some of the flyers, along with Chief Haversham, when we see Tiny turn onto the street. Kavi sees us and pulls to a stop outside the restaurant, exiting to check in with us.

"Whatever you're telling them, keep it up," he says. "I've seen plenty of people leaving town."

"How is it going with your readings?" I ask him.

"Good and bad," he says. "I'm getting plenty of useful data, but I'm also looking at NEXRAD. This thing will be here within the hour, and it's gonna be a son of a bitch. There's no question."

"Any tornado warnings from NWS?" Tristan asks.

"Not for this county. Two counties over, there was a tornado on the ground briefly in a field. They issued the warning, but the funnel petered out quickly."

He continues to talk, but something else catches my attention—a low rumbling sound coming from the north. It sounds familiar, disturbingly familiar. "Guys," I say quietly.

Kavi continues to talk, so I repeat myself, louder. "Guys!"

This time, they turn to me. "What is it?" Kavi asks.

"Listen. Do you hear that sound?"

They pause to listen over the wind. "I hear something," Tristan says.

"Yeah, me too," Kavi agrees.

"Oh my God," I say to them. "It sounds like a freight train. Isn't that the sound a tornado makes? A freight train?"

"Not always," Kavi says. "Sometimes, yes, but not always."

Haversham joins us. "I hear it too."

"What if it's early?" I ask Tristan. "What if it's here now? There's still tons of people in town!"

The freight train rumble gets louder and louder, but I see no sign of a funnel cloud anywhere on the horizon. Before Tristan can answer me, another sound fills the air—the distinctive howl of a train whistle.

"It's a train!" I'm practically giddy with the realization. "The freight train sound is a freight train. Holy shit. Tristan, that's it. That's the answer!"

"What is?"

"What the man said in the park this morning. 'Train the people up in the way that they should go.' Not *teach* them; *train* them. We have to get them on that train."

Realizing that I'm right, he directs an angry glare up to the sky. "Why does everything have to be riddles with you?" he asks. "You know what works well? Direct speech. Something like, 'Hi, Tristan. Hi, Mr. Homeless Man. You know, Tristan, there's a freight train coming through Cedarsburg shortly ahead of the tornado. Oh really? How interesting. Yeah, you might want to get some people on it.' That would've worked too!"

"Chief," I say, "is there any way of stopping that train?"

"It's the 3:30 headed south," Haversham says. "It only stops in town if there's freight or cargo at the depot to pick up."

"How do you let them know that?" Kavi asks.

"There's a signal there."

"Chief," Tristan says, "we can get hundreds of people on that train if there's room in the boxcars, but we have to stop it at the station. Please go quickly; activate the signal."

"Right," he says. He then runs to his squad car, turns on the lights and siren, and heads for the Cedarsburg train depot.

"We did get a gift this morning," Tristan says. "Now let's hope we can use it. Come on, let's get to the train station."

"We have only about a half hour," I remind him. "How can we get people to that train in time?"

"Police cars have speakers mounted to the roof. We can use those. Kavi, you get back to your team. They'll need you. We'll find you again when this is over."

"You two be careful, damn it," Kavi says. "Two of the people you save today had better be you, or I'm going to be seriously pissed off."

Kavi gets back into Tiny and drives off, as Tristan and I return to the Yukon and head over to the train station a few blocks away. Chief Haversham is already there, and he has switched the signal to indicate that there is a pickup. The 3:30 is pulling into the station as we arrive. One of the crew hops off and talks with the chief. We watch their conversation for a minute from the SUV, and it is clear from the crewman's face that he is not pleased with what he is being told.

"We'd better get out there," Tristan says.

"What can we do?" I ask him.

"Improvise. Follow my lead."

As we open the car doors, I hear the crewman telling Haversham, "… way we can take on passengers, even for a short distance. It's against regulations. There's no safety devices on board, and the railroad could face massive liability if we tried."

We approach the men, and Tristan asks, "Chief, what's our status?"

"Mr. Conroy here says he can't help us."

"We don't have time for *can't,* Chief."

"Who is this?" Conroy asks.

To my surprise, Tristan answers, "Agent Shays and Agent Traeger, Homeland Security." I catch a momentary surprised look on Haversham's face; I can't tell if he's caught off guard by the bullshit or thinks this is who we were all along. "We've got a very powerful storm bearing down on this town in the next thirty minutes, Mr. Conroy, and we need a way to get several hundred people to safety now. This train is that way. Homeland Security will assume all risks and all liability. We just need you to take this people to the next station stop south of here. How many boxcars do you have with room in them?"

"Fifteen," he says.

"That'll work. Chief Haversham, dispatch all your police and fire units with rooftop speakers. Have them drive through town, announcing that there's a train at the station that will take people to safety, but it's leaving at 3:55. Any citizens without transportation are advised to be on that train."

"Got it," he says, hurrying off to do just that.

Conroy still looks uneasy about the prospect. "I- I'm still going to need to see some official paperwork," he says.

Tristan walks right up to him, his face a picture of impatience. "You don't have time for that, Mr. Conroy. Right now, I need you to make sure those boxcars are open and easy to get into. You're going to have some passengers very soon. You'll get your paperwork when we get these people to safety. We'll meet up with you at the next town. Now go."

Conroy scurries to the train as Tristan and I return to the Yukon. "You're just full of surprises, aren't you?" I ask him, gently amused.

"Worked, didn't it?"

"We're not actually going to meet the train at the next town, are we?"

"Oh, God no. But it shut him up and let us get back to it. Come on. We can seat six other people at a time in this thing. Let's go round up some stragglers and get them to the train."

For the next fifteen minutes, we do just that, picking up people in front of their homes and bringing them to the train station. Around us, five police cars and a paddy wagon are doing the same thing. Other people are arriving on foot. Still others take their own vehicles out of town. The exodus is happening on schedule.

Overhead, the weather continues to worsen. Winds have picked up to more than forty miles per hour, and to the west, a wall cloud fills the horizon. The tornado is less than twenty minutes away now, and still there are no sirens warning the people. As we make another drop-off at the station, I catch Chief Haversham's attention.

"Chief," I call out, pointing to the west. "Sirens?"

"I can't," he calls back. "We're monitoring NWS at the station, and until there's a sighting in county, I can't sound the sirens." He puts up his hands apologetically and returns to what he's doing.

At 3:52, we are on our final scouting mission before the train leaves. On a residential street, we see a man in his seventies, standing on his front lawn and looking at the menacing skies to the west. Tristan pulls to a stop in front of his house, and we get out to help him to the Yukon.

"Sir," Tristan says, "we're with the evacuation team. We have room in our vehicle. We'll take you to the train station."

"Thank you," he says, "but I'm not going."

"Excuse me?" I ask.

"This has been my home for forty-five years. I've weathered storms before."

"This isn't a weatherable storm," Tristan tells him. "A tornado will tear through Cedarsburg in the next fifteen minutes, and the destruction will be extreme. We have a train standing by at the station to take people out of town, and it's urgent that you be on it."

"Young man, I listened to the radio today. I heard everything you had to say. Thank you for your offer, but I know in my heart that God will protect me."

I watch as the last shred of patience evaporates from Tristan's face. "God will protect you?" he says to the man. Then, taking a step toward him, Tristan looks him directly in the eye and says, "Who do you think fucking sent me?" The man appears stunned by the question as Tristan continues. "This is no longer an offer. You get in that car, or I'll pick you up and put you in it myself."

Clearly uneasy with that option, the man gets into the Yukon and we speed to the train station, arriving at 3:55. The last wave of people boards the train. "That's it!" Tristan calls out. "That's everybody. Get them out of here."

The boxcar doors close, the train whistle sounds, and the sixty-car train slowly pulls out of the station. My relief is short-lived, though, because the train's whistle is followed immediately by another sound, the shrill cry of a tornado siren. Tristan and I exchange a knowing look, and we both look to the west. In the distance, past the edge of town, we get the first glimpse of what is to come. A black funnel has swept down from the sky and is making its way through farmland. I feel my heart stop for a moment, as I realize that in all the preparation, we haven't made plans for our own safety.

Before I can ask Tristan what we plan to do, I feel the first hailstones falling.

Haversham gets on his radio. "All units, code seven. Repeat, code seven."

"Let's get to the Yukon," Tristan says.

We hurry back to the car, pelted by marble-size hail as we run. Once inside, I hear Kavi's voice on the two-way. "Rebecca, do you copy?"

"We copy," I tell him.

"We have visual on a funnel cloud," he says. "Bearing 275, range six miles. It's a funnel now, but it's building strength. We're likely to see a wedge by the time it gets here."

"Okay. What does that mean?" I ask him.

"It means get the fuck out of Dodge! We're going to intercept."

"Roger, we copy. Just be careful, please."

"Ten-four. Go south. Go now."

Tristan starts the SUV, and we head for the south side of town. I look out the window and get a clear view of the tornado in its full force. Movies, photographs, and Discovery Channel series don't compare to what I see approaching Cedarsburg. The sun is blotted out; hail continues to fall. And the funnel cloud looms, growing bigger and thicker. I feel like I'm staring at nature's penis, and it's about to fuck everything in its path.

"We need to be somewhere else," I tell Tristan as calmly as possible.

"Working on that," he says. "I'm looking for anybody who's still here. We can take five other people to safety."

But there's no one in sight. With the tornado siren providing an unceasing soundtrack to the approaching cavalcade of destruction, the people have scattered. Many have evacuated; others are holing up in their basements and storm cellars. Remembering something, I turn on the car radio and tune to KVKC. A tear forms in my eye as I hear the voice of Arnie Delmar. " …cloud is on the ground now, according to our weather watchers. Just outside of town and making its way here as I speak. I'll stay on the air as long as I can. But right now, we need everyone to get to safety, a basement, a cellar, an inside room with no windows. Get the kids and the pets and get to safe—"

Static. The sound of no speech, no signal, nothing.

"Tristan," I cry.

"It's the transmitter," he tells me. "Typically, they're out in the country for a better signal. The tornado must have hit the transmitter. That's good news. Arnie will know he's off the air, and he can get to safety in time."

What he says makes sense, and I hope that Arnie does just that. Kavi's voice interrupts my fear. "This is Tiny. What's your location?"

"We're a half mile south of town," I reply. "Where are you?"

"In paradise!" I can hear the excitement in his voice. "We're westbound on an intercept course with the cloud. It's beautiful, Bec. I'm glad you're not here to see it, but the readings we're getting are incredible. We're going to do an intercept, then circle around behind it to get readings on its dissipation factor and conditions."

"Oh my God, please be careful."

"You bet. I've got my team with me, and we're good."

"What's the wind speed?" Tristan asks.

"We're looking at 170 to 175," Kavi answers. "That's an EF4. You guys were right. Anything this bastard touches is reduced to the molecular level."

"Are you seeing any people still in town?" I ask him.

"That's a negative. Haven't seen a soul since the siren went off. I think we can say mission accomplished on that one. You definitely gave them more warning."

"What's the range on these radios?" Tristan asks. "Will you be able to hear us?"

"Thirty miles. So you can get to safety. We'll meet up again when all this is over."

"You're not going away, are you?" I ask.

"We're gonna be a little busy here," he replies. "So I'd better sign off now. See you on the other side."

"They'll be fine," Tristan tells me as we finally escape the hail on our path southward out of town. "They're basically in a tank. And we've given them the chance of a lifetime to get the readings they need to get. Personally, I'm glad you're here with me." He gives my hand a reassuring squeeze. "Let's go find someplace to wait this out."

The place we find is a roadside picnic area nine miles south of Cedarsburg. Human companionship feels overwhelming at the moment, so we opt for a place of safety and solitude, where we can still see the town in the distance. The tornado stays on the ground for twenty-two minutes, maintaining what looks like a straight course through the town until finally it breaks up, leaving clear skies in its wake. I sprint to the Yukon and grab the radio. "Intercept team, come in please." No answer. "Tiny, this is Rebecca. Please respond." Again, I hear nothing. "Kavi? Kavi, can you hear me?"

When my third plea brings no answer, I look to Tristan, the concern written all over my face. "We need to get back there."

"All right," he says, "let's go."

We rush back to Cedarsburg on the nearly deserted highway, the yellow light atop the car still spinning away. I don't want to believe the worst, but now that the tornado has passed, there's no reason for Kavi not to answer. Continued calls to him go unanswered.

After ten minutes, we reach the city limits and the sight that greets us is otherworldly. It truly looks like an enormous bomb has gone off. Trees are ripped from the ground; cars sit at absurd angles, in places they were never meant to be. A school bus is in someone's living room. People's possessions are scattered everywhere. I'm encouraged by the one thing I don't see: human bodies. There are very few people here, and the ones I do see are emerging from underground, surveying the damage. Ahead and to our right I see smoke rising. "Tristan!"

"I see it. Let's go check it out."

As we draw near, the two of us put on an identical look of astonishment as we see the house on fire—the house from Tristan's dream. "Sara," he says, gunning the accelerator as we pull up in front.

Quickly we exit the Yukon and size up the situation. "All right," he says to me, "we already know the layout of the house, the danger areas, and where we'll find her. Let's get in and out as quickly as we can."

"Right," I say, feeling the adrenaline fill me.

Just as we are about to make our dash to the front door, a voice calls out behind us. "Tristan!"

We turn to see CJ emerging from a storm cellar in the side yard. "CJ," he calls, "it's all right. We'll get her out of there."

"No, don't!" she says. "No one's inside. They left town last night."

An intoxicating feeling of relief washes over me. There's to be no fire rescue after all. "So why are you here?" I ask her.

"I had to stay here today to help as many people as I could. My house doesn't have a storm cellar, so I holed up here. But my family is safe thanks to you."

She hugs us, and we return the favor.

"Will you be all right?" I ask.

"I think so. I have a lot to do, but I'm not hurt, thank God."

"Will you excuse us, then? We have to go find our friends."

"Go on," she says. "I hope you find them."

We return to the SUV and negotiate an absolute minefield of debris in the streets of Cedarsburg. There's no traffic to speak of, but stoves don't exactly make for a trouble-free drive.

"Where are they?" I ask, looking left and right at each corner.

"No sign of them yet."

"God, what if something happened? What if ..."

My sentence is interrupted by a voice from the two-way radio. "Chase vehicle, this is Tiny. Do you copy?"

My heart is racing. "Kavi? Is that you?"

"It's us. We're all right. Repeat, we're all right."

"Where the hell have you been?!"

"The radio got damaged, so I had to find a backup with a battery that worked. Are you two all right?"

"We're fine," I tell him. "We're back in town. Did Tiny make it through okay?"

"She's banged up a bit," he says, "but she kept us safe. And I got about six months worth of research done in half an hour. The biggest blow in Kansas is history, and I think it's time to head back to Lawrence and celebrate!"

Chapter 6

After confirming that Arnie made it to safety, we go back to Lawrence, park Tiny at the university, and head out as a group to a bar called The Day After. The team sits together at a large round table in a corner of the place, with two pitchers of beer filling steins in front of all of us. Paul is regaling the group with the day's exploits.

"You should've seen it," he says. "I'm behind the wheel, and I'm telling Kavi, 'Uh, dude, it's right there.' And Kavi's all, 'Yeah, I know. Keep going.'" This evokes big laughs from the chase team.

"Chance of a lifetime," Kavi says with a shrug and a smirk. "What can I say?"

Paul continues. "At this point, Shafiq reminds him that the current wind speed is 177, and Tiny's rated for encounters up to 150. But we just keep going."

"Did you actually drive into it?" I ask.

"We got within fifty feet of the front of it," Shafiq says. "Then we skirted the side of it and drove up behind it, following it through town."

"What made you do that?"

"Two things," Kavi answers. "First of all, it gets us out of the suck zone, which is not a place you want to be for a long period of time. And secondly, it put me in a good position to take the readings I needed for Project Wind Shear."

"What kind of readings did you get?" Tristan asks.

"Well, my research is based on the theory that a tornado needs instability and large-scale rotation to keep going, and it's surrounded by forces within the storm cloud that can rob it of those things. The factors I've been looking at are cold outflow and stable rear-flank downdraft. Ordinarily, these forces are kept at bay by the instability and vorticity of the tornado until it dies down. Today, I was able to get readings concerning prime zones of cold outflow and RFD surrounding the funnel cloud itself. This will give me a ton of useful information about gathering or creating those factors and forcing them at the tornado to dissipate it faster."

"Like a weapon?" I ask.

"Exactly like a weapon. A gun of cold, stable air that I can shoot at a tornado and make it go away."

His teammates laugh knowingly as he says this.

"Hey, screw you guys," he responds playfully. "You know the science is valid."

"Yeah," Delia says, "and if we had a big enough hose, we could turn the deserts of Africa into farmland."

Kavi explains to us, "They're teasing me about scalability. They don't think it's possible to create something large enough to get enough air to dissipate a tornado. I happen to disagree. Which means when I win the Nobel Prize, I won't include them in my acceptance speech."

"Do you think it's possible?" Tristan asks him.

"Yeah, I really do. It'll take some time and effort, and probably some taxpayer money, but I think it can be done. Especially after today. Following that tornado, that huge wedge as it moved across Cedarsburg, I was tracking all the atmospheric conditions needed to dissipate it. All I lacked was something to scoop them up and something to shoot it out. But hey, even without that, we still managed to save everybody." He lifts his glass triumphantly, and his three team members meet it with theirs.

"Not everybody," Tristan says quietly. "Excuse me."

He gets up from the table and steps outside. Kavi gives me a concerned look, but I wave him off and follow Tristan outside. He stands watching the traffic on Central Avenue go by.

"You did so much good today," I remind him.

"Four people died," he answers. "Four I couldn't save."

"Yes, they did. But because of you, because of all of us, 11,334 people *didn't* die. I think that's far more significant."

"Save everyone. That's what I was told to do. And I tried."

"Of course you tried. That's why we were able to save so many. Arnie's all right. CJ's all right. Everyone in the police department is fine. Everyone we met or interacted with survived this tornado. Yes, they've got a lot of rebuilding to do, but because we were there today, they're alive to do it. And the four people who died just couldn't or didn't get to safety. You need to let them go, and not shoulder the guilt for their fate." I touch his face gently and offer him a comforting look. "It really is a time to celebrate, and those people in there want us with them. Can we go back in?"

"Yes."

He leads us back inside, where we rejoin the others at our table. "Sorry," Tristan says. "Just needed some air."

"No problem," Kavi replies. "Just remembering some of the high points. So what happens now for you two?"

"Hard to say," I answer. "Most of the time, I go where I'm needed. So far, we don't know where that is yet."

"Any chance you can stay another day? My friend Jason is free tomorrow, and I know he'd like to talk to you."

Tristan thinks about it for a moment. "I suppose if I don't get a new assignment tonight, I could talk to him tomorrow."

"Even if you do get a new one tonight," Kavi says, "I'm sure he'd like to go with you and watch you work."

"Yeah, I suppose. For now, I'm kind of tired. I think I'll head back to the hotel."

"Do you want me to go with you?" I ask him.

"No, no, it's fine. Stay here with your friends. The old man just needs his sleep, that's all."

"Okay. I'll be quiet when I come back."

"That's fine," he says. "Just don't get a ride from anyone who's been drinking."

It's sweet. He cares; even if he sounds like my father when he talks like that. "I'll get a cab."

Tristan rises in preparation to go. I stand as well, putting my arms around him, and offer a quick kiss; nothing passionate, just caring. He addresses the team. "I want to thank every one of you for what you did out there today. It was very courageous, and you helped us save a lot of lives today."

"It was an honor to work with you, Dr. Shays," Shafiq says. "Your intel on the storm was amazing. I'd love to know how you predicted it so accurately."

"I got very lucky," he replies. "In a lot of ways. Good night, everyone. Rest up; you've earned it."

The group calls out their good-byes to him and he exits the bar. Kavi watches him go, then turns to me. "He's taking it pretty hard for a guy who just saved 11,000 people."

"It's the four we couldn't save that he's focusing on," I explain.

"That's pretty hardcore self-punishment. Is he always this intense?"

"I don't know about always, but for as long as I've known him, yeah." I don't want to let his mood affect mine, so I deliberately change the subject. "But enough sad talk. This is a party! Let's celebrate."

By 10:30 PM, the conquering heroes are tired, and split up to get some rest. "Do you have to get back to your hotel right away?" Kavi asks me.

"I could spend some more time with you if you wanted," I tell him.

Buzzed as he is, I drive us back to his apartment, and he lets us in. No one appears to be there. "Where's Riley?" I ask.

"Hard to say. He usually doesn't come back home until after midnight. So welcome to my home."

"Thank you. I would say it's lovely, but, you know ..."

"Yeah." He staggers a little in the living room.

"You're a little drunked up there, mister," I inform him.

"Impossible," he slurs, continuing to stagger. "Hey, maybe that's my superpower—an unnatural ability to hold my liquor."

"Yeah, I'm gonna say no on that one."

"Walls, then. The ability to walk through walls." I watch in amazement as he walks over to the living room wall and walks face-first into it. I can't help but laugh. He looks so amazed when it doesn't work.

"Oh-for-two," I tell him.

"Invisibility?"

"Probably not," I say, sitting on the couch. "Come here and sit with me before you decide that you can fly and we end up in the emergency room."

He makes ridiculous arms-out flying motions and an equally ridiculous whooshing sound as he "flies" over to my side on the couch and plops down next to me. "Besides," I say to him, "I already know what your superpower is."

"You do? What is it?"

"You have the power to stop tornadoes in their tracks. And so, to most of the world, you are Kavi Ariashi, mild-mannered student at a major metropolitan university. But I alone know your secret identity. You are Weather Man."

"Weatherman? Like on the TV news?"

"No, that's weatherman. You are *Weather* Man, protector of cities, farms, and trailer parks across the Midwest."

He's wearing the most adorable smile. "I like that."

"I thought you might."

He rests his head on my shoulder; I like how it feels. "God, I've missed you," he says. "It's so amazing that you're here now like this."

"I would say it's a coincidence, but everything I've seen in the last week is showing me that there may be no such thing."

"So what exactly have you been through in that week?" he asks.

I tell him about meeting Tristan at the club in Key West. He's surprised to hear that I was working as an exotic dancer, but there's no judgment in his tone when we talk about it. I describe Tristan's message to me, and how it began our drive to Ohio. He learns about Stelios and everything he taught me, and then about our detour to Atlanta and how Tristan was unable to stop Jeffrey Casner from dying. Kavi is amazed to hear how my knowledge from my law classes kept Tristan from being held for murder in that case.

He's particularly interested in my story of Wyandotte, Pennsylvania, and how my father's company turned it into a ghost town. By the time I get to the story of meeting up with my father again, Kavi is completely transfixed and may even have sobered up a bit.

"That is the most amazing thing I've ever heard," he says.

"Every word of it is true."

"You know, I don't even doubt that. If somebody else tried to tell me that, I might. But because it's you, and because of everything I've seen and experienced in the last two days, I believe you completely."

"Then you're doing better than I am," I reply. "Sometimes I can't believe it myself."

"It makes sense, though. Everything you're describing deals with the untried potential of the human mind. If the public at large found out about what it can do, it could disrupt everything we know and understand. So naturally, the government would want to keep it quiet."

"Please don't tell me you're suggesting a massive government conspiracy of silence."

"Nothing as dramatic as that," he says, "but it's definitely in their best interest to make these things sound like implausible science fiction. If word got out about you and Tristan, you could end up in some danger."

"Yeah, I guess so."

"Are you going to stay with him?" he asks.

I give it some thought. "I don't know. I think so. At least, that was the plan when we left Ohio. We were going to come here, help the people of Cedarsburg, and then travel together. I would help him each time he gets a new assignment."

"Let me propose another idea: stay here. Come back to me."

And there it is, the thought that I've been working so hard to suppress ever since we got to Kansas. I let myself focus on the task at hand—the tornado, saving the people of Cedarsburg—in part so I wouldn't let in any thoughts of my past with Kavi. But now, alone with him, those thoughts come rushing in, and I have to stop them before I say or do something I'll regret.

"Kavi …"

"It doesn't have to be forever. But give us another chance. I've missed you so much. And maybe what you said is right—there are no coincidences, and you're here because we were meant to be together."

"I'm with Tristan now."

"Do you love him?"

I'm truly caught off guard by the question. "I'm not sure that's any of your business."

"Three years ago, you told me you were in love with me. I'm *still* in love with you. Now you're back; you're in my apartment, and you tell me you're with this other guy. I'm prepared to respect that if you tell me that you love him and that you don't have feelings for me anymore."

Everything is happening so fast. "I don't know," I answer quietly.

"About your feelings for him or for me?"

"Both."

In an instant, he puts one hand behind my head and pulls me closer to him. He kisses me before I can utter a single word of protest, and within seconds, any desire to utter one has completely fled. His kisses are warm and strong, and they're filled with so much desire and longing—much more than a lover of a single week can offer. Minute after minute, he continues to kiss me, caress my face, brush my neck and shoulders with his fingertips. And I allow it. No, *allow* isn't even the right word. I welcome it, savoring every kiss, every touch, remembering just how close we once were, how intimate in so many ways.

"There hasn't been anyone else since you," he tells me.

I smile and caress his cheek. I cannot respond truthfully in kind.

"Just say the word," he continues, "and we can try again. You can live in Lawrence, go to school at the university, and be far away from your father."

I have no words; the offer sounds so reasonable, so enticing, so very possible. He kisses me again, and with one hand, he begins to unbutton my shirt. At this, I pull back. He is immediately contrite. "I'm sorry, I'm sorry. Too fast?"

"It's not that," I tell him, re-buttoning. "It's just that you've got a very important question on the table, and I'm afraid if I have sex with you tonight, I'll make my decision based on how that feels."

"I can live with that," he offers, with a little half-smile.

"I could too. That's what scares me. I need tonight to think about this, and in order to make the right decision, I can't let myself be influenced by how much I want you sexually right now."

"You do?"

"Yes. You're the best lover I've ever known."

"Oh, Bec, so are you."

I stand at this point, against every feeling of yearning and arousal that's coursing through me. I know I have to leave here now and think about this, or within minutes, I'll be in Kavi's bed, overcome with the powerful sensations that he was always so good at bringing me.

"I'll have an answer for you tomorrow," I say.

"Thank you. And thank you for considering this. Can I drive you back to the hotel?"

"No, that's okay. It's been a long day; you should rest. I'll get a cab."

"I love you," he says sincerely.

"Thank you," I reply. *Shit, I hate when people do that to me. No graceful exit now.*

Fortunately, a taxi is dropping someone off at Kavi's apartment complex as I'm leaving, and the driver agrees to take me to the hotel. Mercifully, he's in no mood for small talk, because I can't even fathom having to talk about my day. He drops me off in front of the hotel, and I give him the fare and a good tip. I make my way quietly to our room, deciding as I go that tonight is not the time to talk with Tristan about this. With any luck, he'll already be asleep, and we can talk tomorrow, after I've made my decision.

As I quietly open the door to the room, I see that the lights are off, but a glow from the TV illuminates a third of the space. Tristan is seated in a chair several feet from the screen, watching a cable news broadcast of the aftermath of our tornado. The footage looks about like I remember it from earlier in the day. Upon hearing me enter, he mutes the program but does not turn it off or even look away from the screen.

"I thought you'd be asleep," I say to him.

"The news crews were in Cedarsburg this evening. People are coming back, surveying the damage."

"Did anyone talk about us?"

"Yes, actually. Quite a few people. Nobody could remember our names, but they talked about a crew from the University of Kansas who came in earlier in the day and warned people to evacuate. I've heard the word 'miracle' used several times."

That makes me smile. "I like that word. So, any sign of a new assignment yet?"

"Nothing yet. I may actually get a good night's sleep tonight."

"When you decide to turn off the news, you might. I have a feeling we have a more complete story of what went on today than the TV can provide."

"So how was your evening?" he asks.

"Fine," I answer. "Nothing terribly exciting."

He looks at me and a curious look crosses his face. "Is everything all right?"

"Sure. Why do you ask?"

"I may not be able to read minds, but I can tell when something's on yours. Do you want to talk about it?"

"Oh, it's nothing. It's been such a long day. I think we should both just get some sleep. We can talk in the morning."

Now he turns off the TV. "If something's bothering you, I don't think I'll sleep well until I know what it is. Was there trouble of some sort?"

I sit on the bed and he sits next to me. "No, it's nothing like that. I spent time with the group. Then I hung out with Kavi for a while afterward, catching up."

"That certainly sounds fine."

"It's just—he told me how much he misses me."

"I imagine so, after years apart."

"And … he kind of asked me to get back together with him."

"Wait a second. *Back* together? Meaning that you used to be together with him?"

"Yeah. I thought I mentioned that."

"No, I definitely would have remembered if you had mentioned that little detail. You told me that you and he were friends a few years ago."

"We were."

"You neglected to include the part where you were a couple. How long were you together that way?"

"Eleven months."

"Eleven months? That's a long time. Why were you hiding this from me?"

"Jesus, Tristan, I wasn't hiding it from you. Like I said, I thought I'd told you that we used to date. I kind of had a lot on my mind, and I thought you knew. Anyway, it was years ago, so I didn't think it was that important."

"And yet here we are, and he wants you to come back to him. What did you tell him?"

I am so not in the mood for this tonight, but there's no putting it aside now. "I told him I'd have to think about it."

"So you didn't say no."

"And, if you'll notice, I didn't say yes."

"It's bad enough that you have to think about it. Are you actually considering getting back together with him, after everything we've shared?"

He's starting to push my buttons, and it's pissing me off. I didn't want this to be a fight after everything we've been through today, but if he's going to start using words like that, game on.

"Everything we've shared?" I counter. "Tristan, we've been together a week, and if you'll recall, the first few days of that week weren't exactly kittens and picnics. Yes, I'll grant you that the circumstances of this week have been unusual, and that's brought us closer together, but I don't remember putting on your class ring and announcing that we're going steady." I regret the word choice as soon as I say it. So does he, apparently.

"Going steady?" he repeats incredulously. "Holy shit, Rebecca, we're not sixteen-year-olds here. We made love, and I thought that meant something."

"It *did* mean something, and it *does* mean something. I'm not here to end this relationship."

"Did you sleep with him tonight?" he asks point blank.

"No," I reply, thinking that it's not his business but knowing that it is.

"But you have in the past."

"Yes, if you must know. I have."

"God," he says, "I'm so stupid. I let myself believe that I mean as much to you as you mean to me."

"Jesus Christ, Tristan, I just need some time to find out if you do, that's all. This thing with Kavi was bad timing. You want to know what I really wanted to happen? I wanted to come back to this hotel room and find you waiting up for me in bed. Then I would crawl into your arms, make love with you for hours, and fall asleep by your side. Then, in the morning, I would know I was with the right man. Instead, I find you sitting in the dark, sullenly watching a news report about what you've just been through. Then you launch into this … this … interrogation about where I've been and what I've been doing!"

"Well, excuse the hell out of me for wanting to know what's troubling the woman I love."

"The woman you love. God, what is it with men? Why do you take the slightest attention and blow it all out of proportion? A woman says *good morning.* A man hears *I love you.* Sometimes *good morning* just means *good morning.*"

"Oh, spare me the bullshit, please," he snaps. "You of all people complaining because men read too much into women's attention? Wasn't that how you made so much money when you were dancing? Didn't those men give you more when they thought your looks and your words conveyed real affection for them?"

"Don't do this."

"Did you run your fingers through their hair and smile at them and call them by their first name when you were trying to get them into the corner booth for a lap dance?"

"That was business and you know it."

"Oh, right. I forgot, it's business. So that makes it all right. Only, *surprise,* one poor soul actually did fall in love with you, and not because you put your tits in his face or gyrated on his crotch. He fell in love with you— *I* fell in love with you because of who you are. Because of your mind and your heart and your humanity, and a smile that sustained me, even when the pain was unbearable."

His words disarm me. I don't like to admit when I'm wrong, but as I stand there, facing this good, decent man who saved an entire town today, I realize that his only crime was falling in love with me and thinking that it was entirely mutual. I am sincerely seconds away from apologizing to him for everything. But then he keeps talking.

"So please, don't stand there and tell me that men are easily confused attention sponges, when you know very well that you exploited that as a stripper."

The word is a dagger in me, and in an instant, the apology I was warming up goes cold. "What did you call me?" I ask.

I see in his eyes the regret at his word, but all the same, it's out there. "Shit, I'm sorry," he says quietly. "It slipped out in anger. I didn't mean …"

"No, I kind of think you did. I think you meant everything you said to me tonight."

"It was stupid. I- I was afraid of losing you."

"So you thought that a good reconciliation tactic would be to use a word you know I hate? Good choice. Do you want to throw *whore* in there as a verbal bouquet of flowers too?"

"Rebecca, I—I know that an apology doesn't begin to make up for it."

"I can forgive you for saying that word, Tristan Shays. But I can't forget that you said it. I'm very tired, and fighting with you has given me a terrible headache."

"I've got ibuprofen in the bathroom," he says.

"Thank you."

"If you want, I can get another room for the night."

"No. It's late, and we both need the sleep. We can figure things out tomorrow."

Without another word, I go into the bathroom and close the door behind me. I'm not going to cry, privately or in front of him. Instead, I look at my haggard face in the bathroom mirror, under the dreadful glow of fluorescent lights, and realize that I look as bad as I feel. *Kavi wanted to have sex with this?* I shake my head in amazement and fill a glass with cold water. Opening the ibuprofen bottle, I shake two out into my hand and swallow them. Giving it a moment's thought, I take two more and do the same.

He called me a stripper when he knows how I hate that word. How could he do that? All I wanted was for him to be the person I'm looking for. He doesn't even have to love me. I've told him that.

Fuck it. I'm going to bed. I don't want to talk about this anymore.

PART TWO

A MAN HEARS *I LOVE YOU*

As Tristan tells it

7 HOURS LATER

Chapter 7

My name is Tristan Shays, and I am an asshole. Now, this isn't my traditional appraisal of myself, but as I lie awake in a hotel room in Lawrence, Kansas, next to the sleeping form of the woman who means the world to me and currently won't speak to me, *asshole* is a pretty accurate assessment of things.

I screwed up, plain and simple. I let male ego and macho bullshit get in the way of some important things. This isn't to say that she's completely blameless in the whole thing. Contemplating starting up an old relationship isn't a great way to inspire confidence in your current relationship. But maybe I did get ahead of myself. Wouldn't be the first time. You spend enough time with someone and you can start to get false signals. Maybe I got a little obsessive in my affection for her. Or maybe in my mind, a sexual relationship presupposes love between two people. Is that old-fashioned or just naïve?

And then there's yesterday—"tornado day"—we've been calling it. I know I should have an unbelievable feeling of joy and relief that more than 11,000 people were saved because of our actions. I suspect that'll come later. For now, I can't get past the four people who died. Though the rational part of me knows that it wasn't my fault, there is something inside of me shouldering the blame, telling myself that I could have done more. It's entirely unreasonable, but I can't get the thought out of my mind. It, along with my feelings of guilt about how I treated Rebecca last night, made for a very brief and unrewarding night's sleep.

Now it is morning, and the digital clock on the bedside table says it is 8:18. Rebecca is turned away from me, occupying a sliver of her side of the bed, as far from me as she can be without ending up on the floor. I'm glad I can't read her thoughts, the way she can read mine. I suspect I'd learn some things about myself that I don't want to know.

One thing the night didn't bring is a new assignment. I have to wonder if, after the extreme nature of the one I just completed, I'm being given a chance to rest up before something new arrives. This, of course, leaves the question of where to go. Kavi's friend Jason wants to talk to me today; that's fine. Maybe it'll offer some answers about why I have to do these assignments. But once that's over, then what? Without a new assignment, I could fly home to Maryland. Will Rebecca go with me? That depends entirely on her. Even after our fight last night, I still want to be with her. It just remains to be seen if she wants to be with me. It sounds like the answer to a bad riddle. What's worse than having a mind-reading girlfriend? Having a mind-reading girlfriend who's pissed at you. Ha ha, very funny; until it's true.

Is that what is really is to me, a girlfriend? It sounds so junior high to say it that way, but what other words apply? *Lover* sounds seedy; *companion* sounds like something out of science fiction; *friends with benefits* just makes me want to gag. So is this woman friend my girlfriend? After last night, the point may well be moot.

She stirs and after a few moments, turns over and opens her eyes, looking at me. "Hi," she says, barely awake.

"Hi. Sleep all right?"

"Not great but all right. You?"

"Some. Not much."

"What time is it?" she asks.

"Little after 8:15. You can sleep more if you want. We're not expected until later."

"It's all right. I'm up." As if to prove it, she moves to a seated position and then gets out of bed. The awkwardness in the room is thick enough to be spread on a bagel and served as a very uncomfortable breakfast item. Without another word in my direction, she goes to use the bathroom. Granted, I'm not sure which words would be appropriate to precede such an event, but the absence of any words leaves me feeling very alone.

A few minutes later, she emerges and stands at the foot of the bed, where I am lying on top of the covers. We look at each other for a few seconds. "So," she says.

"So."

"New assignment?"

"No."

"Hmm. So what do we do with ourselves today?"

"Go talk to this Jason person, I imagine." I hesitate before continuing, but then venture, "Should we talk about last night?"

She also hesitates before answering. "Can we do it without raised voices?"

"I think so," I answer, sitting up in bed.

She sits on the edge of the bed, and for almost a minute, neither of us wants to be the one to start the discussion. Finally, she quietly tells me, "You hurt me last night."

"I know. I'm sorry. I really wasn't trying to. Sometimes I say things in anger that come out before my brain has a chance to let me reconsider."

"You're not like anybody I've ever met. I have a feeling that if I stay with you, I'll learn so much about myself and about the world, and I like that. But at the same time, I feel like you want something lasting, something permanent, and I don't know if I'm ready for that. I don't want to lead you on, but I also don't want to commit to a relationship just because I feel like it's the only way I can travel with you and spend time with you."

I take a moment to absorb all of this. "I guess I misread the situation. You know I haven't been in a lot of relationships in my life. And the ones I've been in, love always preceded sex. When that got reversed last week, it threw me off. It made me wonder if I was pushing my principles aside or if I was capable of falling in love with someone that quickly. Being me, I decided that I wouldn't push my principles aside just for the sake of sex, so therefore, I must have fallen in love with you at first sight. So, good-bye indulgence in casual sex, hello madly in love with the woman I just met. I think that's pretty healthy mentally, don't you?"

She smiles at that, and I can feel the awkwardness melting. "I wish you'd told me all of this before," she says.

"I thought I didn't have to," I remind her, tapping the side of my head.

"I'm in there far less than you think. And if we're going to stay together, I need you to tell me things, and not rely on my ability to pick up on them. We have to be able to communicate."

"*Are* we going to stay together?" I ask.

"I don't know. Seeing Kavi again brought back a lot of strong memories and feelings. I'm sorry if that's hard for you to hear, but it's true. And when he asked me to stay here with him, he was offering me a relationship, a safe place to live, and a chance to finish my degree. I hope you can see why that was such a tempting offer."

"Yeah. I just wasn't ready to let you go so soon."

"I haven't made up my mind yet. I need to do some more thinking today. I'd like it if you and I can spend today together as good friends, without all the boyfriend/girlfriend pressure hanging over us. It'll help me decide what to do."

"I think that's reasonable."

At 10:00, we arrive at the psychology building on the university campus, in answer to Kavi's invitation to come in and talk to his friend. Entering the designated room, we're greeted by a thin, fair-haired man of about twenty-five, dressed casually and sporting a smile of anticipation. "You must be Tristan and Rebecca," he says, shaking my hand enthusiastically. "I'm Jason Gaskill. I'm a graduate student in psychology, specializing in parapsychology. Please, have a seat."

The room itself is rather small. From the looks of it, it's used for psych experiments in which minimally briefed subjects sit down and are subjected to a battery of bizarre tests, proving or disproving God knows what. As we sit down on one side of a plain six-foot-long table, I notice that someone else is in the room, a woman in her early twenties with red hair and—once I get a look at them—powerfully green eyes. Jason sits next to her and makes the introduction. "This is an associate of mine, Miranda DeLosi. She's going to be taking notes today while we talk."

I notice that she has a digital voice recorder and a pad and paper. I start to wonder if I'm one of those minimally briefed subjects, here to prove or disprove God knows what.

"Nice to meet you," Miranda says to us.

"Let's start recording," Jason says. "So, just to make sure I have the facts right, Kavi tells me that for the past two years, you've been receiving detailed messages about individuals in peril, along with a pain-based physical motivation to go and warn them about this peril. Is that accurate?"

"Yes, that's right."

"And the first occasion was with a friend of yours?"

"Yes."

"How about the ones since then? Have any of them been about people you already knew?"

"No."

"Okay, that may be significant. Let me ask you this: how often is the information that you receive about these assignments accurate?"

The question is a bit confusing. "Well, the directions on how to get there are always right, and the person I'm looking for is always at the place I expect them to be."

"That's good, but how often is the description of the particular peril correct?"

"I'm not really sure. Usually, I stay with the person long enough to deliver the message, and then I move on. On a couple of occasions, I've seen them escape from it, and it was accurate. And there have been a few times when the person didn't listen to me, and that peril happened to them."

"So from what you've observed, it seems to be on target every time, but there have been a number of times when you couldn't be sure."

"Yeah. That sounds right."

Rebecca chimes in at this point. "And we found out that other people can send him assignments, making him think that they're real. Is that important?"

Jason gives me a confused look, so I explain. "Last week, I got the assignment to tell Rebecca that she had to leave Florida and return to college in Ohio. Only it turns out that her father hired some people to send that message to me."

"Huh. Did you know her father?"

"No, I'd never met him until after the fact. But her father had been working with a team of researchers, and somehow, they knew that I could receive these assignments, and they planted one falsely. On top of that, the next assignment I received was real, but it led me to help someone who planted *another* false assignment in me."

"All in one week?"

I nod.

"Busy week. Prior to the incident with her father, had you ever, to your knowledge, received a false assignment like that before?"

"Not that I know of. But it seems like every assignment I've received since then has been tied to Rebecca in some way, even the one that brought me here to help the people of Cedarsburg. Of all the tornadoes that strike all over the country every day, I was sent to a place where we could be helped by a friend of hers."

"Yeah, I heard about what you all did yesterday. Congratulations. That was—that was amazing. On the news last night, some of the people in that town called you messengers of God."

"That word keeps coming up," Rebecca says. "Messenger. Does it mean something?"

"That's what I'm working to find out," Jason says. "I've heard it used a lot in stories of others like you, Tristan. People who are helped refer to these messengers who swoop in, deliver the message, and leave without asking for any reward or payment or anything."

"How many of them do you know of?" I ask.

"About a dozen, with almost twenty case histories. A few of the people I've talked to describe the same person."

"Did any of them describe someone who looks like me?"

"Hard to say. You don't have any really distinguishing features."

"I left the second head back at the hotel room," I answer. Miranda gets a little laugh out of that one.

"Then, of course, there's Ha Tesha."

"Hot what?" Rebecca asks.

"*Ha* Tesha. It's Hebrew; it means 'The Nine.' I've been trying like hell to find them. There's records of them on the Internet, with stories of their existence dating back a hundred years or more, but nobody seems to know where they are or even *who* they are. The most I've been able to figure out is that they're a group of messengers who work together, assisting each other in delivering their messages."

"So why the secrecy?" she asks.

"I don't know. Maybe privacy, maybe a desire to be kept out of the spotlight. I know they're in this country, but much more than that ..."

A thought strikes me. "You say they help each other deliver messages?"

"Yeah, from what I understand. Why?"

"Yesterday morning, we were in a park, and a homeless man gave us information that helped us save hundreds of lives during that tornado."

"Holy shit," Jason says. "What did he say to you?"

"He told us—kind of cryptically, but he told us—to put people on an empty freight train that would be coming through town. He knew who we were, and he knew hours ahead of time how to help us."

"Okay, that's big. What did he look like?"

"Six-two, Armani suit, designer haircut. He looked like a homeless guy! Old, scruffy, ragged clothes, and sporting the aroma of dispossession. You think he could be one of The Nine?"

"I'm thinking maybe."

"Tristan," Rebecca cuts in, "tell him the rest. What he called you."

"Oh, yeah yeah. He didn't address me by my name. He called me Hamesh. I don't know what that means."

"I do," Jason says. "It's Hebrew. It means *five*."

For many seconds, no one can speak. All eyes are on me, which makes me feel like I should say something, but as God is my witness (and potentially my employer), I have no idea what to say to that. Jason finally breaks the silence.

"Okay," he says quietly, "this is significant. It suggests that you're one of them."

"Isn't that a bit of a leap?" I ask, not really wanting to be one of them.

"I'm open to alternative explanations."

"Well, the homeless guy might have mistaken me for a friend of his named Hamesh, and he wanted to give his friend a message about a train that he had to catch—and put some people on."

The three of them are just staring at me, and it borders on amusing, except I know I'm fighting a losing battle. "If I'm part of this secret society," I say, "which I'm not saying that I am, then why haven't I been invited to join it?"

"Maybe you have and you just haven't received the invitation. Maybe they've been trying to reach out to you but they've been unsuccessful. Now that I have this information, I can help them." He pulls out a very fancy phone and starts typing on the keyboard.

"What are you writing?" I ask him.

"I belong to several list-servs for paranormal activity. I'm sending a message out there that says: Ha Tesha, Hamesh has made contact and is with me. Please contact me for details."

"You think that'll work?" Rebecca asks.

"We'll find out," he says.

The interview continues for another twenty minutes, during which Jason listens with fascination as I describe the pain that wracks me each time a new assignment comes in, followed by the thorough details of what I am to do. He asks excellent questions about how and why I carry out these assignments, and probes deeper about what causes some assignments to fail.

At the end of the questions, he turns to Rebecca and says, "Now, if I'm not mistaken, Tristan isn't the only one in the room with gifts. Kavi tells me you have some psychic ability of your own."

"I guess. I just learned about it a few days ago."

"Would you be willing to tell me about it, maybe try a few tests?"

"I suppose."

This is something I really don't need to watch; I'm already a little overwhelmed with the information I've received this morning. "If it's all right with you, I'll sit this one out."

"That's fine," Jason replies. There's some couches in the lobby of the building if you want to relax for a bit."

"Thanks."

"I need to step out for a bit too," Miranda tells him. "I'll leave the recorder running."

I open the door and step out into the hallway, Miranda a few steps behind me. I'm peripherally aware that she is heading the same direction I am, toward the lobby. Just before I reach it, she says to me, "Could I talk to you for a few minutes?"

"Yeah, sure."

I continue to the lobby, and she follows me there. "It's about what Jason was saying in there."

"If you're looking to hire me to help someone, I'm afraid I don't get much choice about who I'm asked to help."

"No, it's not like that. I'm actually here to help *you*."

"Okay, you've got my attention."

"Jason's my friend," she says, "and he's a good guy and a bright student. But the whole paranormal thing, I really think he's barking up the wrong tree."

"Go on."

"So much of his research is based on speculation, anecdotal evidence, and hearsay. That drops it right in the realm of the theoretical. He was so excited to talk to you because he finally thought he'd have something concrete as a foundation for his research, to justify that it might be possible."

"Well, correct me if I'm wrong, but what I just told him seems to do a pretty good job of that. The homeless guy, what he called me; the secret society. Didn't that sound pretty compelling to you?"

"If I wanted to believe in it, yes. I'm a psychology grad student too, only my research is more grounded in fact. And from what you told me, I believe that I can help you so that you never have to take another assignment again, and you won't feel any pain."

"Now you definitely have my attention. If Jason's wrong and there's no paranormal explanation for what's happening, then what does that leave?"

"Please don't be offended when I ask you this, but how much do you know about schizophrenia?"

"Schizophrenia? You think I have schizophrenia?"

"I'm not jumping to any conclusions. I just want to know how much you know about the disorder, and then we can talk about whether it's a possible explanation."

I give the matter some thought. "Well, it's a mental illness. People get paranoid or they see and hear things that aren't really there. But I really don't see how—"

She interrupts. "It's more common than people think. And it *is* treatable, through a combination of medication and behavioral therapy. Doctors look for a set of symptoms in making the diagnosis. The person has delusions, hallucinations, disorganized thought patterns. Patients frequently believe that others can control their thoughts and even send them messages, instructions to do things that they wouldn't ordinarily do. Tristan, open your mind up to outside possibilities and ask yourself—does any of this sound familiar?"

It's a leading question and we both know it, but when she phrases it like that, I can't help but see it that way as well. But still—schizophrenia? It sounds so unlikely. "Yes, I suppose if someone didn't know the circumstances, it could appear to be schizophrenia-like symptoms, but these thoughts don't come from within me. They're sent to me; the instructions on what to do are sent to me."

Very calmly, she tells me, "That's one of the most common symptoms of the illness."

"I'm not mentally ill!" I say loudly enough to convince anyone in earshot that I actually am mentally ill.

"I'm sorry. I'm not trying to suggest that you are or you aren't."

"Well, it certainly sounds like you are. Besides, I have the best evidence of all that it's not schizophrenia—the people I've helped and saved over the past two years. Tell the 11,000 people in Cedarsburg that Tristan Shays is imagining it. See what they tell you."

Again, she offers an irritatingly calm counter-argument. "A lot of times, schizophrenia sufferers read about current events and believe that they could have prevented them. After 9/11, there was a wave of people who were traumatized because they couldn't do anything to help the victims, even if these people were thousands of miles away. The mind is a very powerful force when it wants to believe something. It's possible that you heard about the rash of tornadoes we've had in Kansas this season, and it came to you as one of your assignments that you had to come here and warn people. When you got here, you got the precise location of an upcoming trouble spot, and you acted on the impulse to go and help."

"They didn't tell me where to go. I told *them* where to go. Two days before that tornado hit, I knew the exact time and place, and the severity of it. You can ask Rebecca. She was there to witness it."

"Rebecca. The same Rebecca who's in with Jason now, telling him how she can read minds?"

"Oh, so we're both crazy, is that it?"

"No one's saying *crazy*. It's just a matter of having a reliable witness."

She's causing me to lose my calm and my patience. "What do you get out of this? Why is it so important to you that I have schizophrenia? You don't even know me."

"This study is my life. It's what I want to do for the world. You save people from tornadoes. I save people from this. My father suffered from schizophrenia for twenty years, and for most of that time, he was in denial. But he kept on suffering from it. He couldn't go past a lake or a river or any body of water without being convinced that someone was in it, drowning, and they needed him to save them. Well, one day, he tried to do that, and he drowned; saving someone who wasn't even there. Because nobody could save him. Not from drowning, not from schizophrenia, not from any of it. So I pledged my life to helping people who have this illness. And you're right, Mr. Shays, I don't know you. But I'd like to. Because I listened to Jason and Kavi talk about you; and I listened to you talk in that room. There's something interesting about you. Maybe fascinating, I don't know. And maybe I'm wrong; maybe you really are sent by God or angels or somebody with knowledge of the future. But I tend to shave with Occam's razor. The simplest explanation tends to be the one that usually fits."

Twice in twelve hours, a beautiful young woman has shut me down with her words. I look intently at Miranda DeLosi, standing there with her feelings laid bare and difficult truths on her lips. She offers me a difficult diagnosis about my mental faculties, to be swapped one-for-one with an impossible and potentially lifelong burden imposed by celestial forces beyond my comprehension. *Which crazy is crazier? Could she be right? Could this all be my imagination?*

"I'm sorry about your father," I tell her. "And I'm sorry for losing my temper with you."

"Thank you. And it's okay. It's not the first time I've received that reaction. It's not something that's easy to hear."

"I'm not saying I believe it. But if you have some time, I'd like to hear more."

"Out on the quad, there's the most amazing oak tree with a bench under it. I'd like it if we got a couple lattes and sat on that bench and talked to each other for a while."

A smile lights my face for the first time in what feels like days. "I'd like that too." Then I remember, "Oh, what about Rebecca?"

"Write her a note. Pick a time and a place to meet her, and I'll get it to her. But give us some time, if you would. I don't want us to rush."

I quickly write:

Rebecca,

I'm exploring some theories in psychology with Jason's assistant, Miranda.

Since we have no new assignment, today is a free day. Let's meet up again at the hotel room for dinner around 6:00. Call my cell phone if you need anything. I'll see you later.

—Tristan

I realize that I am giving her an entire day to spend with Kavi, on a day when he will be campaigning his ass off to win her back. I may very well be offering her the opportunity to fall in love with him again, but the unselfish part of me decides that it's all right. If that's the decision she needs to make in order to be happy, then so be it. If you love someone, set them free, and all that shit. In the meantime, I have a date for coffee and psychoanalysis.

The latte comes from the Student Union in the center of campus. It is a short walk from the tree she described, which is as magnificent as she presented it. A few stray leaves are just beginning to try on the hues of autumn, while the rest, still in summer's deep green, tremble and flutter in the late-morning breeze. Students walk by on their way to and from various places, but essentially we are alone.

She spends the first twenty minutes talking about herself, which is only fair, given how deep into my psyche she plans to delve. Miss Miranda DeLosi, of the Des Moines, Iowa DeLosis. All of twenty-three years old, she is the only child of a stay-at-home mother and a military father—now deceased, of course. All through her childhood, she struggled to cope with her father's bizarre and frightening behaviors, while her mother built up a wall of excuses and deliberate disregard, rather than risk admitting that her strong and capable husband could be mentally ill.

"I cried a lot," Miranda tells me. "But always to myself, where no one could hear. Crying isn't dignified, or so my father would tell me.

But I knew that he cried too; he only thought I couldn't hear. He cried because of the things he did, the things he couldn't stop doing. They scared him, and he wasn't a man who was used to being scared."

"How long ago did he die?"

"Five years ago. Before I had the knowledge to try to help him."

"You told me about his obsession about water, about saving people. What other things did he deal with? If it's not too painful to talk about."

"It is. But I owe you this. He had security fears—making sure the door was locked; making sure the stove wasn't on. He could be standing in front of the stove and see that it was off, but he wouldn't believe it. Even after he left the house, he would come back sometimes and check. My mother and I would tell him it's fine, everything's as it should be, but he couldn't take a chance. And he was a military man, so a lot of his issues were about security. If he walked by a room with a closed door, he had to open it because he thought there was someone inside who was injured or dead. It was a litany of little things, where if it was just one of them, it might not be so bad. But over the years, it built up and built up, one after another, until it practically took over his whole life. And then, one day, it killed him."

"I'm so sorry."

"When I found out later that day, I fell apart. But somewhere in the middle of it, I got this thought in my head that I couldn't get rid of: *it's over*. And I hated myself for thinking that. I still hate myself for thinking it. How selfish to think like that. It's over? For who, him or me?"

"For both of you," I reply. "This couldn't have been easy on him either. It's like any other chronic, debilitating disease. When someone you love finally succumbs to it, there's a feeling of great loss, of course, but it's perfectly natural to have feelings of relief too. I don't know how much comfort this brings, but consider this: in his own mind, your father died trying to save someone's life. It doesn't matter if the rest of the world knows there was no one out there to save. He gave his life in the service of others."

At this, she puts her hands to her face and loses the battle with the tears she's been holding back. They flow now, and I feel terribly responsible for making her cry, so I put a sympathetic arm around her shoulder and allow her to cry on mine. I feel my shirt getting wetter as she releases all the emotions that her scientific mind has forced her to suppress.

"And now," I continue, "you've dedicated your life to helping other people battle this illness. That's the most selfless thing I've heard of in a very long time."

"Says the man who saved 11,000 lives yesterday," she says with a little laugh through her tears.

"Right place, right time," I tell her. "I think anyone with the information I had would have made the same decision. I'm sure your father would have."

"Thank you," she says quietly.

"But you see, everything you've told me about your father makes me even more certain that what's happening to me isn't schizophrenia. I don't know what it is, but I feel confident that the information I get is reliable."

"This is what makes me think that if you *do* have it, it's in the very early stages, at a point where you could fight it back and never have to worry about it again."

"I'd need some pretty compelling evidence if I'm going to believe you're right," I tell her.

"The part that really tips the scales for me is the physical pain you describe when each new assignment comes in. You get these thoughts, this information, and you say they're not your original thoughts, and you focus on them, get all the details. And if you don't follow the prescribed course of action exactly, the terrible physical pain continues. Is that right?"

"Yes, that's pretty accurate."

"And this pattern repeats itself over and over. How many times did you say this has happened in the last two years?"

"Almost a hundred."

"That's about once a week," she says. "That must make it very difficult for you to hold down a job."

"I don't work."

"You see? It's disrupting your life."

I could tell her about my money at this point, but she doesn't really give me the opportunity. "It doesn't hit all at once," she continues, "with full force. It builds slowly over time. And an important part of my research is that early detection and treatment can help prevent people from experiencing the worst symptoms of it. That's why I want to help you, Tristan. If I'm wrong, then I'm wrong, and I'll make it up to you if I can. But I really don't think I could live with myself if I was right and I just let you walk out of here without my trying to help you."

"What can I do?" I ask her.

"Back at my apartment, I have case studies. Would you go there with me and look at them?"

"Sure. Lead the way."

Chapter 8

It's a two-block walk from campus to Miranda's apartment, and the weather is beautiful. With the devastation of yesterday, I was expecting at least rain today, but everything has cleared up, and it is a mild, bright September day. Miranda and I don't say much as we make our way; what she's just shared with me was very personal, and I'm sure, difficult to admit.

Ordinarily, I would find her tireless insistence that I have a mental illness off-putting at best, outright rude at worst. But there's something in her tone, a selfless compassion for a stranger, that makes me think that she wants to help me just for the sake of helping me. A moment's analysis tells me that she's me without the external messages. And what scares me just a little is that I can't be absolutely certain that what she's saying isn't true. In my own mind, I know that these messages come from another source, but if my own mind is faulty in some way, wouldn't that skew everything? There are schizophrenics who swear that they see and hear people the rest of the world doesn't acknowledge. Is it possible that I suffer from the early stages of schizophrenia and it's making me believe that I have to travel the country, warning people about perils that may or may not be real?

I was wrong about Rebecca; she didn't really have to leave Key West. But I was misled on that one. I was right about Stelios's boat; at least I *think* I was. I never did have any evidence that it was damaged, other than what he told me. But then there's the Harbisons' house in Wyandotte. I knew the exact time it was going to collapse. How could

I have known something like that? Everything rational in me wants to believe in external influence, which feels crazy, because Miranda's explanation is truly the simplest.

It is this uncertainty that motivates me to follow her and at least hear what she has to say. And, as much as I don't want to admit it, I truly want a reason to stop this two-year fool's errand I've been on.

We arrive at her apartment, and it is such a stark contrast to Kavi's. Where chaos ruled his, order predominates at hers. It's not obsessively clean, but it is extremely presentable, with a mature young woman's sense of style. "This is lovely," I tell her.

"Thank you. I try to keep the place orderly, so I have a haven from all the work."

"Do you live alone?"

"Yep. Just me. I had a roommate last year, but she kept odd hours, and I need my sleep. So I saved up and got a place of my own. Can I get you anything?"

"No, thanks. I'm still fine from the latte."

"Have a seat on the living room couch," she invites. "I'll get some of my case files."

As I make myself comfortable, she disappears briefly into another room. Looking around the apartment, I realize that for all its cleanliness and order, it lacks anything personal to make it uniquely Miranda's. It's like sitting in the model unit that the rental company decorates to entice prospective tenants. Everything is entirely functional and completely impersonal. I look for photographs of friends and family and find none. I look for mementoes, favorite coffee table books, souvenirs; nothing. Even the few framed posters on the wall are general nature scenes. I don't know why, but it makes me sad for her.

Before I can explore that emotion further, Miranda returns with a small stack of manila folders and sits next to me on the couch. "I found five cases that reminded me of yours," she says.

"I'm a case now?" I ask, gently teasing her.

"Pardon me," she says with a smile. "Five cases that reminded me of your *circumstances*. Is that better?"

"Much. Can I ask you something?"

"Of course," she says.

"Forgive me for saying so, but there's plenty of existing knowledge on schizophrenia, and even a range of medications to treat it. Why dedicate your studies to something that's so well understood already?"

"Because I believe the behavioral therapy is flawed and the medications have a range of unpleasant side effects. I'm working on more radical behavioral treatment that avoids the need for drug therapy."

"Is it working?"

"So far I'm having some luck with people in the early stages of the illness. Once it's had a chance to take hold, it's not as easy to combat it."

"I see. So, these case files. Do you want me to read through these, or will you give me the guided tour?"

"Guided tour, of course." She opens the first folder. "Dennis, age forty-four. One day, without any apparent reason, he began having thoughts that there was someone living in his house when he wasn't there during the day. He would stop home unexpectedly but never find anyone. He set up cameras, motion sensors, microphones. Never once did he find anything out of the ordinary. But the thoughts wouldn't go away. He went to a doctor for treatment. A combination of therapy and medication relieved him of these thoughts within two months."

She opens the second folder. "Julia, age twenty-six. She became convinced that her co-workers at the grocery store were stealing from their employer. Though she admits she never saw or heard of any of them doing it, she began accusing them, and then started going to the police to report them, sometimes two or three times a day. It cost her the job, and though we tried to protect her under the Americans with Disabilities Act, we couldn't because the actions directly interfered with the safe and successful completion of her duties."

Opening the third folder, she begins, "Bruce, age thirty."

Before she can say anything more, I look at the subject's picture and stop her. "Oh my God. I've met him."

"What?"

"This man, Bruce. Seven months ago, I delivered a message to him."

"Tristan, that's not funny."

"I'm not kidding. I don't even remember where it was, but I remember his face, and the name Bruce. I warned him that he would be paralyzed in a car accident if he left at a certain time."

She looks at me, momentarily at a loss for words. "There are 300 million people in this country. I brought out five folders, and you recognize one of the five people. Do you know the sheer odds against that?"

"Yes, of course, but Miranda, this is why you have to believe me. Since I met Rebecca, I've experienced a chain of interconnected assignments. People and places that should have no connection turn out to be related somehow, in ways you wouldn't expect. I think that's why I'm in Lawrence. I was sent to help the people of Cedarsburg because Rebecca's friend Kavi is in Lawrence, and he could introduce me to Jason, who would help me find The Nine." I hesitate long enough to see strong doubt on her face. "You think I'm talking crazy, don't you?"

"No, of course not. It's just …"

"What?"

"Bruce's case history. He was fine, no symptoms, no abnormalities, until one day, he began looking for patterns in his interactions with people. He was convinced that people he met for the first time knew him from somewhere, even if he didn't know them. He was sure they were working with other people he knew, to try to hurt him. Pretty soon, it was all he could think about."

"What happened to him?"

"He's in a mental hospital now. He tried to kill himself."

"And because I said I remember him, my attempts to prove to you that I'm sane had just the opposite effect. That went well."

"Tristan, please don't be angry. I'm not trying to make any value judgments about you. I'm just trying to get as much information as I can, and either confirm or deny a hypothesis. If I'm right and there's a way I can help you, I want to do that. I don't know how long you'll be here, and I at least want to tell you what I find out before you leave again."

"What makes you so sure I'm going to leave again?"

"It's what you do. If I can't convince you to stay here and do this research with me, then you'll get another assignment and then go off somewhere ... with *her*."

"That's a very telling pronoun," I reply. "Do we have a problem with *her*?"

She gives a dismissive shake of her head. "I don't even know her. Hell, I don't even know *you*. But I saw the two of you together this morning, and I just don't know what you see in her."

"It's complicated. I know everybody says their relationship is complicated, but in this case, I can't think of a better word for it. We've only been together a week."

"That's it?"

"That's it. But in that time, each of us has saved the other's skin a couple of times. On top of that, we've spent almost every hour of that week in each other's company. Today is the first real amount of time we've spent apart."

"I just ... I see her kind all over this campus. Tanned, good-looking."

"You don't think you're good-looking?"

"Not that way," she answers.

"You shouldn't sell yourself short."

"Thank you," she says shyly. "And then there's you. You're this *figure*."

"I'm a figure?"

"I don't know what else to call you."

"My friends call me Tristan."

"I just don't know if ... Do you love her?"

I'm surprised by her forthrightness. "That's a very personal question, don't you think?"

"Yes, it is. I'm sorry. No, to hell with it. I'm not sorry. I just don't know if, given what you might be going through, if it's a good idea for you to fall in love with her."

"Would you be surprised to hear that you're not the first to suggest that?"

"I'm not?"

"Crazy people need love too," I remind her. She grimaces at the word. "I'm sorry; that was insensitive, given everything." I sigh and decide to be honest. "I thought I was in love with her, but now I'm not sure. We had a fight last night. Things were said. Mostly by me. We made up, kind of; but she's busy deciding if she wants to go back to her former boyfriend."

"Kavi?"

"Was it in the campus newspaper or something?"

"No, it's just—Kavi talks to Jason; Jason talks to me. Do you think she'll go back to him?"

"I don't know. It seems like a reasonable thing to do. Stay here where it's safe, returning to a young, good-looking guy who might be able to rip tornadoes apart with his bare hands. Or travel across the country in rented cars with a middle-aged man who may or may not be mentally ill, rescuing people who may or may not need rescuing. Which would you choose?"

"You," she says.

I offer a smile and a little laugh at her answer, but then I look in her eyes and realize how serious she is. "Should we look at more case files?" I ask nervously.

"I don't want to look at more case files."

I realize now that she is uncomfortably close to me on the couch, and what makes it all the more uncomfortable is that I want her to be this close to me. She starts to do that thing that women sometimes do to men who are usually not me, that inching closer thing until one of us decides to kiss the other. I sit there stunned as she draws nearer, but it's significant to note that I'm not too stunned to try to stop her when at last she does press her lips to mine. *This isn't right,* my helpful little brain immediately tells me. *This definitely isn't right. Twenty or thirty more seconds of this, and I'm definitely going to consider pulling away.*

When the kiss ends, I look at her in disbelief, feeling flushed. "What was that?" I ask her.

"It was what I've wanted to do all day."

"You're joking me."

"No. I'm not."

It dawns on me. "Wait a second. Was this just a ruse to get me over here alone? All the case files, the schizophrenia stuff?"

"No, no, I swear to you that's not the case. Yes, I was attracted to you when I first met you this morning, and the more I heard you talk, the more interested in you I became. But the schizophrenia research is genuine. I really think it may be a possibility. Tristan, I've already lost one person I care about to this illness. I think I'm starting to care about you, and I want you to stay here in Lawrence for a while and let me work with you to figure it out. Please tell me you'll stay."

Everything is moving very fast, and her interest in me, her desire for me to stay have both hit me from out of nowhere. And yet, what reason do I have for leaving here sooner? "I suppose I can stay, unless I get my next assignment. Then I have to go and take care of it."

"When will that be?"

"I don't know. It could be a day; it could be a month."

"But you'll stay until then?"

"I'll stay for a while. Until we can get some answers."

"Thank you," she says.

"So what do we do now?" I ask.

"I'm not sure, but I really hope the answer is that we go to my bedroom."

"What?"

"God, Tristan, I haven't even kissed a man in three years. I've been so wrapped up in my work and in my grief that I ignored some very important things. I'm not asking you to fall in love with me and spend the rest of your life with me. I just want to be held, to feel like someone thinks I'm pretty."

"You *are* pretty," I tell her, barely believing that this is happening. If this is actually the schizophrenia talking, I'm not sure I want to be cured.

"I've been so lonely," she continues. "Being intimate with you would remind me that I'm alive, that I'm capable of physical bonding with another person. And I promise you, I don't do this with everybody I meet—or even *anybody* I meet. I saw something special in you. Something giving and tender, and I want to know you this way."

"I'm with Rebecca," I remind her.

"But is *she* with *you*?"

I have to answer honestly. "I don't know. It's a little up in the air right now."

Rather than replying, she kisses me again, more enthusiastically this time, and I make no effort to resist her. My hands explore her hair and her face and neck. After a few minutes, I stand and take her hand, guiding her to her feet. She steps past me, still holding my hand, and leads me to her bedroom. Without saying a word, I lower the window shade and begin to help her out of her clothes.

Two remarkable hours pass in Miranda's company. She's an amazing combination of shyness and assertiveness at the same time. And for someone who hasn't been with a man in three years, she hasn't forgotten a thing. I'll be fortunate if I don't walk with a limp for the rest of the day. Still, I can't help but wonder at how easily I allowed her to talk me into this. I didn't resist, I didn't hesitate. I didn't even weigh the pros and cons, which is a favorite activity of mine for many years standing. She said *jump me,* and I said *how high?* Now that she is lying naked in my arms, I find myself going through those thoughts I should have gone through earlier. And the guilt I'm trying and failing to suppress is overpowering.

Did I rush into something with Rebecca? She's wonderful and amazing, and I can very easily see myself traveling with her in the near future. But is she soul mate material? And more to the point, do I even believe in soul mates? If so, why was it so easy to be with Miranda this way? I know I don't love her. I *said* I love Rebecca, but was she right in what she accused me of last night? Do I fall in love too easily? Did I really hear *I love you* when all she said was *good morning?*

"You okay?" Miranda asks, snapping me out of it.

"Hmm? Oh, I'm fine."

"You look far away."

"Just a little bit lost in my own thoughts."

"You're not regretting being with me this way, are you?"

"No, no, it's nothing like that. The invitation was just a bit unexpected, that's all."

"I hope you don't think I'm slutty or anything like that."

"Not at all."

"Good." She picks up her head to kiss me again, and I marvel once more at how soft her bare skin feels against mine.

"I guess I'm just feeling … slightly unfaithful to Rebecca."

"I don't want to complicate your life," she says. "What we just shared was amazing, and if you told me you wanted to continue a physical relationship, I wouldn't even have to think about it. But if you told me that we couldn't be together sexually, and we should just be friends or even keep our relationship strictly professional, I would understand and accept that. You've already made me feel better, physically and emotionally, than I've felt in a long time. I at least owe you that consideration."

This time, I kiss her, both to thank her for saying that and to experience the warmth of her lips again. "You're pretty amazing. I really didn't expect this. And honestly, I don't know what's going to happen yet. A lot depends on what Rebecca decides. She and I exchanged some strong words last night, and she's got some thinking to do. I don't want you to feel like a fallback plan or a consolation prize, because I swear to you that's not how I see you. And I don't want you to think this was rebound sex either. You're beautiful and desirable and fascinating to talk to. As for what happens next, it's hard to say. For the past two years, I haven't considered my life to be my own to do with as I please."

"I'm willing to take it a day at a time, if that's what you need." As I get out of bed to find my clothes on the floor, she says, "Can we meet up again tomorrow morning?"

"I don't see why not."

"I'd like to start doing more formal questions and answers to see if my theory is on target. How about 10:00 in the psych building?"

"Wow, from sex to psychoanalysis in one fell swoop. That was quite a segue."

She laughs at this. "I guess you've discovered that subtlety isn't my strong point."

"Got that feeling, yeah."

"Look on the bright side—we can totally skip over any awkward questions about sexual dysfunction or diminished libido."

"You researchers and your unconventional testing techniques."

After a moment, she looks right at me and says, "I really like you, Tristan Shays. I'm a hell of a long way from understanding you, but there's something very likeable about you."

"Thank you," I answer sincerely. "I feel the same way about you. And for the record, I'm very glad we were together this way."

I leave Miranda's apartment in the early afternoon, which gives me several hours to be alone with my thoughts and, more importantly, my actions. I return to the city park across from the hotel—the same one where, just yesterday morning, the homeless man gave me the information I needed to help save the people of Cedarsburg. As I suspected, he isn't there now. With everything Miranda and I talked about today, I have to wonder if he was ever there at all.

All this free time gives me plenty of opportunity to explore the one topic I'd rather stay away from: warming up to the concept of Tristan Shays, crazy person. I've never known anyone with schizophrenia, but I've read books, seen movies. It doesn't look pleasant. At least technology will make it easier. If I start talking to people who aren't there, I can just wear a Bluetooth headset on my ear and look terribly important.

It's a funny mental image, but the humor masks something darker, the reality that Miranda might be right. As I sit on the park bench formerly occupied by my prophetic assistant, I think back over my life. The past two years are very much on my mind, thinking over all the assignments that I've been on. It strikes me that in more than 90 percent of them, I have left the scene without ever confirming whether what I told them was accurate. Occasionally, I would learn that I had made a difference or conversely that my message had been ignored and bad things had happened. But it's entirely possible that the very act of my delivering the message could have affected the outcome. The very real truth of the matter is that these messages in my mind could have come *from* my mind, and I've been delusional for two years.

The realization is staggering, and I don't know what to do with that knowledge. My mind, my thoughts are at the heart of everything I do; if they can't be trusted, where does that leave me?

When Miranda first proposed the idea of schizophrenia this morning, it sounded absolutely absurd and impossible. But the more she told me, the more everything sounded familiar. That's what scares me the most—how very plausible it could all be. Maybe I was meant to meet her. I let myself be convinced that Kavi was the reason we were sent to this area, so he could help us. Maybe Miranda is the real reason; I came here to learn the truth about my own mind and to get some help.

She spoke of the possibility of ending the assignments. If she can suppress the voices, stop the pain, get me off this ride that's stolen my life for two years, I could start over, find a new purpose. Do I want that new life to be with Miranda? With Rebecca? I don't know; maybe neither of them. Maybe I need to take care of me for a while and not worry about anyone else. I know that sounds incredibly selfish, but after helping 11,000 people yesterday, I think I've earned some me time.

But what to do about Rebecca? In just a few hours, I'll see her again, and she'll want to know about my day. I can tell her about Miranda's theory, about the possibility of schizophrenia. I can't tell her about what I've done, though. I mean, really, why should I? Either she's going to stay here with Kavi—in which case, our relationship is over anyway—or she'll choose to go with me, and learning about my infidelity would be hurtful to her. It's settled, then. Telling Rebecca would be a very bad idea, and I'm doing her a favor by keeping that information to myself. She doesn't need to know, and since Miranda won't say anything about it, there's no way she can find out.

"Oh my fucking God, you slept with her?"

I receive this cheerful greeting roughly ten seconds after meeting up with Rebecca at our hotel room, in preparation for dinner together. In all my plans of silence and covertness, I forgot that my traveling companion has an all-access pass to my cerebrum, and the simple act of trying very diligently *not* to think about my sexual encounter with Miranda effectively created a movie of the event in my thoughts that Rebecca could pick up without even trying. The question leaves me speechless, completely unready to answer, because she already knows the answer.

"Say something," she says.

"How was your day?" I ask, knowing the complete awfulness of the query.

Her reaction is one of disbelief. "How was my day? You're seriously asking me how my day was?"

"I don't know what else to say right now."

"You had sex with this Miranda chick today? One day after you and I had a long, supposedly meaningful talk about our relationship?"

"I didn't want to say anything to you about it."

"You didn't have to, Tristan. It was pouring out of your thoughts like a goddamn peep show. Why would you do this to me? Why? Why? And if you utter the words 'we were on a break,' I'm pretty sure I will staple your head to the floor."

"I didn't plan this. She wanted to talk to me about … Oh, to hell with it. You can see it faster than I can say it. Just read me."

I close my eyes and go over the details of my day in my thoughts. She enters those thoughts, and in less than a minute, she knows everything I've been through today. I only hope she can plainly see the guilt I've been feeling all day.

"Schizophrenia? Holy shit, Tristan. Why would you let her convince you of something ridiculous like that?"

"Why is it so ridiculous? I let her talk to me about it because I think it might be possible."

"It's ridiculous because your assignments are accurate. They send you to people who are in danger, people who need you to help them. Crazy people don't get that kind of accuracy. They get random shit about … fuck, I don't know … demons and pumpkin pie and Bozo the clown."

"Bozo?"

"My point is, she's leading you on."

"No, she's not."

"She lured you over to her place so she could make you feel vulnerable and then take advantage of you sexually."

"That's not what happened," I counter.

"Where is she now?"

"Why? What are you going to do?"

"I don't know. Talk to her, have some tea, kick her ass. Whatever."

"Rebecca, please. Don't do this. Don't blame her for what happened. If anything, it's my fault."

"Umm, I got the whole thing, scene by scene. You weren't exactly raped, but I know when a woman is using a man for sex."

I feel as if I'm being pulled apart at the seams. Two strong women have a hold of me, and every decision I can make will hurt at least one of them.

"Rebecca, I'm sorry. I know that sounds hollow and pathetic in the face of what I've done, but I'm sorry. I never meant to hurt you."

She pauses as she takes this in. "That's a start," she says quietly. "You really surprised me with this. You were so shy and hesitant about being intimate with me, and then, a week later, you jump into bed with this woman like it's nothing. Like *I'm* nothing."

"That's because ..." I have difficulty saying more.

"Because what? Say it."

"It's because I was falling in love with you. Because you really mean something to me. And with Miranda, it was just sex. She wanted to fuck me, and I responded like a big, stupid boy and said *why not?* You may have noticed as you were rooting around in my brain that I'm pretty torn up over this whole thing. I'm afraid I've succeeded in pushing you away from me by doing this. And ... shit, I don't know. If she's right about my mental health, maybe the best thing you can do is to push away."

After a few moments, she continues, "I probably shouldn't even tell you this now, but I told Kavi my decision today. I told him I'm not ready to stay here and be with him. I told him I'd rather travel with you. Now I'm wondering if I made a mistake."

"Rebecca, I don't know what to say. Maybe I was sure that I was about to lose you. I don't know; that sounds like an excuse, like a rationalization. But I was pretty certain that Kavi would be your choice."

"Then maybe you don't know me as well as you thought you did."

For many painful seconds, neither of us says a word. I have a thought, but I don't know quite how to articulate it. After a half dozen false starts, I decide to just spit it out. "I have an idea. I haven't received a new assignment yet. I'd like to propose that we stay in Lawrence until I do. You can spend as much time with Kavi as you want. Spend some time on campus, learning about their programs, and decide if you want to go to school here. I'll stay out of your way if you want."

"And what will you do?"

"Miranda wants to run some tests on me, to see if what's happening to me really is schizophrenia."

"Tristan, I really *really* hate that you're buying into this."

"I know. But she offered me the possibility that the assignments can stop. And as much as I want to help people and travel with you, the pain of it, the burden of it, the crushing responsibility is tearing me up inside. This is a chance to end that, and if I don't at least learn more, it'll haunt me for the rest of my life."

My words seem to have disarmed her somewhat. She paces a few steps in silence. "Can you forgive me for what I did?" I ask her.

"I'm not sure. Do you plan to keep having sex with her?"

"If you want a relationship with me, then I'll never even look at her that way again."

"I really think I want a relationship with you," she says quietly.

"Then my interactions with Miranda will be strictly clinical from here on out."

"Thank you."

I put my arms around her and she accepts the embrace, letting me hold her and convince her of my sincerity. "I'm just so worn out emotionally," she says. "Everything we've been through has exhausted me."

"I'm pretty hungry," I tell her. "Would you let me buy you dinner?"

"Yeah, that sounds good. Make it someplace fancy. You still have to make it up to me."

Dinner is indeed fancy; I owe her that. I try not to feel bad for the sea creatures that gave their lives as a sacrifice to my sexual appetites, but in the final analysis, better them than me. Over dinner, she tells me about her day on campus.

"Jason is pretty intense," she says.

"I got that impression."

"He ran all kinds of tests on me, to see what my abilities are. He had this deck of cards with different shapes on each card, and he asked me to pick which shape he was holding up behind a barrier."

"How'd you do?"

"At first I bombed on it, because he would hold up the card without looking at the shape. But then he started looking at the shape as he held up the card, and then I got it every time by seeing it in his thoughts."

"So you're officially spooky?"

"Limited spooky. We've determined that my abilities extend to perceiving the thoughts of people in my immediate vicinity if I'm concentrating or if they're projecting those thoughts."

"What about what happened the other night—the dream and the soot?"

"I asked him about that, and he didn't have an answer. He's never seen or heard of anything like that. He's going to do some more research, but I think I've stumped him with it."

"A medical mystery. Congratulations."

"Thanks, I think."

I hesitate before approaching the next topic. "Do you want to talk about what happened with Kavi?"

"Not in detail. I just decided that I'm not done traveling yet. I think I want to go on more assignments with you. Unless, of course, that's going to stop now."

"I just don't know. Miranda is pretty well convinced that I'm not right in the head, and that's what's causing me to get these assignments."

"And what do *you* think?"

"At first, I thought it was impossible. But the more I thought about it, the more I realized I can't completely rule out the possibility. All along, I've trusted the source on these assignments, even if I didn't know exactly what it was. But what if I'm wrong? What if it's some kind of chemical imbalance in my own head? It could be convincing me to take on all these assignments, when there's really nothing that needs to be done."

"But what about Wyandotte?" she asks. "We went to the Harbisons' home, knowing that it was going to collapse, and it did. How could something that precise be a chemical imbalance?"

"I spent a lot of time thinking about that today. The only theory that supports the diagnosis is that somehow, you remembered these people from your childhood. You knew that they still lived in Wyandotte and that they might need help. By that point in our travels, our thought patterns were very much in synch. Somehow, you projected the need to go see them into my mind, and I followed it there."

She looks at me in disbelief. "That's a hell of a stretch."

"I know. I didn't say I believe it; I'm just not ready to rule it out."

"Tristan, I know how much you're looking for anything that will bring these assignments to an end. But I don't want you starting treatment for a mental illness if you don't really have one. Just be careful. I don't trust this Miranda person. I trust her even less now that she's had sex with you."

Our waiter chooses this opportune moment to approach our table and check on us, precisely in time to hear Rebecca's last statement. He pauses, giving an almost comical look of surprise and a hint of admiration. "Can I get you anything else?" he inquires.

"We're fine," Rebecca answers.

He leaves the table, now free to savor the tidbit he has overheard.

"I'm not ready to commit myself to an institution yet," I tell her. "There are some tests I can take. If they come back positive, then I can start some form of treatment. If they come back negative, then I guess I'm God's little messenger, and I can continue to deal with that."

"Just please, whatever you do, be very sure about it. If you stop taking these assignments and they're legitimate, innocent people could die."

Rebecca's warning stays with me for the rest of the evening. We finish dinner and spend some more time in the hotel room, letting basic cable TV fill in the long stretches of silence that this day has brought upon us. I'm tempted to watch the news, to see if there's any progress in Cedarsburg, but I know that the nature of the media is such that the tornado is already old news. At some point in the middle of the televised entertainment—such as it is—we decide that it is time to go to bed. There's no intimacy in the room, no closeness. We are more like two friends who have decided to split the room to save a little money. It feels strange, given how close we were just last week. And it makes me wonder if my dalliance with Miranda has cost me Rebecca's trust permanently. Is there a period of penance I can endure to prove myself to her or am I doomed to be doubted for the rest of our time together?

Despite my overactive thoughts, I fall into sleep sometime after 2:00 in the morning, dimly aware that Rebecca is asleep on her half of the bed as well. That should be the end of it, the end of a very long and strange day. But something has other plans for me. My current state of uncertainty keeps me from knowing if it's divine providence or mental illness, but the sensations are very familiar.

It starts in my teeth this time, which is unusual. The pain radiates out through my jaw, down my neck, and shoots through both arms. I am jolted awake with a start, and I cry out with the unexpectedness of the sensation. This awakens Rebecca, who has apparently become used to seeing this in me, and she holds on to me, to keep me from shaking and twitching off the bed. This goes on for more than a minute, and the images I see, the information I receive—it's almost more than I can bear. When at last the pain subsides, I am trembling and panting to catch my breath again.

Rebecca wipes the sweat off my forehead with the edge of the pillowcase. "I guess it was too much to hope for, not getting an assignment," she says. "So where are we going this time?"

My answer is laced with fear. "Nowhere."

"Nowhere? You mean the next assignment is here in Lawrence?"

All I can do is nod in response.

"Tristan, what's wrong? What aren't you telling me? Who are you supposed to warn?"

"It's Miranda," I answer, still not believing it myself. "She's going to die tomorrow if I don't stop her."

Chapter 9

Rebecca looks at me in disbelief. "Miranda? *That* Miranda?"

"Yes."

"What are you going to do?"

"What do you mean? I'm going to warn her."

"But what about the schizophrenia thing and the tests?" she asks. "I thought you were doubting the assignments now."

"I can't take that chance," I tell her, sitting up in bed unsteadily. "Until it's been conclusively proven that I'm mentally ill, I have to go based on the belief that this is real, and I need to keep warning people who are in danger."

"What will she think of that?"

"Well, I hope to hell that since she's the subject, she'll be grateful and she'll listen to me."

"Yeah, no kidding."

"What time is it?" I ask.

"About 4:15. It's still dark out."

"I should try to get some more sleep," I decide.

"Do you want me to go with you when you tell her?"

"No," I say too quickly. Then, more calmly, I add, "Thank you, but I need to do this alone. I'm supposed to meet with her at 10:00 this morning. I'll tell her then."

Any sleep that follows is fitful at best. I lie awake for many minutes, staring and the ceiling and replaying the details of what may happen today. When I eventually slip back out of consciousness, I turn over again and again, searching for elusive physical comfort amid the overpowering emotional discomfort. As daylight saturates the room early in the 8:00 hour, I realize that there's no further hope for sleep, so I get out of bed and start my day. Rebecca does likewise a few minutes later.

"Are you doing all right?" she asks, already knowing the answer, from the sound of her voice.

"No, I'm a wreck. I want to go over to her place now and tell her, get it over with."

"What time is … you know … *it* supposed to happen?"

"At 3:05 this afternoon."

"Then you have time. Give yourself a chance to work out what you're going to say. She's not expecting you until 10:00. Coming over early, all in a panic, won't do much to dispel her beliefs about your mental state, right?"

She's making infinite sense. "You've got a lot of nerve being so rational when I'm in this state of mind," I chide gently.

"I think one of us is the keeper of the rational thoughts at all times," she decides. "This morning, it's just my turn. I don't suppose I could buy you breakfast?"

"Thank you, but no. I'm too shook up to eat. I'm just going to walk for a while before I meet with her."

"Walk or pace?" she asks.

"Pacing is a kind of walking. I'll be in the park across the street."

"You want some company?"

"Not this time. Sorry."

Now dressed and ready, I hurry out of the hotel room and into the park. I wasn't entirely honest with Rebecca. Yes, I need some time to myself, to walk and think, but the choice of destination isn't random. I'm looking for somebody.

There are a few people in the park at this hour, but no sign of the one I seek. Without a name to call, I am left with general queries, and I shout them to anyone who can hear me. "Where are you? Are you here? Please, answer me!"

The volume and vehemence of my calls startles passersby, and very likely makes them question my sanity almost as much as I have in the last day. But at the moment, I don't care. I need to see him again, and if I can call him to me, I'll do whatever it takes. "It's me, Tristan! It's Hamesh—I need you!"

Still, no one responds. Then it occurs to me: I *do* have a name I can call, if I could just remember it. *What the hell did he say it was? Otis? Rufus? Moses? No, I remember—Amos.*

I let out a staccato burst of whistling sounds, then call, "Amos! Come here, boy. Where's that big dog? Where's Amos?"

I am truly a portrait of street theatre this morning to everyone who can see and hear me. From calling to people who aren't there, I have moved on to calling dogs that aren't there. For my next trick, ladies and gentlemen …

With no one responding, I am on the verge of giving up. Then, from across the park, a familiar face approaches, running the best he can, given his advanced age. Amos bounds over to me and leans against my legs, wagging his tail as he lets me pet him. "I am so glad to see you, you smelly old beast. Yes I am. Now, where's your daddy?" He tilts his head the way dogs so often do at the sound of a question directed at them. "Where's your daddy this morning?"

He lets out a little boof and points his nose east. "Take me there," I instruct, and he begins a much slower trot across the park. I follow behind him, hoping desperately that the dog isn't out here by himself.

"There *are* leash laws, you know," an officious man in a sweater vest says as Amos and I pass by him.

"Blow me," I reply, miles from interested.

As we traverse a small hill, I see another familiar face in the distance, seated on a park bench. It's him, my prophet of the other day. Upon seeing him, I quicken my pace until I am standing before him. He looks up at me.

My first words to him barely make sense to me. "Are you real?"

"Are *you?*" he replies.

I have to laugh a bit at the question. "I think so."

"Then I guess I am too."

"Do you remember me?" I ask.

"You know the answer to that. If you thought I didn't, you wouldn't be here."

133

"Yes, but why are *you* here? Are you here because I asked you to be? Do you live here? Who are you really?"

He shakes his head a bit. "So many questions, when you really came here to ask me just one."

"Is it true, what I saw, what's going to happen today?"

"I can't answer that for you. It hasn't been decided yet."

"So you know what I saw? You know what I'm supposed to do?"

"I know what your mission is," he says. "What you're supposed to do is less clear."

"Please, I need you. You have the gift."

"Gift? We all have gifts, Hamesh. What matters is how we use them."

"I'm so uncertain. I don't know if I can even trust my own mind."

"Why would you doubt? You trust me, and you don't even know who I am. You're so quick to trust others, so why would you not trust yourself? You know what the past two years have held. So many missions finished, so many people."

"But what I've learned lately; I'm unsure of my sanity."

"What is sanity? If you were in a room with a thousand people, and everyone but you saw flying pink elephants, would they be insane or would you?"

"I … I guess I don't know."

"Sanity is just the product of mass perception. It's for you to decide if you believe others or believe yourself."

"You call me Hamesh; that means *five*. Am I one of Ha Tesha? Am I one of The Nine?"

He smiles warmly at me. "Amos likes you. He never lets strangers pet him."

"Why does Miranda have to die?"

His smile fades at the question, and his eyes pierce mine. "She doesn't. God sent one to shield her and one to shepherd her. Which one will get there first?"

"Me. I'm the shield. That's right, isn't it?"

"I'm hungry," he says. "I hate to trouble you, but do you have a few dollars so I could get some breakfast? They have french toast this morning."

I pull twenty dollars out of my pocket and give it to him. "Get a side of sausage too." With that, I turn and start to walk away. Remembering, I turn back to him and add, "Thanks for the train thing the other day. It worked."

The minutes until 10:00 pass far too slowly, and I am wracked with anxiety the whole time. As with many of my assignments, I rehearse what I am going to say, but I know that when the moment arrives, what comes out will most likely be spontaneous. At the appointed time, I enter the psychology building and rush to the room where Miranda said she would be. It is a small meeting room, and she is inside, setting up some recording equipment for our tests.

Forgetting myself, I sprint to her side and enfold her in my arms, breathing heavily from running and from the total wreck I've made of myself in the last six hours. She puts a hand on my shoulder and says in a surprised voice, "I'm glad to see you too."

As I pull away, gently embarrassed by the scene I'm making, she gets a good look at my face. "You look terrible," she says. "What happened?"

"Can we sit down?" I ask.

"Sure." She sits, and I sit in the chair next to hers. "Tell me what's going on. Did something happen since I saw you?"

"Yes. Miranda, in the middle of the night ... I got a new assignment."

"I see. And that means you won't be able to stay and work with me."

"No, it's not like that. The assignment is here in Lawrence."

"Well then, that's good."

"No, it isn't." I can't put it off any longer. "Miranda, the person I was told to warn is you."

She looks surprised at this announcement, but not as surprised as I expected. "It's me? What are you supposed to warn me about?"

"This afternoon at 3:00, you're going to go to your bank, Union Consolidated just off campus. While you're there, a man is going to enter the bank, intending to rob it. He'll have a gun, and he'll be very nervous, almost panicky. There's going to be an off-duty cop in the bank too, and he's going to try to stop this guy. I saw gunfire, and ...

Miranda, if you go to that bank this afternoon, you're not going to come out of it alive."

The worst silence I've ever experienced fills that room. Her expression is inscrutable. I've delivered dozens of messages like this before; there's no easy way to tell someone their life is in danger. In the past, I've been met with disbelief, fear, hostility, and all manner of emotional outbursts. Miranda is giving me nothing, a stony silence that defies analysis.

Many seconds later, she replies quietly, "Thank you for telling me about this. I can't imagine how difficult it was for you to know this and have to tell it to someone who's close to you. Do you think you'll be up to doing the tests this morning?"

"What?"

"I'd still like to proceed with the tests we have planned."

"Miranda, it's okay to react to what I told you."

She smiles an awkward little smile and averts her gaze. "I'm not sure quite how to react to something like that."

"That's fine. Please just tell me that you won't go to the bank this afternoon."

"I don't know."

"You don't know? After what you just heard, you don't know?"

"Tristan, think about it. This message came to you in your sleep, after the day you and I shared yesterday. You had some anxiety about starting a relationship with me, coupled with anxiety about the prospects of a schizophrenia diagnosis. It would be only natural for your mind to come up with a scenario in which you had to prove to me that you *were* actually getting these messages, and at the same time 'save me' from danger, so you could convince both of us that they're genuine."

"Just tell me this: were you planning to go to the bank this afternoon?"

"Yes."

"You see? How could I know that if the messages aren't real?"

She opens her purse and brings out a check and a deposit slip for that bank. "This was on my bedside table yesterday when you were in my room. It's the deposit I'm going to make later today. You must have seen it yesterday and the detail stuck in your mind."

I stare at the document in her hand, trying hard to remember if I really did see it yesterday. I know how real the pain was this morning. This was no dream; it was as real as any assignment I've ever received—which still raises the question, how real was any assignment I've ever received?

"But we haven't done a single test," I remind her. "Nothing's been proven. This could very easily be everything I say it is. At least tell me you won't go to the bank this afternoon."

"I have to make this deposit."

"Then at least go at a different time. Please."

"Tristan," she says gently, "as dedicated as you are to these visions being real, that's how dedicated I am to my belief in the pursuit of this diagnosis. If I were to alter my plans because of what you told me, I'd feel like I was being untrue to my research."

"But you could die if you go there."

"I'll go in there knowing what you told me, and I'll know what to look out for. If things get bad, I'll just duck. And then, when I come back safe and sound, I'll be a lot more willing to believe in something paranormal. If I'm not there at that time, how will I know if your vision was accurate?"

"Miranda, please—even if you go five minutes earlier or later, please don't gamble with your life like that. If you want me to, I'll skip giving the next message to someone, and we can see what happens."

"Why should my life matter more than someone else's?"

"Because it does!" I shout, growing frustrated with her unflappable calm. I've given her the equivalent of a death sentence, complete with escape clause, and she insists on going to the execution anyway. It doesn't make sense.

"I'm sorry," she says. "I'm upsetting you. I tell you what: I'll give it some thought, and make up my mind later this afternoon about whether to go. For now, I'd really like to begin those tests together. Are you still willing to try?"

Knowing that I am unable to sway her, I quietly answer, "Yes."

She brings out a book called *Diagnostic and Statistical Manual of Mental Disorders,* which clearly looks like hours of fun reading, and turns to the relevant section. And the questions begin. For the next hour, she bombards me with yes-or-no questions, what-if scenarios, recaps of countless assignments I've been on, and general questions about me and my family, particularly our medical history.

In the middle of it all, she asks, "Did you tell Rebecca about what you and I shared?"

"Is this part of the diagnostic process?"

"No, but I've finally worked up the courage to ask."

"I didn't tell her."

"Oh."

"But she knows."

"Oh." After a moment, she asks, "How did she find out?"

"Women's intuition or psychic thought transference. Whichever one fits in with your world view."

"How did she take the news?"

"Well, I'm walking without a limp, so that's a start."

"She wasn't happy about it, then?"

My tone turns more serious. "No, she wasn't."

"I'm sorry, Tristan. I didn't mean to screw up your relationship."

"You haven't. I made the decision, and I knew what it could mean for me and Rebecca. We talked last night, and she wants us to stay together."

"I'm guessing by *us,* you're not referring to you and me."

"No, not so much. But I want to be your friend. And as your friend, I want to ask you again to reconsider going to the bank this afternoon."

"If you're concerned," she says, "you could call the police and tell them what's going to happen."

"I can't. For one thing, they'd ask how I know. And for another, it's the presence of one cop that leads to the gunfire. I can't imagine how much worse it would make it if more guns were present."

"That must be awful for you," she says, "the burden of wondering what you can change, and whether your intervention will make things better or worse. You see, this is precisely why I want that schizophrenia diagnosis to be right. I want to work with you to relieve that burden, so you don't have to go through the fear you're going through now with me."

"What do your tests tell you? Do I have it?"

She looks down at the book as she speaks. "It's too soon to say for sure, but from what you've told me, your behavior patterns are consistent with a patient who has schizophrenia. You're older than the typical onset age, but it's possible that you had minor symptoms years ago that you didn't even realize."

"So what do we do now?" I ask.

"I have a friend in town who's a psychiatrist. If you're willing to stay, you can talk to him tomorrow, ask him any questions you have. He's going to want to start you on medication, but I think we can make great progress without it. But it's up to you."

"Oh." I wish I knew what else to say, but the tone of her voice is one of certainty, of finality. It's difficult to go from heroic to treatable in one morning.

She sees the look on my face and approaches me, putting her arms around me in a comforting gesture. "I'm sorry to introduce this to your life," she says gently, "but it's important that you know."

"It's not your fault," I reply, not entirely convinced of that.

"Try to look at the good side. You're free now. You can look at those assignments for what they are: your mind trying to convince you to do things that you don't need to do. You can settle down now, stop traveling so much, find a job that you want to keep. Maybe even start a family with Rebecca, if that's what you want." I'm intrigued to note a little hitch in her voice at the end as she says that. "And you don't have to worry about my being in any danger just for going to the bank this afternoon."

"At least do this for me—call me when you get home from the bank, so I know you're all right."

"Of course," she says.

"If you don't mind, I think I need some time alone."

I spend the next several hours walking the streets of Lawrence, Kansas. The thought of human companionship seems overwhelming to me now, so I spend my second day in a row in near isolation, internalizing my feelings—just as Miranda said this illness would make me do. It's so hard to reconcile everything that's happened with everything she told me. The assignments when I didn't stay long enough to learn the outcome—*that* I can accept. But what about the ones when

I did? What about Cedarsburg? How could a mental illness tell me to be in exactly the right place and time to help those people?

At this precise moment, a man walks by, talking into a cell phone. I hear him say the words, "Just because I'm crazy doesn't mean that I'm not right," in a playful tone. The words stop me in my tracks. Was I meant to hear them? After a few seconds, I turn around to look at the man, and to my dismay, he's nowhere to be seen. *Oh, brain, don't do this to me now.* I'm relieved to catch a glimpse of him entering a building. But what if what he said applies to me? Do schizophrenia and the assignments have to be mutually exclusive? It's something I'll have to discuss with Miranda tomorrow.

The thought of her makes me check my watch. It is 2:40 in the afternoon; I've been walking the streets for hours, looking like a well-dressed transient. I have to wonder if she's been to the bank already and simply forgot to call, whether she still plans to go at the regular time, or whether she'll put it off, in deference to what I told her. I want to believe, truly want to believe, that it's the illness talking, that she's in no danger, no matter when she goes. But just because I'm crazy, does that mean I'm not right?

Minute after minute drags by. I watch as 3:00 becomes 3:15, with no call from Miranda. Inside, I am in anguish, unsure of what to do, until I see two Lawrence police cars go zooming by, lights and sirens going. They are heading toward campus, toward the very bank where Miranda was going. It is six blocks away from where I am now, and nothing can stop me from going there.

I break into a run, or at least as close to a run as I can get with my current energy level, and I cover the distance in about five minutes. By the time I get there, four police cars have the entire block cordoned off to vehicular traffic. As I feared, they have all converged on the bank, some heading inside, others keeping the public back from out front. My heart races with terror as I see this, and my instinct tells me to disregard safety and go inside the bank myself. I am across the street from it, about to sprint over there, when I am surprised to feel a hand reach out and hold me by the arm. Startled, I turn to see a man, maybe twenty-five years old, wearing an old army fatigue jacket of olive green and a pair of tan pants. His features are pleasant, but his eyes have a look that denies his few years.

"She's already gone, Tristan," he says gently.

"What? What are you talking about?"

"Miranda. She's gone from here."

I should be astonished at his level of knowledge, but things I have seen and heard in the past week allow me to continue the conversation. "Then why didn't she call me? She was supposed to call me when she left the bank."

"No, Tristan, you don't understand. I'm sorry, but … she's gone in the way you warned her about."

Now the astonishment begins to creep in. "No. You're not real," I tell him, surprised at my own certainty.

"I'm afraid I am. I could punch you in the arm if that would help, but I think you've been punched enough."

"Who are you?" I ask.

"My name is Alan."

"How do you know what happened? Were you in the bank too?"

"No, I was out here."

"Then how could you—?"

He interrupts. "I guided her to the other side."

My head feels like it is in a fog. The most incredible words continue to pour from his lips, and I am too stunned to grieve or to even doubt him. I have to know what's happening, what this all means. "Are you an angel?"

He smiles pleasantly. It's obviously a question he's heard before. "No, I'm not an angel."

"Some kind of, what, grim reaper then? What?"

"No, Tristan, I'm a person, just like you. My gifts are just a little different than yours. Sometimes when people die before they're ready, they don't know where to go. I can see them, and I help guide them to the other side."

The tears I have been fighting begin to show. "Miranda?"

"Yes. I'm sorry, my friend. I know it's not much consolation, but you should know she was at peace when I escorted her."

My head drops to my chest as despair washes over me. Alan puts a comforting arm around my shoulder. "Come on, let's walk," he says. "Let's get away from this place."

I don't even know where we walk; my mind is somewhere else, everywhere else, anywhere but here. "How long have you been doing this?" I ask him.

"Almost ten years now. I've probably helped more than five hundred people since then."

"Doesn't it bother you?"

"It did at first," he replies. "But before too long, I looked at it as a gift, a chance to do something for people who can't possibly repay the kindness. And that helped me feel really good about myself. Before it all started, I was just an outcast in high school. The other kids thought I was weird. They had no idea how right they were. Then one day, there was an accident outside the school. One of the jocks collapsed on the football field during practice. And then, just like that, he came to me; he told me he had to go somewhere but he didn't know how. For a few seconds, it freaked me out. Then my mind filled with the knowledge of what to tell him, and I helped him move on. Since that day, I've kept using that knowledge."

"So do you see—ghosts—everywhere?"

"No, it's not like that, fortunately. The ones I see are meant especially for me. And you're not dead either, so don't go getting all Bruce Willis on me."

"Then how did you know to expect me?" I ask.

"When I escort a soul, I have access to certain thoughts. You were among those thoughts. I got to experience the day you spent together."

I hesitate a moment and offer him a concerned look. "All of it?"

His knowing smile is my answer. "Yeah, that too. Don't worry, I've gotten good at keeping my mouth shut."

I have to know. "Did she say anything to you?"

"Yes, she did. She said, 'Tell Tristan I'm sorry I forgot to duck.'"

Despite myself, I have to laugh a little at the absurdity of the message.

"She also said she's sorry she doubted you," he adds.

"Alan, do you know where she is now?"

"No. Sorry. I don't get to see that part. But I know that every feeling that runs through me when I help someone there is strong and peaceful."

"Can I ask you something? What happens to you if you refuse to help someone?"

He looks surprised at the question. "Why would I refuse?"

"I don't know. You're busy, you're tired, you're sick to death of helping?"

"I've never thought about it," he says. "I imagine the person would stay with me until I could escort them. But I'm always happy to do it, so I've never refused."

I shake my head, fighting off more anguish that wants to escape from me. "I could have saved her. I tried to stop her."

"I know you did. She made her choice. You didn't do a single thing wrong."

"So it's true then," I say to him. "These gifts of mine, they're real. I'm not schizophrenic."

"No, of course you're not. *She* was."

This stops me in my tracks and I stare at him in disbelief. "What?"

"She had the illness. She had a fairly tentative grasp on reality."

I'm astonished by the news. "Did she know?"

"I'm not sure. If she did, she was strongly in denial about it. She was so focused on helping others, she forgot to help herself."

"How could you know that about her, if she didn't even know it about herself?"

"I can pick things up about people just by being near them. It's how I learned about her, and how I'm learning about you right now. If what I'm seeing is correct, I should feel honored to be in your presence."

"No, please don't talk like that. Alan, I'm so confused by everything that's going on. I don't know what to do, where to go, or even who to trust."

"You trust me. Now trust yourself, Tristan. There's nothing wrong with your mind. Far from it. You're going to be very important to a lot of people in the days ahead. But you have to leave Kansas. Find The Nine."

"You know about them?"

"Of course. And I know that you have to go to them."

"But I don't know where they are."

"You'll find out. Someone's reached out to them on your behalf."

Jason. His message must have reached them.

"I should stay for Miranda's …" The next word catches painfully in my throat. "Funeral."

"No. You shouldn't. I know that sounds cold, but it's the reality of the situation. You're needed elsewhere. I'll go, and I'll offer your condolences."

He's such a mystery to me, this person I've only met minutes ago. He's reaching out to me, offering acts of kindness for no apparent reason. I have to know. "Why are you doing all this for me?"

"We're different from other people. Most of the time, we do what we do alone, in isolation, and there's almost no one who understands. When we have the chance to meet each other, it's important that we reach out. It's also important that you keep Rebecca close to you."

"It is?"

"Her part in this isn't over. Take her with you."

"I'll try. We had a fight."

"Fix things again. Without her there, you could be in very great danger."

He puts his arms around me at this point, in a way that no one ever has before. More than a friend, less than a lover. I imagine this is what a dear brother's embrace would feel like. And I don't want him to let go. When at last we separate, I tell him, "I don't know how to thank you for everything you've done."

"You already did. Find The Nine, and be safe."

By the time I make it back to my hotel room, I feel dizzy and light-headed. It could be shock; I don't know. Staggering into the bathroom, I quickly drink two glasses of water, but even that is too much for my system to take, and I throw them up into the sink and switch to a cold, wet washcloth for my head. Taking it with me, I find my way to the bed and fall down heavily on my back. For a blissful moment, I feel like I could lose consciousness, but the feeling quickly leaves me, and I am left in an intermediate state—deprived of the nepenthe of unconsciousness but too far from lucidity to be of any use to anyone. I become aware of my own sobs, but I'm unclear of the reason for them. Are they because Miranda and I were so recently intimate? Am I feeling guilty over her fate? Or am I just weeping for myself, from the exhaustion of one more crisis I'm ill-equipped to handle? Whatever the cause, it is many minutes before the anguish finds an end to its release.

Not long after that, in the dazed semi-awareness that follows, I hear the door to the hotel room open, and Rebecca enters, coming straight to my bedside. "I heard what happened," she says quietly. "Are you all right?"

"I wasn't there. I tried to stop her, but she wouldn't listen."

"Are you feeling sick?"

"I don't know. I don't know what I'm feeling. I wish I couldn't feel anything at all."

"Shh," she whispers. "It's okay. Everything you're feeling, everything you're going through. Just let it come out."

"I don't have schizophrenia. The assignments are real."

"That's good. I'm glad you found that out. How did you know?"

"I met someone who told me. He's like us, but different. Rebecca, I'm starting to think that what we can do—this sort of thing—it's more widespread than we realized."

"I'm just glad you're all right. I was worried about you when I heard what happened at the bank."

"If you want to say 'I told you so,'" I offer, half in jest, "now would be the time."

"I hope you know me better than that," she scolds gently. "I'm just grateful not to lose you."

"This person I met, Alan, he said I have to leave here and find Ha Tesha. He said you need to come with me. That I'd need you. That is … if you still want to be with me."

She's silent for a moment, then says, "These past few days have hurt. When you chose to be with her, it really stung me. I know you and I haven't been together for a long time, but I'd like to believe that everything we've been through together meant something."

"It did," I say quietly, struggling to get to a seated position. "And it does."

"It's going to mess with my head if you spend the next few days grieving for someone you just met. If you're going to be falling apart with guilt, tell me now, because I don't think I can watch that."

It's hard to admit that she's right. "She's not mine to grieve. She's somebody I met who died. End of story. If you come with me, I'll find a way to think of her as another assignment that didn't succeed. It's unfortunate, it's tragic, but it's not my tragedy."

"I'm sorry to sound cold about this, Tristan, but I need you at full capacity. If you're undercut by misplaced emotions, we could get hurt. Everything that Stelios told us about is still happening, and like it or not, we could very easily get dragged into the middle of it."

"Will you be able to trust me again after everything that's happened?" I ask.

"Every time you give me reason to trust you, I will. But it's not automatic. If I keep doubting you, there's only so much I can take."

"I understand."

"Did this person you met tell you where to find Ha Tesha?"

"He didn't know, but he said that I would find out."

We are both startled by the ringing of Rebecca's cell phone in the quiet of the room. She fumbles for it momentarily and then produces it from her pocket. "Hello? ... Jason, hi. ... I'm fine. ... Yes, he's here, but he's not in much of a shape to talk. We both found out what happened. I'm so sorry about your friend. ... Yes, I think so. ... Sure, we'll be there. I'll tell him. ... See you then." She ends the call and looks at me again. "Jason has news."

Chapter 10

Jason has news. Even without hearing it, I know it can only mean one thing: Ha Tesha received his message and made contact, just as Alan said they would. As I rise from my isolation, I prepare myself for what feels like the next part of my journey. I've been in Kansas far too long. I need to meet these people, this council of messengers, and learn the truth of who I am. Now that mental illness has been crossed of the list of suspects, I have only sanity to fall back on, and sanity demands answers.

Rebecca encourages me to rest, but if I cloister myself, the temptation will be to remain cloistered and not face what's ahead. So instead, I get out of bed, let some light back into the room, and try very hard to convince myself that I'm not responsible for Miranda's death. The very thought of it makes me wince. Someone I spoke to this morning is gone from the world; someone I held in my arms yesterday, someone I kissed and touched, someone who shared her intimacy with me has died so unnecessarily. Moments like this, despite all my otherworldly gifts, make me feel like I don't have the first clue how this world truly works.

Within the hour, Rebecca and I are back in the psychology building, meeting Jason. He has chosen a different meeting room this time, and I'm glad. It would be too painful to be in the room where I first met Miranda. Jason's eyes meet mine; his expression instantly tells me that he knows I've gotten close with Miranda, and that he is hurting too.

"Hi," he says quietly. "Thank you for coming."

"Sure. How are you holding up?"

"I don't know. I think I'm still in shock. You?"

"Yeah, I'm right there with you," I tell him. "I'm so sorry this happened. I did my best to talk her out of going—"

"I know," he says, putting up a hand to discourage me from saying more. "She had her reasons, and there was no changing her mind."

"I met someone," I tell him, "someone with gifts similar to mine. He told me that what I'm experiencing is real, and that I have to find The Nine."

"I can help."

"They contacted you?" Rebecca asks.

"Yes. Apparently, they've been looking for you. I know where they are."

"Where are they?" I ask.

"Zion, Illinois."

"Zion? Seriously?"

"It's a small city north of Chicago, almost on the Wisconsin border. They're eager to see you."

"Yeah, I think I'm getting a bit eager to see them too." He hands me a set of directions that he's written out and I ask, "They're expecting me?"

"Yes. I told them your name and that you'd be coming to see them soon."

After a brief pause, I ask, "Will you be going to Miranda's funeral?"

"I think so. There's some things I want to say to her. Things I guess I should have said a long time ago."

"I'm sorry for your loss," I tell him.

"I'm sorry for yours," he replies.

"Jason, if I'd had any idea that you ..."

"No, it's all right. You don't have to say it. My failure to say what should have been said is just something I have to live with. You've got places to be. Be careful out there, finding this group."

"I will."

"And please let me know how it goes?"

"Definitely. I have a feeling that by the time this week is over, I'll have enough material for your doctoral thesis."

"There's more," Jason says. "Rebecca, I did more digging about the dreams and what happened to you with the soot. And I found something."

With surprise painted all over her face, she replies, "You did?"

"Yes. In Hopi Indian medicine, of all places. Hugely discredited by science, of course, but the details were so close that I had to pursue it. I don't know the Hopi words for it, but in English it translates to trans-somnolent manifestation. According to a professor in KU's Native American Studies department, a few of the old Hopi medicine men could train their minds to enter the thoughts of members of the tribe who were very sick, unconscious, even comatose. Once inside, they were able to heal these people by identifying their ailments and manifesting from a dream state the medicines they needed. And here's the cool part: it was said that these medicine men could awaken from this dreamlike state physically carrying the ailment of the sick tribe member in their hands. They would then bury it in sacred ground and pray over it so that it could be returned to the earth."

"Oh my God ..." she says.

Jason looks very proud of his discovery. "That sounds so much like what you described."

"It does, it really does."

"But you have to be careful," he warns. "From what the professor told me, this is a very rare and powerful ability, and it can be dangerous for you. I really recommend that you don't try it again until you know exactly what you're dealing with."

"Thanks, Jason. Thank you for all your help."

"You're welcome. I'm glad I met you, both of you."

"And thank you for the information you shared," I add. "This may just be the answers I've been looking for."

We leave the chemistry building and return to the dampened sunlight of late afternoon. "I guess that's it then," I offer. "We can check out of the hotel, make travel plans, and fly to Chicago."

"I'd ..." she starts, but then stops short.

"What?"

"It's nothing. It's just—I'd like to say good-bye to Kavi."

"Of course. I'm sorry; that makes perfect sense. It just slipped my mind. If you'd like some privacy, I can meet you back at the hotel."

"No, I actually think this'll be easier if you're with me. Would you come with?"

"Of course. I'd like to say good-bye to him too."

We walk the short distance back to the meteorology lab, where, after a brief search, we find Kavi in front of a computer monitor, hard at work. He looks up and sees us, and immediately stops what he's doing to come and speak with us privately. "Hey, you two," he says. "It's good to see you."

"Good to see you too," Rebecca replies.

"Tristan, I heard what happened. I'm really sorry."

"Thank you. I'll be all right."

"We've come to say good-bye," Rebecca tells him, her voice obviously fighting back a wave of strong emotion.

"Yeah, I was afraid you'd say that."

"Jason found The Nine, and we have to go meet them, figure out who they are and what they want with Tristan."

He nods in understanding, and I think I detect a similar wave of emotion that he's working hard to suppress. "It was amazing to see you again. I can't even tell you how great."

"You too," she says.

At this awkward moment, I awkwardly chime in. "I can't thank you enough for all the help you gave us in Cedarsburg. I don't think we could have saved nearly as many lives if it weren't for you and your team."

"Glad to do it," he replies. "The data I was able to collect is incredible. If all goes well, we may be saving a lot more lives with what we've learned."

"So, your hearing is coming up in a couple of days?" Rebecca asks.

"Next Monday. I'll remember everything you told me, and I'll be nice to the judge."

"You should be fine."

"I just hate to see you go so soon."

"This isn't good-bye forever," she tells him. "I'll call you. And who knows? Maybe the urge to go back to school will hit again."

"I know you're with someone else now, and I don't want to interfere with that. But having you near reminded me of how much I treasure your friendship."

She hugs him upon hearing this, and holds him close to her for many long seconds. I wish I could be elsewhere for this moment, not because it is difficult to watch but because I feel like an intruder in a very private exchange. So I find things in the room to look at instead—computer monitors, bulletin boards, ceiling tiles (138 of them in the room, I determine).

When their embrace ends, he looks into her eyes. "Rebecca Traeger," he says quietly, "you know how to make an impression on a guy."

She smiles at these words. "You're not so forgettable yourself, Kavi Ariashi."

"Please be careful, both of you. From what Rebecca tells me, the things you do can get a little dangerous."

"We will," she answers. "I'll call you once we get settled."

With the good-byes behind us, we return to the hotel and check out, taking one last look at Lawrence, Kansas, our home for the past week. So much has happened; it's difficult to wrap my mind around it. Of all the places I've been and the things I've done in the last two years, this week has felt the most significant. And now it's time to meet The Nine, whoever they are, and try to get some answers.

We return the SUV to the rental company at Kansas City's airport, then make our way to the terminal. We find seats on a 7:15 PM flight to Chicago and settle in. It's a ninety-minute flight, so we'll have just enough time to rest and take a few deep breaths without feeling confined in our seats. And when we get there, then what? Will they be expecting me to stay with them? If I truly am one of their nine, they're incomplete without me. But who knows how long they've been working without me there? What if I don't like them or the work they do? What if it's no better than a cult, and they want me as their newest member? These questions flood my mind, keeping me from getting comfortable during the flight.

Rebecca is preoccupied looking out the window as the Midwest passes thousands of feet below us. Our time in Lawrence couldn't have been easy for her. Seeing Kavi after all these years, then the ordeal of the tornado, our argument, and my regrettable decision to spend time with Miranda. Even if she forgives me, I wonder if I can forgive myself.

"I'm fine," she says, startling me out of my reverie. "Don't punish yourself."

"I thought you weren't going to poke around in my thoughts," I remind her as she turns to face me.

"I don't have to," she replies. "What's going through your head is so loud, it's like someone's narrating an audiobook."

"Sorry."

"You're right, this week has been difficult. But I don't regret it. It's obvious that I was meant to go with you. I know that now. I also know that there's going to be problems and challenges along the way. I think the best thing we can do for each other is work as a team. I don't know what's going to happen when we get there, but I have a strange feeling that something bad is waiting for us."

"I feel it too," I tell her. "Can you tell anything more about what it is?"

"No, not specifically. Just something dangerous. Someone dangerous."

"Great. Haven't had enough of those lately."

Arriving at O'Hare Airport, we retrieve our luggage and go to the rental car area. Though it is only 9:15 at night, I feel very tired after everything that's happened in the last three days. We choose a company based on the presence of a "Cars Available" sign, since we didn't make a reservation ahead of time. The woman behind the desk smiles pleasantly at us as we approach. "How can I help you tonight?"

"We'd like to rent a car," I reply. "I notice you have some available."

She looks at her computer screen. "That's right. Are you looking for something for the weekend or longer?"

"I'd like to start with the weekend and have the option to extend if needed. We're here on business, and we're not sure how long we'll be in town."

"Okay. The daily rate for a compact is $72. If you extend to a full week, we can give you the weekly rate of $355."

"You wouldn't happen to have a convertible, would you?"

She checks availability. "I do have a Chrysler Sebring convertible on the lot. It's $114 a day or $596 for the week. Would you like that?"

Rebecca and I answer in unison. "Yes."

Climbing into the Sebring is like getting together with an old friend. This one is green, rather than the gold that took us from Florida to Ohio last week, but the controls are familiar, and the feeling when that top comes down is like taking a first healing breath after being held underwater for too long. As we head northeast on the I-294 tollway, I feel some of my strength returning to me.

"Now this is more like it," Rebecca comments, her hands held aloft over her head, playing with the breeze. "I may have to get me one of these."

"You're in a good mood," I observe, "given everything that's happened over the past few days."

"I've decided not to dwell on it," she replies. "It is what it is. I can panic and treat it like a life-altering crisis, or I can call it new circumstances and take it as it comes. That's the way I want to roll."

"I wish I shared your outlook. I'm just so preoccupied with The Nine and what might happen. I don't know what to do."

"You said the most important part, Tristan: what *might* happen. I know that living assignment to assignment can make you feel like your future is already written, but you have to keep believing that you have a say in what happens with your life. Things change. You didn't know I'd be traveling with you, right?"

"Right."

"So there you go. There's change right there. Meet these people, hear what they have to say, and decide if this is how you want the next part of your life to play out."

As usual, she makes a lot of sense. I only hope that when the time comes, I can do the reasonable thing.

Interstate 294 becomes Interstate 94, and we follow Jason's directions, getting on smaller state highways as we approach the city of Zion. Normally on an assignment, I know exactly how to get there, but this isn't an assignment, and I have to rely on an actual road map. It's a strange feeling. It's been almost ten years since I've been to Chicago, and nothing looks familiar. Green Bay Road takes us into a residential area, which is mostly devoid of pedestrians and traffic at 10:30 at night. I hate to arrive this late, and I actually contemplate getting a hotel for the night and arriving in the morning, but they are expecting me, so I press on.

Rebecca helps me to navigate to the address Jason gave us, and I pull up in front of a long one-story structure that looks like a nondescript office building. "Is this it?" she asks.

"The address matches. I guess this is the place."

"Is there even anybody here?" she asks. "It looks a little dark and deserted."

"One way to find out." I put the top up and we get out of the car. "Let's leave our things here, just in case we need to make a hasty exit."

"A hasty exit," she repeats with a little grin on her face. "Is that middle-age-speak for 'get the fuck outta here in a hurry'?"

"Something like that, yeah."

As we approach the front door to the building, I see a short sign on the lawn outside the entrance. I can just make out the words Davis Consulting on the sign. Rebecca stops to read the sign. "Who's Davis?" she asks me.

"Well, I imagine they'd be less welcome if the sign said 'Secret Society of Mysterious Prophets and Psychics.' I'm pretty sure there is no Davis."

There is a button next to the door that looks like a bell or a buzzer. The only thing to do is to push it, so I do. A moment later, I hear a buzzer sound within. Seconds pass with no response; I begin to wonder if anyone is there or if we are even at the right place. Almost a full minute after pressing the button, I watch as the front door slowly opens. Behind it stands a man of at least sixty years. The hair he has left is a bright white, and his face is gentle through its wrinkled appearance.

"Welcome," he says in a soothing voice, a rich baritone made tenor over the years.

"I'm Tristan Shays. I was told you are expecting me."

"Of course. We've been awaiting your arrival. Won't you come in?"

I make a move to enter, with Rebecca following. Seeing her move toward the entrance, the man's expression changes to one of caution. "And who is this?" he asks me.

"Rebecca Traeger," I reply. "She's my companion. We travel together. I would ask that you welcome her as well."

"Jason didn't tell us that you would be accompanied," he says calmly. "What transpires here is a matter of discretion and secrecy. It is a risk to open our doors to outsiders."

"We're a package deal," I tell him. "Rebecca has saved my life, and I've saved hers. If you want me to join you, I have to insist that you trust me enough to welcome her here."

The old man looks at Rebecca intently for a moment. Then, unexpectedly, he looks deeper, almost *through* her, and something sparks recognition in him. "This is Persephone," he says.

She looks at him in disbelief. "You know me?"

His tone softens. "I don't know your face, and the name Rebecca is unfamiliar to me, but if you are Persephone, then you are welcome here."

"That was the name I was given as a child. But how could you …?"

He motions for us to follow him. We cross the foyer and enter a dimly lit reading room, with shelves of old books lining each wall, stacks of leather-bound volumes piled on tables, and racks of parchment scrolls in every corner. Our host goes to one corner and searches for a scroll. Finding it after several seconds, he brings it to a table and unrolls it. We gather around, but one important thing stands in the way of comprehension.

"I don't read Hebrew," Rebecca tells him.

On the side of the scroll is a wooden pointer, black with age, and tipped with a carved representation of a pointing human hand. He takes the pointer and holds it up to a section of the scroll, moving it from right to left, and then down with the translation of each new line. "And as the new days commence, from the west shall come Hamesh, keeper of the word of Hosea, he who will bring wholeness to The Nine. Upon the tail of a mighty wind will he arrive, fresh-steeped in grief and newfound wisdom. And by his side shall come Persephone, fair of face and possessed of fire."

He gently places the pointer on the table and looks at us with a soft smile.

"Oh my God," Rebecca says softly.

"I am called Ehad," the old man continues, "keeper of the word of Elijah. And so you see, my friends, you are more than welcome here. You are needed."

"How can this be?" I ask him. "When was that scroll written?"

"It was given to us seventy years ago."

"Seventy?" Rebecca says in disbelief. "That's impossible. Tristan, do you know what this means?"

I am all but frozen with astonishment. "No, Rebecca, I honestly don't."

"You've had a long journey," Ehad says. "You must be tired."

I turn to him. "I have a thousand questions. Please, I know it's late, but if I could spend some time talking with you and the others, it would mean a lot to me."

He nods, rolling up the scroll again. "You'll stay here. While you go and retrieve your things, I'll gather the others."

Rebecca and I head back to the front door, as Ehad moves deeper into the building. Once outside, Rebecca grabs me by the arm and speaks urgently to me, her face pale with fear. "Tristan, we have to get the fuck out of here."

"What? Why?"

"Why? Because there's a scroll in there from seventy years ago that talks about the past three days of our lives. And it calls me 'possessed of fire.' What the shit is that about?"

"I don't know," I answer, with a smile of contentment plastered on my face, "but they do. Isn't that why we're here, to get some answers? Our new friend just whipped out the answer key. It may have been written before we expected it to be, but damned if it doesn't offer some pretty on-target stuff."

"Seventy years ago, Tristan. That was written before our parents were even born. How much else is written in there? Stuff we haven't seen or done yet? It's creeping the living fuck out of me, and I don't know if I can be strong for this." There is a frightened hitch in her voice as her words trail off.

For the moment, I put my own excited anticipation aside and look to her feelings. Putting my arms around her gently, I hold her close to me and say, "I don't think we're in danger here. I have a real feeling of peace inside. When we go in, you can look at their thoughts, see if there's anything to be concerned about. You heard what Ehad told us: we're needed. I'm prepared to trust them until they prove to me that I shouldn't. But I'm not going to drag you into this if you don't want to be here. Tell me you want out, and I'll give you the car keys and enough money for a nice hotel for the night. And there'll be no hard feelings, no disappointment. The choice is yours."

She thinks about it. "You'll stay with me, whatever happens?"

"Of course."

"Okay. Let's see what they say."

We gather our belongings from the car and bring them inside the entrance to the building, where Ehad is waiting for us. "You may leave them there," he says. "Someone will bring them to your rooms. Please, come with me."

The structure is an office building, but it is clear that the group has made extensive modifications over the years, transforming it into a workplace and a living space. Carpeting covers the floors, and beautiful paintings line the walls, scenes from the Old Testament that look like they were painted by a firsthand witness. Rooms along the central corridor are converted from offices to living quarters, while other larger rooms are used for meeting areas and places of business. I am intrigued to note that one large room is decked out as a chapel. *Whoever these guys are, they're serious about this.*

Ehad leads us to a meeting room in the back of the building, where seven other men are seated around a large rectangular table. Upon seeing us, they all rise and approach us. Ehad introduces us to the group. "Brothers, this is a good day. What was long told has come to be. Our brother Hamesh has come to join us. And this is Persephone. Please come and greet them."

One by one, they approach us (in numerical order, I later found out to my amusement). A man in his seventies leads the group. "I am called Shtayim, keeper of the word of Samuel." He puts his hands on my shoulders, then—to my surprise—gently kisses both of my cheeks. He follows suit with Rebecca, as the next man approaches us.

"I am Shalosh," he says, "keeper of the word of Malachi." He greets us in the same way, his touch subdued by his many years.

"I am Arbah, keeper of the word of Zechariah."

And so it continues, with Shesh, keeper of the word of Haggai; Sheva, keeper of the word of Nahum; Shmoneh, keeper of the word of Ezekiel; and Tesha, keeper of the word of Isaiah.

It's like nothing I've ever experienced, this ritualized greeting of theirs, the way they treat me like a long-lost son. Yes, they call me "brother," but since the youngest of them has twenty years on me, I feel like the junior member of the team. "Well, I … uh … I'd introduce myself, but I have the feeling you already know me. My name is Tristan Shays, but while I'm here, I suspect I'm Hamesh, keeper of the word of … who was it again?"

"Hosea," Ehad answers pleasantly.

"Yeah. Him. Whoever he is."

"Hosea was a prophet of the Old Testament," Ehad explains. "And you are his direct descendant, just as each of us is descended from a prophet of old."

Well, now I feel stupid. Perhaps an inane observation would break the ice. "But I'm not even Jewish." *Perfect.*

This evokes a chuckle from the otherwise stoic assembly. "What you believe does not change who you are," Arbah says. "Come, sit with us. I know you have many questions."

We join them around the table, and I'm gently surprised as a young man enters the room, bringing water and trays of fruit for the assembly. Once everyone is seated, Ehad asks me, "What would you like to know?"

Where to begin? "Well, now that I know who you are, I guess the first question is why you've chosen this life. This place seems so separate from the world outside that door. Do you all live here? Is this your life's work? Were you born into this or did you learn your calling later in life?"

"These are all good questions," he replies. "Let me explain what I can. We are all men of faith. Ha Tesha has been in existence for centuries around the world, each chapter peopled by descendants of the ancient prophets. Members come and go, of course, but each chapter must have nine members. Without you here, Hamesh, we were incomplete. Each of us found his calling later in life, at a time when we were needed to replace a departing member."

"So, there was another Hamesh before me?"

"Of course. Many, over the years."

"And what happened to him?"

"He died two years ago."

It's all starting to fall into place. "Right about the time I got my first assignment. That has to be it. I was being called into service, only I didn't know it. Why didn't you just send someone to find me?"

"We were searching for you," he says, "but we were unsure of where you were or even who you were. We prayed that when the time was right, you would come to us, and now you have."

"But wait, if everyone in the society is a descendant of the prophets, wouldn't it just pass down from father to son?"

"Not everyone in the bloodline is called to this task. The prophets had several wives, and thousands of descendants. They are spread all over the world, populating Ha Tesha's twenty-two chapters."

"Can I ask a question?" Rebecca interrupts.

"Of course, Persephone," Ehad replies.

"That scroll you read to us, what is that? And how could somebody seventy years ago know who we are and when we were coming?"

"Seventy?" he repeats. "I said that was when we were *given* that scroll, not when it was written. That scroll is a book of prophecy specifically relating to our chapter. It took many years to reach us, once it was determined that it belonged to us. The best we are able to determine, it was written in Israel more than 240 years ago."

Rebecca and I share a look of astonishment that silences us both. When I'm finally able to speak again, I ask, "You're telling me that our arrival here was foretold in the 1760s?"

"It would seem."

"Then what's the point?" Rebecca says loudly, sounding agitated. "What's the point of any of it? If it was all written centuries ago, and we don't even have any choice—"

"Who says you don't have a choice?" Ehad asks.

"But it's in that scroll."

"Tell me, Persephone, did you choose to come here?"

"I don't even know anymore," she answers. "I think we did, but now I can't be sure."

"Just because something is written doesn't mean that life is without choice. It simply means that someone long ago knew what those choices would be."

"I don't understand," she says.

Tesha takes up the explanation. "All of us, the prophets, the messengers, have been blessed with vision that others don't have. Hamesh, you often see things which have not yet happened. You go to see the people in your visions, and you offer a warning. But they don't always heed that warning, do they?"

"No," I answer somberly.

"So you see, Persephone, we don't see things that *will be,* only things that *might be.* Every one of us has free will; it's God's gift to us. There is plenty of prophecy written that did not come to pass. It's what you might call an occupational hazard of what we do."

"What *do* you do?" she asks. "Are you like Tristan … I mean Hamesh? Do you all get assignments and then go out and help people?"

Shalosh replies, "To some extent, yes. One of us will get a mission, and the others will use the group's resources to help get him there and assist him in completing it."

"Over the years," Shmoneh adds, "we have placed ourselves in various industries and amassed the resources we need, financial and otherwise, to help carry out these missions."

"And do you help each other through the pain?" I ask.

This elicits confused looks. "What pain?" Ehad asks.

"The pain that comes with each new assignment."

The confused looks evolve into a troubled murmur among The Nine. "You feel pain when you receive a mission?" Ehad says.

"Yeah, terrible pain every time, until I'm actively on my way to carry it out. Doesn't everybody here feel that?"

"No," Sheva answers, "none of us. Quite the opposite. Each new mission is accompanied by a feeling of euphoria and inner peace."

"Then why the hell am I in agony every time?"

The others huddle up to discuss it, as Rebecca and I watch in disbelief. After considerable discussion, they return to their seats, and Ehad offers an explanation. "Hamesh, how do you feel about the missions you are given?"

"Honestly? I resent them. I consider them an intrusion into my life and my time, and I wish more than anything else that I never had to do them again."

"There's your answer," he says. "Ha Tesha views these missions as gifts, blessings from God, giving each of us the chance to help others and save lives. We receive each mission with joy and enthusiasm, and the feelings that accompany it are bliss. Your mind, your heart are fighting these gifts, rejecting them. You complete them not because of a desire to do good, but as a remedy to the pain you feel. If you can welcome these missions, embrace the opportunity they afford you, then each one will bring feelings of pleasure, rather than pain."

Rebecca touches my arm excitedly at this news. "That's great!" she says. "This is what you've been waiting for, a chance to end the pain. And all you have to do is accept the assignments willingly."

"You say it like it's easy," I tell her.

"It *can* be easy," Ehad says. "But it has to come from you." In response to my doubtful look, he adds, "You are tired." It is more of a pronouncement than an observation. "You've had a long day. Let me show you to your rooms. There will be time to speak further in the morning."

He escorts Rebecca and me to two rooms on opposite sides of a corridor. From that point forward, the rest of the evening is a blur. Exhausted as I am, it is mere minutes before I am face down on the bed, sound asleep.

A small window at my bedside brings the illumination of morning into the room hours later. Exactly how many hours, I'm not sure, but as I open my eyes and make my initial attempts at getting up, I realize that I feel well-rested for the first time in days. I pick up my wristwatch, expecting the time to be past noon, and to my surprise, it is just after 8:00 in the morning. I contemplate lying down and getting some more sleep, but quickly realize that I don't need any more.

Instead, I get up and use the private bathroom attached to my room. *My room. Is this going to be my new home? Will I have to give up the house in Maryland and take up residence in this place? The prospect isn't exactly appealing. Although I sure did sleep well.*

Post-freshening, I leave my room and step up to Rebecca's door, which is pulled to but not shut. I peek inside and see that she is still asleep. That's fine; she needs the rest too. I return to the meeting room from last night, where I find Ehad seated, reading the *Chicago Tribune*. "That's not exactly the Talmud," I say pleasantly.

He lowers the paper enough to reply, "The Talmud doesn't have a crossword puzzle." I believe I actually see a smile form.

"Very true."

"Good morning, Hamesh. Did you sleep well?"

"Frighteningly well," I reply, sitting with him at the table. Breakfast foods are laid out, and I gesture to them for permission to partake.

"Of course," he says. "What's ours is yours."

I help myself to a banana and a granola bar, and pour a glass of orange juice. I know it sounds crazy, but things smell and taste better here. Ehad puts the newspaper down so we can talk.

"Are you getting settled in?" he asks.

"No, but don't feel bad. I've spent the last two years feeling unsettled, so it's nothing I can remedy overnight."

"I'm sure you've seen and done some incredible things."

I nod. "Things I can't even believe myself. Successes, failures. A whole town. Eleven thousand people saved from a tornado, just this week."

"Astonishing. What a blessing. I'm so thankful you've chosen to come to us."

"Yeah, about that. Ehad, I don't know how long I can stay. You're very courteous and accommodating, but my being here is a matter of chance. Someone I met told me that you existed, and when he contacted you, I found out that you were looking for me."

"You say this, and you still attribute it to chance? Everything you have experienced should tell you that chance is a word used by those who don't understand the workings of the world. All the places you could have gone, all the people you could have met, and yet, here you are. Where you are needed. Hamesh ... *Tristan*—" He catches me off guard with that one. "You've only just arrived. I can't force you to stay. All I can ask is that you not leave in haste. Talk with us, learn what we know, and teach us what *you* know. There's a great deal of prophecy dealing with your arrival. That has to mean something, doesn't it?"

After another bite of the granola bar, I ask, "Don't you find that strange? Stories of your future written centuries ago?"

"Yes, I find it strange," he replies with a smile, "in the same way I find a sunset strange, or the tide, or the birth of a child. Just one of the strange and wonderful gifts that God has chosen to give us. Surely you've felt it? At the moment when one of your missions resulted in the safety of an innocent person?"

I think back to the moment in Wyandotte, Pennsylvania, when the Harbisons' house collapsed, with them safely outside of it because they heeded my warning. "Yes. I have."

"So you see? We are all, every human being, magnificent creatures, cursed with the tiniest of understanding. Just as early man gazed with wonder at the fire that started when lightning struck a tree, we gaze with wonder at the gifts of foreknowledge we are given. We can't know with certainty where they've come from, but we know they're real. And like that fire, they can be a valuable tool or a source of great danger. Ha Tesha exists to ensure that they are used as the valuable tool they are."

"You're good," I tell him. "You should sell insurance."

"I *did* sell insurance for twenty-six years," he says. "You see? We're not that different from you. We're not this group of clandestine rabbinical superheroes. We're men who want to help people in need. And when I look at you, Hamesh, I see the same instincts in you."

I like him. There's something so natural and so genuine about him, and I can't help liking this man. "What's your name?" I ask. "Your pre-number name?"

"Tzvi," he answers. "Tzvi Goldman."

"Nice to meet you, Tzvi. Tristan Shays of Ocean City, Maryland. And from the looks of things around here, I'm going to be your *Shabbos goy.*"

He laughs heartily at this and even smacks my arm playfully with the newspaper. "I have a feeling we're going to have to watch you carefully. *Shabbos goy,* indeed. We have a kid for that."

It feels good to share a laugh with him. He's obviously their number-one man, literally and figuratively. He's like the old Jewish insurance salesman father I never had. "Help me understand this," I say to him when the laughter ebbs. "Help me embrace this, the way you all have, so it doesn't feel like it's tearing my soul apart."

A compassionate expression lights his face. "Oh, Tristan, you're so close to that already. Here, let me show you. Stand up."

"But I'm still eating my banana."

"Your banana will wait. Stand up."

I rise and he does as well. He stands a few feet in front of me and says, "Now, put your arms out in front of you." I oblige, putting both arms straight out in front of me. "Watch what happens when I approach." He steps toward me, makes contact with my outstretched arms, and is deflected to the side. "You see what just happened? You're closed off, blocked. So when I approach, you push me away. Now, open your arms." I spread them a bit. "Wider. Wiiii-der." I extend my arms, appearing as if I'm bragging about catching a very large fish. He approaches again, and this time walks right up to me between my outstretched arms. "Now when I approach, you can embrace what life brings you."

And with that, he puts his arms around me. It is the second time in two days that I have been hugged by a stranger, and it's absolutely comforting. He smells like fabric softener and after-shave lotion, the kind that only older men use. Without realizing it at first, I notice that I have put my arms around him as well, and my head on his shoulder, and I'm letting him comfort me. All of which is good, because I also realize that I am crying gently.

"It's all right," he says. "You're safe here."

"I've been so blind," I tell him, not even knowing where the words come from. "I let myself believe this was some kind of curse."

"Now you know better. Now the pain can be replaced by something good."

To my surprise, I hear Rebecca's voice from behind me. "I could come back if this isn't a good time."

Startled, I quickly remove myself from the embrace as if I'd been caught doing something improper. "No, it's fine. We were talking. It isn't …"

"Tristan, it's all right," she says. "I took a quick peek in your thoughts when I saw you there, just to make sure you were okay." She steps over and offers me a quick kiss. "I'm glad you were able to talk to someone."

"Good morning, Persephone," Ehad says. "I trust you slept well?"

"Like a baby. Whatever's in the water here, you should bottle it and sell it. I haven't felt this good in months."

"I'm pleased to hear it. There's food and drink available. Please help yourself to anything you'd like."

She sits at the table and grabs some toast and coffee. "Thank you."

Ehad approaches her. "So you have the gift of sight? Is that what you were telling Hamesh?"

"I guess so. Just recently, I learned that I have a limited ability to see the thoughts of certain people."

"That's a valuable gift. Is it one you treasure?"

She gives him a polite but firm look. "It helps me know who my friends are. That's what I value."

"I see. Well, if you two will excuse me for a bit, I'll go confer with the others."

He leaves the room, and Rebecca continues with her breakfast. "That was a little rude, wasn't it?" I ask her.

"What, that? He was being kinda, I don't know—spooky."

"These people are our hosts," I remind her. "We should be good to them."

"Geez, did I sleep through the part where you drank the Kool-Aid?"

My response is swift and stern. "Knock off the Kool-Aid shit. It's not like that."

"Sorry," she says, sounding annoyed. "It's just that last night, you were creeped out, and this morning I find you hugging Numero Uno there and spouting the company philosophy. So obviously there was a moment of clarity that I wasn't present for."

"I'm willing to give them a chance. You can read them. Are you reading anything sinister?"

"Sinister? No. Fucking weird, a little. It's like they just drove here from the Bible. I'm as open-minded as the next person, but these guys make the Amish look like a heavy metal band."

"I'll grant you they're a little … traditional. Maybe that's not such a bad thing."

She looks at me in disbelief. "Oh my God, you're going to stay here, aren't you?"

"I haven't made up my mind yet."

"But you're thinking about it."

"I don't know. Rebecca, I just don't know." A thought occurs to me. "Are you jealous?"

"What? Why would I be jealous?"

"I don't know. You tell *me*. Are you afraid they'll take me away from you?"

"Maybe."

"Rebecca ..."

"What do you want me to say? We show up on their doorstep, and you're instantly initiated into this—this *thing* of theirs. Meanwhile, here I am, all talked about in their freaky prophecy scrolls, and yet every member of this kosher sausage festival looks at me like I'm leper of the year. And I just don't know what to do about that."

"Bec, I'm sorry. I didn't think about how this would affect you. But things are happening very fast, and I haven't had a chance to make up my mind yet about what I want to do or where I want to be. We came here because I wanted to learn things. Well, I'm learning them. It's been kind of a whirlwind week, if you'll pardon the expression. But we're here, and it's peaceful, and these people are welcoming us. Right now, that sounds pretty good to me. That door isn't locked. If you don't want to be here, you're free to go anytime you want to. You don't need my permission or anything like that."

"But I'm your destiny. The creepy scroll said so." She actually sounds hurt.

"I'm good with that. You want to stay and be my destiny, that works. You just gotta make nice with the weird old Jewish guys."

"Okay. I did it all the time at the club in Key West."

"Could've lived without that knowledge, but okay. Now finish your breakfast, and we'll—"

The rest of the sentence doesn't emerge. Instead, I am overtaken by the strangest sensation I have ever felt. It starts off as pain, but then, as my conscious mind fights the pain, a new sensation overtakes it—something halfway between the first drop on a very tall roller coaster and a powerful orgasm. But then the pain decides that it's not through with me yet, and the two feelings battle for control inside me. I am vaguely aware that I have fallen out of my chair into a semi-conscious state on the floor, where I am twitching in my present state of pleasure-pain.

I hear Rebecca calling, "Help! Somebody, please help!" Then I hear men's voices entering the room. Rebecca tells them, "Do something. This has never happened to him before."

Ehad kneels at my side and supports my head. Putting his mouth close to my ear, he softly tells me, "I'm here, Hamesh. Banish the pain; let the euphoria wash over you, and follow the instructions you receive."

I struggle to do just that, and in a matter of seconds, any pain and convulsion are gone, replaced by a sensation of warmth and overpowering inner peace. My next assignment is here, and as the details fill my mind, I realize how truly serious the situation is. But the feeling of peace is so powerful, I feel nothing but joy.

When the last of the information comes to me, I open my eyes and see Ehad holding my head, Rebecca standing directly over me, and Shteim and Sheva off to the side.

"Are you all right?" Rebecca asks me.

"I- I'm fine. It was an assignment." I turn to look at Ehad. "It worked; I banished the pain, like you said, and this sense of calm and peace washed over me."

"I'm very pleased," Ehad says. "Your control was excellent. I don't think you'll be plagued with the pain any longer."

"What's the assignment?" Rebecca asks impatiently.

I slowly rise to a sitting position. "Yeah, that. It's big. Gather the others. We've got things to go over."

Chapter 11

Within minutes, the other eight members of Ha Tesha are gathered in the central meeting room, along with Rebecca. All eyes are on me. The new kid has his first homework, and this one won't be graded on a curve.

The metaphor is no accident, as I explain to the group. "I've been called to Libertyville, less than an hour from here. This afternoon, an incident is going to take place at Leonard High School. A fifteen-year-old student is going to bring a weapon to school, with the intention of inflicting violence on classmates and teachers."

"Wouldn't there be metal detectors at every door?" Rebecca asks. "This *is* a high school."

Shalosh tells us, "Libertyville is an upscale area with no history of violence in the school, so there are no metal detectors."

I continue. "The student isn't there now, but will be this afternoon, and right around 1:15 is when everything is going to happen, so we don't have much time. Now, I can't just walk into the school without a reason to be there, so I'll need an identity and a purpose."

Ehad speaks quickly to the others in what I assume is Yiddish. "Arbah will assist with this," Ehad tells me. "This is his area of specialty."

"I'm coming with," Rebecca says.

Ehad looks to her, then to me for confirmation.

"You sure about this?" I ask. "It could get ugly."

"I'm good with ugly," she replies.

"Okay, so we'll need an identity for her as well."

Arbah nods and hurries from the room. Ehad turns back to us. "What resources do you need? Police protection?"

"Actually," I reply, "I want to do this as quietly as possible. We want to keep our shooter as calm as possible, and not let on that we know what's going to happen. If we can head this off quietly before things escalate, we're most likely to get through this without anyone getting hurt. We'll have cell phones with us, so we can call for help if we need it. But if we can talk our troubled teen out of this before any shooting starts, that's the cleanest end to the situation that we can hope for."

"I understand. I just don't want to see you put yourselves at risk."

Rebecca and I share a meaningful glance and a knowing little smile. "It's something we've gotten used to," she tells him.

"When you're finished, return here," Ehad instructs. "Try to keep as low a profile as you can, given the circumstances, and don't mention the group's name. We want to be transparent in this effort."

A few minutes later, Arbah returns with two laminated cards and a set of scrolls. I briefly ponder whether they contain more prophecy about how the day will progress. Arbah quickly sets me straight. "These are blueprints of the layout of Leonard High School," he says, unrolling them on the table in front of us.

"That's amazing," I tell him. "How did you find those so quickly?"

"We have a remarkable amount of information on hand," he says. "Part of our preparation for any eventuality." He looks over the blueprints with us. "It's a two-story building, with very few unused rooms. But if you'll look over here on the first floor, room 134 has been converted from a classroom to an after-school meeting room. During the school day, it's not used, so it could be a place to bring this student, away from other people."

"How do we get into the building?" I ask.

He holds up the badges. "Audiologists," Ehad says. "You're there to conduct hearing tests on some students. That information will get you into the building. Once inside, you can make your way to room 134 and lie low there until you find the student. Above all, look like you belong there. If you appear to belong, people won't ask questions; they'll let you go about your business."

"What about equipment?" I ask. "Audiologists carry testing equipment."

"We have cases and authentic equipment."

"What about a weapon?" Rebecca asks. "Should we be armed?"

The members of the group look uneasy at the suggestion, until I put their worries to rest. "No, no guns. It's bad enough with one in the picture. More than one will lead to all sorts of trouble. We're doing this unarmed."

"All right, then," Ehad says. "You have about two hours before you need to be there. I suggest we run some scenario drills. We will assume the roles of people you're likely to meet, and you can practice what you'll say and do if complications arise. Let's begin."

The scenario drills are actually quite helpful. The members of Ha Tesha portray security guards, teachers, office staff, and students, as Rebecca and I plan a road map of how the assignment will proceed. When a complication arises that stalls us on what to do, a member of the group comes up with a suggestion. They're quick and they're smart. They've clearly helped each other through difficult situations for years. It makes me wish we could send the whole team in for this one, but that's neither practical nor discreet. So once again, Rebecca and I will go it alone to face the situation.

Once the drills are over, we don our best audiologist-looking apparel, pausing to pose for digital pictures of our faces, to go on the ID badges. We take the assembled badges and the genuine-looking equipment with us to the front door of the building. Ehad meets us there, to see us off.

"Be safe," he says, more of an order than a wish. "Call the police in if you need to, and call us if we can be of help."

"We will," I assure him. "Save us a couple of places at the dinner table. We have every intention of being back here."

"Just be back by sundown," he says with a smile. "It is Friday, after all."

With that, we exit the building and load the equipment into the Sebring. As I get behind the wheel, I feel this assignment is different from all the ones that came before it. Better in some ways but worse in others. I have strategies and preparation at my disposal that I've never had before. But there's so much at stake. I think about the news reports of school shootings in recent years—the widespread carnage, so many young lives lost so needlessly, all because one or two individuals felt tormented or cast out or just wanted to get their names in the news before they died. In my mind, I see the faces of the witnesses, those who barely escaped the slaughter. I hear their sobs, the terror in their voices as they confront their mortality, most for the first time ever. And I try to find a good reason why I am willingly putting myself in the middle of this upcoming horror. The answer is swift and obvious: *because I'm the only one who can prevent it.*

"Are you all right?" Rebecca asks, snapping me out of it. I am surprised to realize that I've driven us several miles without even being aware of it. *Thank God for putting the brain on autopilot.*

"Yeah, I'm just thinking too much. How about you? You okay?"

"I guess. I'm trying to decide if I'm getting used to this or if I'm just in denial that this is my life now."

"If you come up with an answer, let me know. I've been asking that question for almost two years."

"The training was helpful, though," she observes.

"Can't argue with you there. I feel like a freelancer who's just been hired by a very powerful company. Suddenly, we have to do things by their rules, but they've got all the good toys."

After a few moments of silence, she looks up. "Huh."

"What?"

"I just realized," she says. "We didn't even put the top down."

"You're right; we didn't. Guess we had other things on our minds."

"I really don't want to get shot," she says, and I can hear the fear in her voice. She sounds so young, barely older than the students we're going to protect, and I can't help flashing back to those news reports. Seeing the pretty, popular girl in tears, knowing that these qualities that boosted her to the pinnacle of high school society are the very things that made her a target in the eyes of the under caste.

I reach out to her and hold her hand tightly in mine. "We'll do everything we need to do to stay safe. Besides, we're audiologists. Everybody loves us."

She smiles, despite herself. "Thank you for that."

Mile follows mile, and we both do our best to distract ourselves from thinking too much about what's ahead. After the discovery of Rebecca's mind-reading ability, twenty questions has lost its appeal, so we content ourselves with the radio and sightseeing Chicago's northern suburbs. Far sooner than we want, the sight of Libertyville's Leonard High School fills our view. I want desperately to turn around and drive, just drive anywhere but here; to take Rebecca someplace safe and forget about the assignments, The Nine, all of it. Now that I know how to fight the pain, I can just ignore the assignments when they come in. Let someone else do it.

But I know that's not possible. Even without physical pain, I don't think I could live with the emotional pain of ignoring tasks that are mine to fulfill.

I pull into a visitor parking space at 12:55 PM and take a deep breath. "You ready?" I ask.

"If I say no, can we stay here?"

"Fraid not."

"Then I guess I'm ready."

We gather our materials and make our way to the front entrance to Leonard High School, the door closest to the main office. An unarmed security guard stops us at the door, and we show him our ID and ask to be shown to the office. He points the way, and we proceed to the next obstacle: approval.

As we enter the office, an older woman behind the desk asks, "Can I help you?"

"Crown Audiology," I answer. "We're here to do hearing tests for some of the students."

She looks distressed at this; she's clearly not a woman who enjoys surprises. "It's not on my calendar."

"That's strange," I reply. "This was all set up a week ago by District. They gave us a list of fifteen students who need testing."

"Well, I don't have anyone available to help right now."

"Quite all right," I tell her with a smile. "We were told we could set up in room 134. We'll call for the students ourselves. You'll barely even know we're here."

This seems to put her at ease. "Thank you. I appreciate that. Please come see me when you're finished, and we'll get the paperwork taken care of."

"We'll sure do that, Mrs. ...?"

"It's *Miss*," she says, turning on what I'm gently afraid could be the charm. "Canaday."

"Pleasure to meet you, Miss Canaday. You have a good afternoon, and we'll see you in a bit."

As we're leaving the office, Rebecca discreetly says to me, "You sure have your act worked out. No wonder I fell for you."

"Can't suppress the natural Shays mystique," I reply, scanning the halls for our target. "Time?"

She checks her watch. "It's 1:06."

"That's cutting it close. Let's get to room 134."

We walk briskly down the hall to the unused room, open it up, and set up the equipment in a hurry. "What now?" she asks.

"We find our quarry."

"Can I help?"

"You could if you knew who to look for. Unfortunately, it's got to be me. You wait here and look like an audiologist. Once I come back, hopefully accompanied, we have to be convincing."

I grab a clipboard and pad and head for the door. She stops me. "Tristan ... be careful."

"I will."

Time is tight, very tight, and this school has 1,800 faces in it. Courtesy of the assignment, I've memorized the face I'm looking for, but with students in the halls for the passing period, it's needles and haystacks until I can narrow it down. *Think, Tristan. Not a crowd; this is someone walking alone, looking nervous or tense. Probably carrying a bag or wearing a long coat. Someone focused, someone purposeful. Someone ... there.*

Fortune is on my side, as I spot the prospective shooter entering the school building holding, as I suspected, a fairly large backpack. My first instinct is to run over and grab the backpack, taking it out of the school and someplace safe, but I fight that impulse and calmly make my approach, clipboard in hand and story in place.

"Excuse me, are you Cassie Haiduk?"

She freezes at the question; well aware of what she is just minutes from doing, to be approached this way by a stranger must be extremely daunting. I watch her as she decides whether to lie. "Yes."

"Hi," I say with a pleasant smile, "I'm Dr. White. I'm here doing hearing tests on the students, and we've got you on the list for 1:00. Can you spare about five minutes to take the test?"

She looks inconvenienced but not suspicious. "I really need to get to class."

"Your teacher knows you're on the list. It'll literally take five minutes."

"There's really nothing wrong with my hearing."

"It's a routine test. It won't even hurt. Please, Cassie, just a few minutes and we can get you all taken care of."

She emits the sigh of teenage surrender. "Fine. Where are we doing this?"

"Room 134. Shall we?"

She holds her backpack tightly and walks by my side. I size up the bag, deciding that it's not long enough to hide an assault rifle or any kind of machine gun. She may be carrying multiple automatic or semi-automatic handguns. Judging by how carefully she's protecting that bag, the weapons must be in there. At the moment, I don't know who's more nervous, her or me.

Cassie Haiduk, just fifteen years old. From the information I am privy to, she's very intelligent but very troubled. Moved from place to place; some family trouble with the law. And I'm very concerned that she wants to die today and take as many people with her as possible. When the assignment came in, I was bracing myself for a male subject. Cassie's face was a surprise; for a girl to carry out an act of violence on this scale is rare, almost unheard of. It makes me all the more wary of her as I escort her to room 134, where Rebecca is waiting.

We enter the room and I close the door behind us. Rebecca puts on her bravest smile as she sees us enter. "This is Rebecca, my assistant," I announce. "Rebecca, this is patient nine, Cassie Haiduk."

"Hi, Cassie," she says, marking a piece of paper in front of her in an effort to keep up the façade. We have one more stratagem to try within our cover before we have to go for broke. "Have a seat here at the table, please."

On the table is a pair of large headphones, attached by a cord to an impressive-looking machine. I have only the most rudimentary information on how to operate it, so I hope to hell our gambit pays off, because if I have to actually test this girl's hearing, the jig is up.

"The machine is going to generate a series of tones," I tell her, reciting what I remember from the scenario drills. "You'll raise your hand when you hear the tones and put your hand down when you stop hearing them. Sound good?"

"Sure," she says noncommittally.

"We need to make sure there are no electronic devices that will interfere with the machine—MP3 players, cell phones, pagers—so I'm going to ask you to leave your bag in the far corner of the room, please."

She resists this suggestion. "No. I don't have any of that sort of thing in my bag. I need to keep it with me."

"I promise you it'll be safe. It'll be right over there where you can see it."

"No! If you want me to do this, the bag stays with me."

"Cassie, please," I insist. "It's important. For your hearing."

She looks at me, then at Rebecca, then back at me. For a moment, it looks like she is about to acquiesce; then I see her eyes light on my identification badge and stay there. "What did you say your name was again?" she asks.

Fuck, what did I say my name was? It comes to me with a degree of certainty. "Dr. White," I tell her, "from the audiology clinic."

"Then why does your ID say your name is Dr. *Weitz?*"

A dozen plausible explanations immediately spring to mind, but before I can utter a single one of them, I see her eyes narrow as she asks, "Who are you?"

"Cassie, wait," Rebecca says as the girl gets out of her chair, clutching the bag.

"I said *who are you?!*"

It's over, and it's time. Cards on the table. "Two friends who don't want to see you die today," I say simply.

She looks stunned at the revelation. "What is this? Why are you here?"

"Cassie, we know what you're planning to do," Rebecca says. "We don't want to hurt you. We just want to ask you not to do it."

Her amazement continues. "How could you possibly know? I never told anyone about this. I didn't write about it. Nothing."

"The explanation is complicated," I answer. "And I'm happy to tell you all about it once we're all safe. But for now, would you please consider handing me the gun?"

"What gun?" she asks, looking as confused by my question as I am by hers.

"We know you brought a gun to school today," Rebecca says, "to hurt some people and then hurt yourself."

"I don't have a gun."

"Then what's in the bag?" I ask her.

Being as aware as I am that we are at endgame, she slowly unzips the bag and pulls the contents out carefully, placing them on the table in front of her. My eyes widen as my heart races out of control at the sight of it.

"Tristan," Rebecca says slowly, her voice a symphony of fear, "that's not a gun. You said gun."

"I saw violence and I assumed gun," I tell her. "I didn't see *this.*"

The object on the table is clearly homemade, but so skillfully done that it could pass for something found in any military bunker in the world. "It's C4," Cassie says in answer to our unspoken question. "Fifteen pounds of it. Placed in exactly the right spot, it will start a chain reaction that will take down the school."

"Shit," I whisper, still baffled at the inaccuracy of my vision. Gun to bomb isn't a spur-of-the-moment change. This was something she was planning all along. *So why couldn't I see it?*

"I have the detonator on me, so don't think about rushing at me or anything like that. I can set this off right here, before you get near me. In fact, I think I want the two of you over there, in the corner."

Rebecca and I take two chairs into a corner of the room and sit there, while Cassie stands guard over the explosive.

"How does a high school student buy that much C4?" I ask.

"She doesn't," Cassie answers. "She finds the recipe on the Internet and she makes it out of common household ingredients and not-so-common ingredients she manages to steal from her high school's chemistry department, where she's been working as a lab assistant. Once you have the ingredients, the recipe isn't hard to follow. It's kind of like making chocolate chip cookies."

"Swell," I say.

"Now, I'm ready to hear the part about how you knew about this," she continues. "Because I'd really like to know."

"The standard disclaimer is that you'll find this hard to believe," I begin, "but it's true. And it's also true that neither of us wants to hurt you. Quite the opposite. There are people in this world—more of them than you'd suspect—who have learned to use what might be called extrasensory or psychic ability. I'm one of those people. Sometimes I get messages in my mind—images of things that are going to happen, and I'm compelled to help the people in those images, to stop these bad things from happening. This morning, I got an image of you bringing a gun to this school and killing a lot of people before killing yourself. Rebecca and I came here to stop that from happening. To help you to live."

There is less disbelief in her voice than I expect when she asks, "Then why the disguises, the equipment, the fake identity that you couldn't quite remember?"

"We had help this time around," I reply. "From some people with good intentions and a little more organization than they know what to do with. But their intention, like ours, was your safety. Your life."

"So what do we do now?" she asks. "Because I'm still going to do this."

"Will you at least tell us why?" Rebecca says.

"What for? It won't change anything."

"Because I for one would like to know why an intelligent woman wants to kill almost 2,000 people. You've got the bomb; you're in control here. But for what it's worth, Tristan gets these messages when somebody—God or whoever—thinks the person is worth saving. And that's why we came here. So if you feel like talking to somebody about this, we're a captive audience, if you'll pardon the expression."

She looks at us intently for several seconds, probably trying to decide if it's a trick or a stall tactic. What she sees on our faces is genuine interest in her. "I don't want to kill anybody. I don't even want to hurt anybody. I didn't pick this time at random. In about fifteen minutes, the entire school is going out to the football stadium for some stupid pep rally or something. There won't be anyone in the building. I'm not trying to hurt people with this."

"But then why try to destroy your school?" I ask.

"I hate this place and everyone in it," she says quietly. "I know how cliché it is to be in high school and feel like nobody likes you. But it's different here. Since I came here a year ago, things have gotten worse and worse. I transferred here in the middle of my freshman year, and I thought it would be a chance to start over, to go somewhere nobody knew about me or my family. But somebody found out, and it spread like a plague all over the school, and now every day is like torture for me."

"What did they find out?" I ask. "What happened to your family?"

Again she hesitates before saying it. "My father is in a federal prison in Florida. He was convicted of selling secrets to the Chinese. But what I know and the rest of the world doesn't care to is that he's innocent. He was charged with this because he knew his employer was about to do something illegal, and he was ready to blow the whistle on them. So the company falsified documents and gathered all kinds of phony evidence, and they got him out of their way. They didn't care about him or his family. All they cared about was their precious oil."

At the sound of the word, Rebecca and I both freeze in our seats. *No, no, no, it can't be possible. After all we've seen and done, the trail can't possibly lead us back where we started. It's time to say something.*

"Oil?" I ask.

"My father is an engineer. He worked for a company that was trying to reduce the country's dependence on OPEC for oil. They were looking for American offshore oil reserves, but not having much luck for the longest time. But then they started closing in on this area in the Gulf of Mexico, off the coast of Florida. The only problem is, there's a drilling ban in place until the year 2022. So the company worked a deal with a Chinese oil company to work together. Somehow, the Chinese had a contract in place that preceded the ban, and they were going to get to do their drilling. But my father found problems with that partnership, legal issues, and he didn't want to be a part of it. So he gathered evidence of his own, and he even put it in a safe-deposit box, with instructions that it should be given to the authorities if he died."

"But wait," Rebecca says, "that still doesn't explain why you wanted to blow up the school. If you didn't want to hurt anyone, including yourself ..."

"It was a diversion," Cassie explains. "I need to go to Florida to help my father clear his name. But I knew my grandmother would never let me go. And if I ran away, she'd have the police looking for me. So I was going to make a big enough explosion to cause damage and confusion ..."

I finish the thought. "And you could conveniently get lost in that confusion, letting you slip away to Florida. You would let your family think that you'd been killed?"

"If I had to. At least long enough to hitchhike or hop a freight train down there to go help him. Once I was done, I'd let everyone know I was all right."

"That's a pretty extreme way to disappear, don't you think?" Rebecca asks her.

"It's what they deserve," she says. "These people. This place. Only now that you two showed up, I've got no explosion and no diversion. So no way to slip out of here."

"Cassie, would you excuse us for a moment while we talk privately?" I ask. She agrees, and I take Rebecca into a corner of the room. I turn to her with renewed purpose in my eyes. "You know what this means?" I ask her in hushed tones. "We have to stop them and help Cassie's father clear her name."

"I can't believe you're going to do this," she answers in similarly sotto voce.

"What choice do we have? After Kansas, I was ready to stay here, work with The Nine, and take what life brought to me. But this? The very first assignment we get relates to Consolidated Offshore. If that's not a message, I don't know what is."

"I know," she says quietly. "But I'm afraid of what it'll take to make that happen."

"It's something we've been avoiding, but I don't think we can avoid it anymore. We have to go to Florida and present the evidence that clears her father and indicts Consolidated."

"And what do we do with Cassie?" Rebecca asks.

"I think we have to take her with us."

"What? We can't take a fifteen-year-old girl across state lines. Least of all one who's just tried to blow up an entire school."

"We need her. She can lead us where we have to go. And what else would we do with her? Turn her in to the police? We stopped her before she carried out her plan, so in the eyes of the law, she hasn't committed a crime yet."

"She's in possession of a very dangerous explosive device, Tristan."

I glance over at the device. The C4 is shaped into a large cube, and on the side of it is a menacing-looking electronic receiver with four LEDs on it. I try not to think about the fraction of a cent I earned for the creation of those lights. "What if she can disable it here?"

"Do we even know if she knows how to disable it?"

At this moment, Cassie walks over to the bomb and calmly pulls the receiver off of it, flipping a switch off on the device. The LEDs go dark as she places it on the table. "There, it's disabled," she says. "And I could hear every word you were saying. It's a really small room."

"We suck at talking privately," Rebecca says.

"We really do," I concur.

"Guess I passed my hearing test, huh?" Cassie asks.

"Looks like it," I reply.

"So you're going to take me to Florida?"

"I really think you can help your father," I tell her. "We were drawn into the Consolidated Offshore battle last week. The local fishermen are trying to keep the oil company from drilling in their fishing waters. With this new discovery, we could end this battle before anyone else gets hurt."

"So we're taking sides?" Rebecca asks.

"At this point, I don't think we have a choice."

"How do we know we're taking the right side? You know what the fishermen have done in the name of their cause."

"Yeah, and I know what Consolidated has done. You familiar with the concept of the lesser of two evils? For my money, that's big fish, not big oil."

Rebecca looks back at Cassie. "The bomb is totally safe now?"

"Yeah, it's C4. Without the detonator, it's inert. You could play volleyball with that chunk of it and nothing would happen."

"What do we do with it?" Rebecca asks me. "We can't just leave it here."

"We take it—and her—back to Ha Tesha. They'll know what to do."

Cassie looks confused. "What's Ha—"

"A bunch of weird old men who helped save your life today," Rebecca answers.

The passing period has ended and the halls are empty when the three of us make our way out of room 134. The dismantled device has been put back in Cassie's backpack, and the audiology equipment is packed up into its case again. We breeze past the main office without drawing the attention of the staff, but as we head for the front door, the security guard stops us.

"Where are you folks going?" he asks.

"Out to our vehicle to get some more equipment," I answer, trying not to sound like I'm totally making it up.

"You have a student with you," he rather astutely observes.

"That's right. She's the reason we need the additional equipment. Her hearing test was abnormal, and we need to have her with us, so we can choose the right size of audio ... manometer for her specific cranio-cochlear permutation."

"Students aren't supposed to leave the building without signing out."

"Look, Officer ..." I read his nametag, "Axton, time is critical here. We're flirting with impending deafness for this girl if we don't get the proper equipment for her. I know I don't want that on my conscience. Do you want it on yours?"

He thinks about it for a few seconds, then says, "Just bring her right back in when you're done."

We thank him and hurry out the door. "That was brilliant," Cassie says with a little smile. "Even *I* believed you."

"Don't get too comfortable," I respond. "It won't work for more than a minute. We have to get to the car and get out of here. Because I'm pretty sure once they realize she's gone, we're kidnappers."

"Oh, that's fun," Rebecca says. "We haven't been *that* yet."

A note of concern enters Cassie's voice as we reach the car. "You two aren't going to rape me and leave my body somewhere, are you?"

"Why does everybody who hitches a ride with me ask me that? No, we're not going to do anything weird to you. Now get in the back seat and hide while we drive past security."

Certain as I am that we are going to get caught, we manage to leave the school grounds undetected. More importantly, Cassie's plan for retribution has not only been stopped, but it has gone unnoticed, so there will be no need for her to be arrested or institutionalized. Now, an astute observer might suggest that someone wanting to blow up a building filled with 1,800 people probably *should be* institutionalized, rather than, say, taken across the country. But I understand what overwhelming desperation can do to a person. So I'm willing to let the first attempt at urban terrorism off with a warning. A second attempt will result in sterner measures. That's my story, and I am—needless to say—sticking to it.

The first stop has to be Ha Tesha, to check in, get packed, break the bad news, and most importantly, get the fucking bomb out of my rental car, which I am almost positive does *not* have fucking bomb insurance. As much as I like the Sebring, I have no desire to pay thirty grand for the pleasure of handing the pieces of one over to the rental company.

So we make the drive back to Zion with our new passenger, a troubled young woman who probably expected to be fleeing the scene of destruction at this hour, but instead has the opportunity to correct an injustice and help us bring down Consolidated Offshore as an added bonus. Then we'll fly to Pensacola and end this with a minimum of fuss.

In less than an hour, we pull up in front of the headquarters of Davis Consulting, which looks as nondescript and unassuming by day as it did by night. The three of us get out of the convertible. "I'll need the bag," I tell Cassie.

She actually hesitates a moment before deciding to hand it over. I take her eventual acceptance as a sign of trust. She looks at the building before us and asks, "What is this place anyway?"

"It's kind of the Bat Cave for the Psychic Friends Network," I answer. "Or a synagogue full of crusaders, if that makes you feel more at ease. Don't worry; they don't bite."

We approach the door and I ring the buzzer, not having been given a key. Ehad opens the door and looks pleased to see us. He notices Cassie and his expression changes. "Who's this?" he asks.

"This is our bomber," I answer as the three of us enter.

"What bomber? I heard shooter."

"As did I," I retort. "An interesting bit of information, wouldn't you say? But gun there was not, and bomb there was."

"Did it go off?" he asks, quite concerned.

"I'm pleased to report that it did not, especially because we were in the room with it the whole time." I hand him the sealed bag.

"What's this?" he inquires.

"The bomb. It's okay, it's been disabled. But I'm hoping your team can break it down into harmless component parts and get rid of them discreetly."

Ehad hands the bag off to two members of the team, and then says to me, "Hamesh, may I speak to you in private?"

As I'm walking away with him, I catch Rebecca whispering the word *busted* to Cassie. "Come on," Rebecca says to her. "I'll show you around."

Ehad takes me into his private living space and speaks in quiet but clearly perturbed tones. "I thought it was understood that bringing the young woman here was not a good idea."

"I'm sorry, Ehad. We didn't have much choice. We managed to get her out of the school without anyone finding out that she even had the bomb. Ehad, she needs us. Her father is in a federal prison in Florida, accused of a crime he didn't commit. She's the only one who can help him. We have to get her on a plane to Florida, and we have to go with her."

"Hamesh, this is a very bad idea. You completed your mission and no one was harmed, and for that we are thankful. But to insert yourselves into this girl's life puts you and her and others at risk. If you leave her with us, we can see that she gets the counseling she needs."

"Cassie doesn't need counseling."

"She meant to kill hundreds of people," he reminds me.

"No she didn't. And now that I know what she did mean, I know that she's not a threat to herself or others. She needs to do this, and we need to help her. You remember what I told you last night, how all of my recent assignments were linked to Rebecca somehow? Well, this one is too. Cassie's father worked for Rebecca's father; he tried to do the right thing and it landed him in prison. For days now, I've felt that all these assignments are leading up to something, and I really believe this is it. I'm sorry, truly sorry to walk out of here so soon after arriving, but I know that this is something I have to do. All I can ask is that you understand and that you give me your blessing."

"Will you come back to us when you've finished?" he asks, his voice trying to hide the disappointment.

"I don't know. I'll come back if it's my destiny to, I guess."

"You have my blessing. Just, please, be safe. All of you."

I hug him in an expression of my gratitude, then return to Rebecca and Cassie to let them know of our plans. We need to pack our things quickly and make our way to the airport as soon as possible, to catch the next available flight to Pensacola. I'm aware that Cassie doesn't have anything but the clothes on her back, but stopping at her home would be too risky. Anything she needs I can buy her, should the trip prove to be longer than an overnight.

Rebecca and I bid our good-byes to the members of Ha Tesha. It's a shame, really, having to leave so soon. I'm really starting to like them, and without question, their resources are useful. But there's no doubt in my mind that this errand is vital. If Calvin Traeger is willing to imprison an innocent man for the sake of a potential oil well, he's capable of just about anything.

We make our way to the highway, headed toward O'Hare Airport. I didn't count on Friday afternoon rush-hour traffic starting as early as 3:00, but Chicagoans like their weekends, and apparently they want them to start as soon as possible. As a result, we do more sitting than moving. In the rearview mirror, I see Cassie taking out her cell phone, which makes me a bit nervous. "Who are you calling?"

"My grandmother," she answers.

"I don't think that's a good idea," I reply.

"I disappeared from school, and now I'm about to get on an airplane and go to Florida. I have to tell her what's happening."

"I thought the whole idea behind today was to disappear without the family knowing where you are," I remind her.

"Well, things have changed," she declares. "You ought to know; you're the one who changed them. I want her to know why I'm doing this, why this is so important to me. Maybe she won't stand up for her own son, but I will."

I don't argue the point. Her grandmother has a right to know. Cassie's bound to leave some of the details out—the high explosives part springs to mind—so I imagine she'll be discreet about other sensitive details as well.

"Grammy, it's Cassie. ... I'm fine, everything's okay, but listen, I have to tell you something important. I'm not in school. ... No, it's fine. I met these two people, and they're going to help me get Dad released. ... No, they're adults. ... Grammy, please, I can't go back there. Not until this is resolved. ... We're going to the airport. They're going to take me to Florida. ... But why? ... You don't understand. We can help him. We can get the judge to see that he ... Okay. ... *Okay!*" She hands me her phone. "She wants to talk to you."

Anxiously, I take the telephone. If her tone is any indicator, Grammy is old-school pissed off. "Good afternoon, ma'am," I begin politely. "My name is Hamesh," I answer her first query. *Close enough, anyway.* "I'm with the, uh ... Justice ... League ... of America." *Wow, that went well. Apparently I'm Aquaman now.* "We've been working on inconsistencies and judicial errors in your son's case, and we believe we have the evidence we need to persuade the court to release him. But we need Cassie's testimony in court, and she's agreed to accompany us to Pensacola, Florida for a few days to testify. With your kind permission, of course. The League will pay for all her expenses, and she'll be very well taken care of. ... I see. ... I understand. ... That's very reasonable. ... Thank you for your time. ... Bye-bye."

I close the phone and hand it back to Cassie.

"Did she buy it?" Rebecca asks.

"No, not a word. She's calling the police and the FBI now. I expect there'll be an Amber Alert within the hour."

"Shit," Cassie says. "I'm sorry. She can be stubborn."

"Quite all right," I answer, changing lanes.

"What do we do now?" Rebecca asks.

"Well, we *don't* go to the airport, for starters," I reply. "That's the first place they'll be looking for her. Next thing we do is get off the interstates, since that's the second place they'll be looking for her."

"We could go to another airport, maybe Indianapolis, and fly out of there," Rebecca suggests.

"We could, but by the time we reach there, the alert will have spread to neighboring airports."

"Are you saying that we're driving to Florida?" Cassie asks.

"That's what it's looking like," I tell her. "At least until we can come up with a better plan."

"Damn it," Cassie says. "Maybe if I call the police and explain things, they'll cancel this and we can fly there."

"Too risky. Someone could be coercing you into saying it. We have to stay under the radar on this one until we help your father. Then we can make our explanations and hope they don't arrest us for kidnapping anyway."

Chapter 12

"This is all my fault," Cassie says dolefully.

"No it isn't," I reply, then give the matter some thought. "Well, okay, yes it is, but I'm willing to accept that you had a good reason."

"So what do we do?" she asks.

"We keep driving. It'll take a while, but eventually, we'll get to Florida, and then we'll do what we can to help your father."

"Cassie," Rebecca says, "do you have something specific in mind, a way to help him? Not to be rude or anything, but we're taking a very big risk here, going down there. I kind of need to know that there's a plan of action in place."

"Everything we need is in the safe-deposit box," she replies. "And the only person who can get it out of there besides him is me. I'll get the evidence and we'll give it to the judge. We have to. We have to stop Consolidated Offshore before they do what they're planning to do."

I couldn't agree with her more, and though I'm not delighted that we're the ones who have to do it, I can't shirk this responsibility. I look over at Rebecca, long enough to see her processing the implications of doing battle with her father. And what will Cassie think when she learns that one of her rescuers is the daughter of her father's worst enemy? Should make for some lively conversation around the breakfast table, once that news gets out.

I continue to make my way south on two-lane state highways. The interstate would be much faster, but I can't risk it. As soon as the authorities hear about Cassie's disappearance, they'll patrol the airports and major roads heading toward Florida. It will take us at least two days to get there on secondary roads, but it's the safest bet we have. Minute follows tense minute as we continue on in silence. The state roads do have one advantage: traffic is lighter, and we are able to proceed at a steady pace, out of the bumper-to-bumper madness of the main arteries.

At the top of the hour, I turn on the car's radio and scan the dial for a news station. I quickly find one and patiently wait through the national news stories, hoping that the local news will air without mention of us and our afternoon's activities. My hope is short-lived, as the newscaster reports, "Illinois State Police have issued an Amber Alert for a fifteen-year-old Libertyville girl taken from Leonard High School this afternoon. Cassandra Haiduk is a sophomore at the school. The girl's grandmother reports receiving a phone call from Haiduk within the last hour, stating that she was bound for Florida with two adults. Sixty-two-year-old Yelena Haiduk became suspicious after talking to the girl and one of the adults, and called the authorities."

"At least they don't know who we are," Rebecca says, clinging to hope.

"Calls to Leonard High School confirm that Haiduk was seen leaving the school with two individuals posing as audiologists. One is a white male, approximately six feet tall, 180 pounds, with dark hair and dark eyes, 35 to 45 years old. The other is a white female, roughly five feet nine inches tall, with blonde hair, and between twenty and thirty years old. They were seen leaving in a dark green convertible with Illinois plates. Anyone with information on this incident is urged to call CrimeStoppers, at—"

I quickly turn the radio off. "We're fucked," Rebecca decides.

"Not entirely," I counter.

She looks at me incredulously. "How not entirely? Short of our names, they know everything about us, including exactly what we look like and what we're driving. We have to ditch the car."

"We can't ditch the car," I remind her. "It's a rental, and now it's on everybody's radar." Fortunately, at this moment, a billboard catches my eye, and a half-dazed little laugh escapes my lips. "Doesn't mean we can't disguise it, though."

She gives me a puzzled look, then looks up in time to see the same billboard, which reads: Darius's Auto Body and Paint Shop.

"What?" I say to her. "We always liked the Sebring better in gold anyway."

"And when we return the rental car a different color than it was when we picked it up?"

"My darling girl," I say in all seriousness, "if we live long enough to return this rental car, the color of it is going to be the last thing on everyone's mind."

The South Side of Chicago, as legend tells it, is the baddest part of town. My travels have taken me into some dangerous places, and this is definitely one of them. I can scarcely blame the Englewood residents for eyeing us with suspicion as we drive past. We're three white people in a shiny new convertible, cruising purposefully through an area struggling with poverty and a strained infrastructure. I'd be glaring at us too.

We make our way to Darius's Auto Body and Paint Shop and pull the Sebring into one of the bays. A technician waves us forward and then signals us to stop when we're in the right place. I put it in park and step out to talk to him. "What can I do for you folks today?" he asks pleasantly.

"Well," I answer, "I just got tired of looking at the green, and I'm thinking she'd look better in a metallic gold. Can you give her a new paint job this afternoon?"

He looks the car over, nodding his head from time to time. "Yeah, I think we can do that. Goin' from dark to light, though, probably needs two coats. That'll cost you extra."

"I'm not too worried," I tell him. "If you're as good as people tell me, it's worth the price."

He accepts the compliment. "Take me about an hour and a half to finish it. We got a waiting room if you and yours want to get comfortable."

"Thank you very much. I'd like that."

We go to the waiting room, which has a few chairs, some magazines on tables, and a TV in the corner, showing the latest from CNN. I pause long enough to hope that we don't merit inclusion on *that* network on top of everything else. Two other people are also in the room, waiting for their work to be done. The three of us huddle up in a corner of the room, trying very hard not to look like we're actually huddled up.

"Is it safe for us to stay in one place for this long?" Rebecca asks.

"We don't have much of a choice," I reply. "The color of the car is the first thing that's going to stand out when they're looking for us, so once that's taken care of, it buys us some time down the road. Nobody here raised a fuss when we asked them to paint the car, so that suggests to me that the news hasn't reached them yet. We'll wait here, play it cool, pay in cash, and then be on our way. Is anybody hungry?" They both nod. "I am too. There's a place to get takeout down the block. I'll walk over there and get us some dinner."

"We should go with you," Cassie says.

"No, it's risky if the three of us are seen together outside. For safety's sake, I'll go by myself." I take thirty dollars out of my wallet and give the wallet to Rebecca for safekeeping. "I've got my phone with me. If anything goes wrong, I'll call you."

"Be careful," she says.

"I will."

I make my way through the shop and out onto Sixty-third Street. There's plenty of traffic, both vehicular on the roads and pedestrian on the sidewalks. It's the end of the work week, and people are anxious to start their weekend. I feel conspicuous. I'm clearly not a resident of this neighborhood, or even a likely business patron here. And that's not a value judgment or anything of the kind, just simple numbers—I'm the only white face on the block. And since that face is wanted by authorities at several levels, I feel very much like every eye is on me. The actual truth, as I look around, is that people give me a glance at most and then go on their way.

Charlie W's is a chicken and barbecue restaurant half a block down from Darius's. At this time of day, they're doing a bustling business, with nearly every table filled with customers sharing the exploits of the past week. Fortunately, they have a take-out counter, so I get in line and decide what to get for the three of us. There are four people in line ahead of me, so I have the opportunity to look at my options before I get to the counter. Once I step up, a woman in her sixties greets me. "What can I get ya, sugar?"

She called me "sugar." I like that.

"I'm getting dinner for three of us, so I'd like to get a variety of things. Can I please get four pieces of chicken, a pulled pork sandwich, some mashed potatoes, an order of cole slaw, three biscuits, a Coke, a Sprite, and a root beer?"

"Sure thing. Anything else for you today?"

"Yes, if you've got paper plates, and some plastic utensils and some napkins, that'd be great. We're in the waiting room at Darius's Auto Body."

"No problem. It comes to $21.38 with tax." I hand her the cash. "Out of thirty." She hands me my change. "Your number is five. It'll be just a few minutes."

I step to the side to let the next patron approach, and find myself very fidgety as I wait. With all these customers in the restaurant, I feel very exposed. If even one of them heard the news report, I could be found out. I have to remind myself that I'm not with Rebecca and Cassie, not in the green convertible, and not wearing a T-shirt that says, "Hi, I'm the guy from the Amber Alert." To those around me, I'm just a guy waiting for chicken. And I'm okay with that.

The food arrives as promised a few minutes later, and I leave the restaurant complete with plates and plasticware, as requested. Perhaps a little more swiftly than I should, I walk back to the body shop and rejoin my traveling companions. The look of relief on their faces does not escape me, as I probably have a similar look on my own. The life of a fugitive is not as pleasant or glamorous as modern cinema would have one believe.

"Hi, honey, I'm home," I offer as gallows humor. "I've brought dinner. I hope nobody's a vegetarian."

"Hell no," Cassie says. "Bring it on."

And so, with more determination than table manners, we three reduce the bounty to bones and wrappers in short order. Having skipped lunch in favor of saving a school from destruction, we were all hungrier than we realized. It was quite good. If we're ever fleeing through this part of Chicago again, we'll have to stop in at this place.

The minutes wear on as the painter continues his work. By 5:45, we are the last people left in the waiting room, which gives us a little bit of time and room to strategize. I've found a map of Illinois at the shop, and we go over potential routes south that keep us off of the obvious one, Interstate 57.

As we're looking at the map, a young, professional-looking man enters the waiting room carrying a sheet of paper in his hands. We look up, and I immediately default to wondering who he is and what he wants with us. He speaks before I can ponder it too long. "You folks have the Sebring?"

"That's right," I answer.

He extends his right hand and says, "I'm Darius Parker. I'm the owner."

"Nice to meet you," I answer, offering my hand. "I'm Charles. This is my wife Lisa and our niece Danielle."

"The painting's done," he says, taking an empty seat near us. "It'll be dry soon. I wouldn't take it through a car wash in a big hurry, but it's safe enough on the road."

"Thank you."

"I couldn't help noticing a rental car sticker on the back bumper."

Time to think fast. "Yeah, we bought it from the rental company this week. They sell some of their used vehicles, and the price was too good to pass up. Only thing we didn't like was the color, so here we are." I'm praying that the smile on my face masks the terror I feel at his line of questioning.

He nods a little, and there's a look on his face that I can't quite pinpoint; it looks like something important is imminent. His next statement proves how right I am. "I heard the news report," he says simply. The words stop my heart and freeze my blood, leaving my face absolutely ashen. I have no choice but to continue the façade.

"News report?" I ask.

"Let's be honest with each other," he says. "I know you're the ones they're looking for. The girl. The Amber Alert. It's why you're getting your rental car painted."

Dead to rights. The words fill my mind. I hope they're not literal. "Yes," I say quietly. "It's us."

Short of options, I let my eyes wander to the door of the room. Darius sees me and utters a single word in response. "No."

"What do you want with us?" Rebecca asks him.

"I want some answers. I want to know why you came to my shop. Mostly I want to know why I shouldn't turn you in."

"If it's money you want ..." I start, purely out of instinct.

He cuts me off before I can finish. "I *could* choose to be very offended at that. I'm going to chalk it up to fatigue and bad judgment, and forget that you said it."

"Thank you."

"The reason I'm in here with you now—the reason I'm not on the phone to the state police—is because I've seen a lot of bad people in my time. Dudes you would not want to mess with. Men who would think nothing of killing you and everyone you ever cared about."

I do hope he's going someplace happier with this.

"And every one of those men had a look about them. Something in their face that says *this is who I am. This is what I do.* I look at you, and I don't see that look. Here you are, and they say you kidnapped this girl. Took her out of school and away from her family. And here she is, here with you, like they said. I'm wondering why that is, if that's not the kind of people you are. Maybe I should just ask her. It's Cassie, isn't it? Isn't that what they said your name is?"

"Yes," Cassie answers quietly, sounding more like the accused than the victim.

"Cassie, I want you to know that no matter what you tell me, you're safe. I won't harm you nor bother you at all. I'd just like to know how you ended up in the company of these two people today."

"They're helping me," she says simply. "I have to get to Florida to help my father. He's in prison for something he didn't do, and I can help get him released. But I couldn't get there on my own, so they're helping me."

Darius looks to me. "Is that the truth?"

"Yes. That's the truth. We tried to call Cassie's grandmother to notify her, and she overreacted. And now we're on the run."

Darius Parker stands up, looking down at the haggard and pathetic visages of the trio in front of him. For many seconds he just stands, looking. Deciding, perhaps. Then he chooses to trust us. "Seven years ago, I spent almost a year in Joliet for a crime I didn't commit. A robbery of a convenience store. Turns out the only thing convenient was me. They needed a suspect, and there I was. Didn't matter that I had a college degree or a steady job or a stable household. They needed a young black man to play the role of criminal, and I got the part. So I spent more than eleven months in that prison, knowing that I didn't deserve to be there. Finally, they caught the guy who actually robbed the store. He didn't even look anything like me, except, well …" He gestures toward his face with a knowing smile. "So I know what it means to be imprisoned for something you didn't do. Tell me this: if I turn my back and let you drive out of here in your freshly painted metallic gold convertible car, do you swear to me that you'll take this child where she needs to go, and help her do what she needs to do, and not harm her in any way?"

"We swear," Rebecca says.

"We'll protect her with our lives," I add.

"When they ask you where you got such a beautiful paint job, you tell 'em Earl Scheib did it or some such. Because if they catch up with you, you've never heard of Darius's Auto Body, understand?"

I offer my hand, and he shakes it. "Perfectly."

"Then you best get out of here. You've got a long road ahead and plenty of folks lookin' for you."

"Thank you, Darius," I reply. The others rise, and the four of us make our way over to the Sebring, which—as he said—now sports a beautiful fresh coat of metallic gold paint.

I open the driver's door, and he says, "Aren't you forgetting something?"

I am momentarily puzzled.

"Five hundred and seventy-six dollars and eighteen cents. I'm a nice guy, but I'm not *that* nice."

I have to laugh. "Of course."

"Why do I suspect you'll be paying in cash?"

"Because you're a smart guy, too." I get my wallet back from Rebecca and hand him six hundred dollars. "Consider the rest a tip."

"Thank you very kindly. It's been a pleasure having your business. I hope you'll understand if I don't invite you to come back and see us again real soon."

"I think that's fair."

He puts a hand on my shoulder and looks me squarely in the eyes. "And if they do find you, you play it smart. No cowboy shit, you hear me?"

"Yeah, I do. Thank you, Darius. You really helped us."

"Yeah, yeah. Go on."

I start the car and lean my head out the window. "What, no oil change?"

"I'll give you an oil change," he says, hiding a smile. "Get your ass outta here."

With a wave, I exit the building and make my way south and out of the city of Chicago. Darius was right—the road ahead will be very long, and while our new paint job will spare us some initial scrutiny, every stop will be a risk, every encounter an opportunity for someone to play the hero and turn us in.

Interstate 57 is the best route south through Illinois, but state road 45 parallels it closely, so it's the road we choose. After several miles, city gives way to suburbs, and suburbs later give way to cornfields and farmhouses, along with signs advertising herbicide, tractors, and how really wonderful guns are. In case someone is stealing your corn or your tractor, I suppose.

Once the suburbs are behind us, traffic on SR 45 drops to the point where we see only a car or two per mile. It offers a feeling of peace, something I suspect we all need very much. We had listened to one more radio update about the Amber Alert, and there was nothing new, so we decided that would be enough for now. There was no need for periodic reminders of our plight.

We continue to travel with the convertible's top up. As good as wind in the hair feels, it would provide too much exposure at a time when we really can't afford it. We keep the windows open, allowing air in, and providing some sound to fill the vacuum left by our group's dearth of conversation. When Cassie speaks for the first time, more than an hour later, her words are actually startling.

"I could use a bathroom soon," she says.

"So could I," Rebecca adds.

"What is it with women always going to the bathroom together?" I tease.

"Tell me you don't need one too," Rebecca replies.

"Yeah, I suppose it would be a good idea. Unfortunately, the actual roadside rest areas are confined to the interstates." I see a mileage sign ahead. "We're only ten miles from a town called Urbana. We can stop there, if you both can wait that long?"

"That's fine," Cassie says.

The road continues to wind south, and within fifteen minutes, we see a sign that says "Welcome to Urbana, Home of the University of Illinois." Route 45 becomes a street called Cunningham, and just south of the entrance to Interstate 74, I see another sign: "Crystal Lake Park, 1 mile." Where there's park, there's restrooms, and it probably won't be as crowded at this time of day as a gas station or other public establishment. So I follow the signs, detouring briefly off of 45 and over to Crystal Lake Park. As its name suggests, a small lake is the park's central feature, surrounded by playgrounds, hiking trails, and grassy fields. On the shore of the lake is a clubhouse, bearing the very welcoming stick figures denoting restrooms available. I park the Sebring and we all climb out. At this point, I check the paint job to make sure no green is peeking through. I find not a bit. The car looks like it rolled off the assembly line in metallic gold.

As I lock up, I instruct my traveling companions, "Stay together. Don't lose sight of each other. When you're done, meet me back at the car."

"I'd kind of like to stretch my legs," Rebecca says.

"Okay, but let's not take too long here. The sooner we're out of Illinois, the better I'll feel. And remember, stay together."

We all make our way to our respective restrooms. I brace myself upon entering, knowing what chaos can await in a public park's facilities. I'm quite pleased to discover that the place is clean, well-kept, and even smells good. *Good for you, Urbana Park District. You'll forgive us if we don't stay longer.*

My business completed, I wash my hands and exit the room, looking for Rebecca and Cassie, who have not yet emerged. I return to the car to wait for them. That's when I see him and he sees me.

A man and his dog in a city park should not be out of the ordinary, but this man clearly recognizes me, though I have never been to Urbana, Illinois before in my life. He looks relatively young, just shy of thirty,

I'd guess, with sandy brown hair and an overall neat appearance. He's walking a fluffy silvery-black dog of about forty pounds. All the while, this man is looking at me like he knows me or like he should know me. It's making me very uneasy, more so when he begins to approach me. "Excuse me," he says. "Tristan Shays?"

My heart is racing, but I force myself to remain externally calm. "Sorry, pal. You got the wrong guy."

He remains polite but it's clear that he doesn't believe me. "My name is Virgil. I'm sorry to bother you, but I need to talk to you."

"Well, you're welcome to talk, but I'm not the guy you're looking for."

"It's okay. I understand. You didn't expect me here."

Out of the corner of my eye, I see Rebecca and Cassie approaching from the ladies' room. In my mind, I project a thought that I hope is clear enough for Rebecca to pick up across the distance: *stay back!* I watch as she reacts; seeing me with a stranger, she grabs Cassie by the arm and holds her there, far enough away from me.

Virgil continues. "It's been difficult for me to find you. I know you've been traveling. And your car doesn't look like I expected it to."

He just won't let up. It's time to change tactics. I look him straight in the eye and say in a firm but non-threatening tone—in deference to the dog, "Who are you?"

"I'm Virgil," he repeats. Gesturing toward the dog, he adds, "And this is Keesho. He travels with me."

"What do you want with me?"

"I have a message to give you," he says simply. "Something you need to hear."

I'm stunned at these words. "You *what?*"

"Where are the others?" he asks. "This involves them too."

"You're a messenger," I say in quiet disbelief. This changes everything. Though I have met others who share my gifts—Stelios, Alan, the homeless man in the park—I am totally unprepared for Virgil to find me here. I wave to Rebecca and Cassie that it is safe for them to approach. "How did you find me?" I ask him.

"It wasn't easy. You've been on the move because they're looking for you. Keesho here helps me. I know roughly where to go, and when we get close, he tracks down the person I'm supposed to find. He's done search and rescue. Saved a lot of lives."

The others draw near, watching me, to know how to react to this stranger. "Hello," Virgil says to them, "you must be Rebecca."

"That's right," she says. "Who—?"

"This is Virgil," I tell her. "He's a messenger. He's been looking for us."

"And you're Cassie?" he asks. She nods uneasily in response. "I'm very glad I found you. I came up I-57 from the south. Keesho here told me you'd be in this park."

"Virgil, you said you have a message for us. What is it?"

"Right. I'm sorry to have to tell you this, but I'm here to tell you not to go to Pensacola. You're in great danger if you go there."

"Thank you," I reply, as calmly as possible. "I know there's a degree of danger in every assignment I complete."

"Not like this," he says. "Nothing you've done before was like this."

As logical and reasonable as that message is, it still hits me like a speeding truck, sending a shiver through me. "Virgil, if you know who I am, then you know *what* I am. Don't you?"

"Yes. You're … like me."

"I'm called Hamesh, keeper of the word of Hosea," I tell him with all due import.

He just smiles and passes his right hand just above his hair, to indicate that the reference has gone right over his head. So much for *that* calling card. That shit blew their doors off in Zion.

"Let's just say it means that I'm not your average Joe off the street. I've seen some things and been in some dangerous situations. Thank you for the warning, but I'm ready for what's to come."

"No," he replies gravely, "you're not. I was told that you would be confident and unafraid, but I was also told that you don't know the magnitude of what's waiting for you. You're walking into a battle, Tristan. All three of you. Two very powerful sides are at war, and right now, neither side claims you as its own. They would think nothing of killing all three of you. I know why you're going there, but if you go, Cassie's life will be in danger. And if she dies, you'll be blamed—if you survive at all. Everything you've worked for will have been in vain."

I stand silently and just look at him. "I see the look in your eyes," he continues, "and I know it means you're still going. Please consider changing your mind, changing your plans. But if you don't, at least be very careful, more careful than you've ever been before. And trust no one. I'm so sorry to have to deliver this message to you, after everything you've been through."

I put a reassuring hand on his shoulder. "It's okay. You're doing what you have to. I've learned not to kill the messenger."

"Of course," he says with a knowing smile.

"Please don't tell anyone you saw us," I request.

"I won't. I promise. Be safe, and God bless you."

"He has so far," I reply.

Without another word, Virgil and Keesho walk across a grassy field to the parking lot of Crystal Lake Park, get into a blue sedan, and drive away; maybe going home, maybe going on to their next assignment. I meant to ask him what he feels when each new mission arrives, pain or pleasure. I just couldn't find a way to work the question in.

Upon looking at my companions, I realize that they are both very uneasy, almost in a state of shock. "Are you okay?" I ask them.

"Okay?" Cassie asks, perturbed. "What the fuck just happened here? Who was that guy, and how did he know about who we are and where we're going?"

"Cassie," I say gently, "try to stay calm. That man has the same sort of gifts that I have. He gets messages, warnings about people in danger, and he's compelled to tell them, to try to save them. The same way I found you at your school."

"But he said I could die!"

"I know. And if you want to turn around and go home, you say the word and we'll go. Right now. No questions asked."

"But I have to help my father." Her voice is laced with fear and uncertainty. It is yet another enormous decision on a day already filled with enormous decisions for her.

"It's your call," I tell her. "You say go, and we'll go. You say don't go, and we take you home to Grandma and warm up the mother of all reasonable explanations."

She stares at a point in front of her for many seconds, working it all out in her head—weighing the risks and the consequences. Finally, in a quiet but determined voice, she says, "We go."

"We go," I repeat. I next step over to Rebecca, who looks almost as flustered as Cassie. "What about you? I know this isn't what you expected when you signed on to this little road trip. Can I leave you someplace safe?"

"No," she says, sounding surprised at her answer. "I need to be there. I think this is what it's all been leading up to. Everything we've been through together. You found your answers on this part of the trip. I think it's time to find mine."

"Okay."

"I'm scared, Tristan. And the worst part is, I don't even know what I'm scared of."

"The unknown is the scariest part of all. But you've got us, and whatever it is we have to face, we'll face it as a group. All for one, and all that shit. Despite appearances, I think we're a pretty formidable team. We'll work together and do everything we can to keep a low profile. Yeah, it'll be dangerous, but we have an advantage: we've been warned. We know what's coming; the other guys don't."

I realize during this attempt at heartfelt morale-building that both women are staring at me with confused looks on their faces. "What?" I ask.

"I'm just wondering what's so funny about what you just said," Rebecca answers.

This confuses me until I realize, to my own amazement, that I am emitting an unconscious string of stupid giggling laughter. "Nothing's funny. It's just ... oh shit, I'm getting a new assignment."

"What?" Rebecca exclaims. "Oh no, not now!"

I drop to my knees as the sensation continues, wracking me with that same new combination of overpowering pleasure and discomfort. Rebecca hurries to my side to keep me steady, as Cassie watches this trip continue to get stranger. The details come in, as they always do, and I grasp the importance of this new assignment. As important as it is to get to Pensacola and help Cassie's father, this has to come first. Once all the pertinent facts are safely in my head, the sensation leaves me and I'm able to stand again.

"I just can't get used to the way these assignments affect you now," Rebecca says, letting go once she's sure I'm all right.

"What just happened here?" Cassie asks, looking slightly traumatized.

"Homework assignment," I reply. "The same way I learned about your plans for the school this morning, I just found out about someone else who's in danger, someone who needs my help. I'm sorry to delay us, but we have to make a stop on the way to Florida."

"Where are we going?" Rebecca asks.

"New Orleans. There's a police detective whose life is in danger if we don't warn her by tomorrow night."

"So we're going?" Rebecca says, apparently far less certain of the answer than I am.

"Of course we're going. How could you even ask?"

"Well, it's just that … we're already on an assignment, and this will take us out of our way."

"Not by much. New Orleans is just up the coast from Pensacola. We can keep working our way south, stop off there long enough to give the warning, and head right to Florida."

"Yes, but Tristan … warning a cop? We're already wanted for kidnapping. Going and seeking out the police in a major city is very risky, isn't it?"

"Yeah, I guess it is. But I don't see how we have a choice in the matter. I got the assignment, and I know what's going to happen to her if I don't warn her."

Rebecca's next words surprise me. "But you're not in any pain. It's not like before, where you'd be in agony if you didn't take the assignment. Cops risk their lives every day, especially in a dangerous place like New Orleans."

"What are you saying?"

"I'm saying that maybe this time, we need to put our needs first, and let this person in New Orleans fend for herself."

I really don't know what to say. I can't deny that there's something very reasonable in what she said. New Orleans, while technically on the way to Pensacola, would be a diversion from our route. And the idea of seeking out a member of law enforcement for a conversation at this point in our journey would invite scrutiny and could very well lead to our capture.

Then there's the part that Virgil added. The battle; the danger; the chance that Cassie or all three of us could be killed in a war that's not even ours to fight. But did he know about the new assignment when he warned us not to go to Florida? There's no way to know.

Can I really let this police detective go unwarned, when I know very well that my message could save her life? "No," I decide, "we have to go to New Orleans. We have to warn her. We've disguised the car. If I go see her alone, she has no reason to even suspect that we're the people in the Amber Alert. And that's if the alert even made it all the way to Louisiana in a single day. We'll be careful, we'll be cautious, but I can't live with myself if I can save this woman's life and I do nothing."

They look at each other and then look at me. "My earlier offer still stands. If anyone wants out in light of this, let me know now, and I'll get you home." Neither of them responds to the offer. "Okay then. Let's get back on the road. We've got a lot of ground to cover."

We get back into the car and make our way back to route 45, headed southbound. It disturbs me a little to know that I actually considered not taking this assignment. Yes, the pain I used to feel is gone now, but not because these assignments aren't my problem. It's gone because I've acknowledged my responsibility. I am a messenger, and whether I stay with them or not, I am one of The Nine, keeper of prophecies that date back more than 2,000 years. I will continue to do this work until it is no longer mine to do.

As we drive, I find my cell phone in my pocket and dig it out. I turn it on and wait for it to find a signal. I notice that Rebecca is watching me very intently. "What are you doing?" she asks.

"You heard what Virgil said. We're walking into a very dangerous situation." I search my pockets for the slip of paper I need, and find it in my wallet. "We can't go into this alone."

I suspect that she is about to read my thoughts, and her next statement confirms it. "Tristan, no. We can't call him. You remember what happened at our last meeting. And you heard the guy: he said we should trust no one. Why all of a sudden do we want to trust him now?"

"Because … because we've got no one else."

I dial the number from the slip of paper, and listen as a phone rings twice on the other end. A familiar voice says, "Hello?"

"Stelios, it's Tristan Shays. I think we're in trouble, and I need your help. We're on our way to Pensacola, Florida right now. Is there any way you could meet us there?"

With a new assignment ahead, we press on. I try to stay optimistic, believing that we are on the side of right, but deep inside I fear there is no right and wrong in the battle ahead, only two sides, greedy and relentless, with the three of us in the middle, trying to stay alive. I don't know if I've ever been this frightened.

Oil and water shall combine with blood, and
set the messenger adrift into battle.

Printed in the United States
by Baker & Taylor Publisher Services